SWING, SWING TOGETHER

SWING, SWING TOGETHER

Peter Lovesey

Chivers Press
Bath, England

Thorndike Press
Waterville, Maine USA

This Large Print edition is published by Chivers Press, England, and by Thorndike Press, USA.

Published in 2002 in the U.K. by arrangement with the author.

Published in 2002 in the U.S. by arrangement with Gelfman Schneider Literary Agents, Inc.

U.K. Hardcover ISBN 0–7540–4985–X (Chivers Large Print)
U.K. Softcover ISBN 0–7540–4986–8 (Camden Large Print)
U.S. Softcover ISBN 0–7862–4408–9 (General Series Edition)

The text of this Large Print edition is unabridged.
Other aspects of the book may vary from the original edition.

Set in 16 pt. New Times Roman.

Printed in Great Britain on acid-free paper.

British Library Cataloguing in Publication Data available

Library of Congress Cataloging-in-Publication Data

Lovesey, Peter.
Swing, swing together / Peter Lovesey.
p. cm.
ISBN 0–7862–4408–9 (lg. print : sc : alk. paper)
1. Cribb, Sergeant (Fictitious character)—Fiction. 2. Police—England—London—Fiction. 3. London (England)—Fiction. 4. Large type books. I. Title.
PR6062.O86 S95 2002
823'.914—dc21 2002067281

Jolly boating weather,
And a hay-harvest breeze;
Blade on the feather,
Shade off the trees,
Swing, swing together,
With your bodies between your knees,
Swing, swing together,
With your bodies between your knees.

Eton Boating Song
William Johnson Cory (c.1863)

CHAPTER ONE

Original use of butter—Respecting the Rules—Down to the Thames

'Naked?' Harriet Shaw inquired.

'Completely, darling. In the buff. It's awfully good fun. Words can't describe it. You'll come, won't you?'

'I believe I might.'

'Splendid! We'll meet in the common room at a quarter past midnight. Can you get some butter?'

'What do we want with butter, for goodness' sake?'

'We rub it on the sides of the window to stop it from squeaking. Otherwise it makes enough noise to rouse the entire college. And you'll need a towel, of course. There's a stack of them in the linen store. Slip in there this afternoon when the maids are not about. Jane and I still have the ones we took last time. Oh, and don't breathe a word to anyone else. People aren't to be trusted. Certain of our fellow-students would like nothing better than the Plum to catch us red-handed.'

'If she does, I shall be red all over, never mind my hands.'

In Elfrida College for the Training of Female Elementary Teachers, Miss Plummer had a well-justified reputation for securing the highest standards of behaviour in her young ladies. Any reckless enough to flout her Rules and Regulations, a copy of which hung above the spiritual text over each student's bed, incurred more than displeasure. There was a scale of penalties ranging from restriction of diet (for minor offences, such as speaking out of turn) to instant expulsion (for offences not clearly specified in the Rules, but darkly implied by the phrase 'intemperate, indecorous or unladylike conduct'). As a system it worked well, and the young ladies received their training in an orderly manner appropriate to the profession they were entering. That is not to say that the Rules were never disobeyed: that was too much to ask of thirty girls of seventeen and upwards. But Miss Plummer's discipline was such that girls with insubordinate tendencies kept them under control for the greater part by far of their time at Elfrida College. The flaw in the system was that if they *did* decide to kick over the traces they kicked with all the gusto of the front line of the chorus.

And that was how Harriet Shaw was persuaded to take a midnight bathe with Jane Morrison and Molly Stevens on the night of Tuesday, 27 August 1889.

The College was located beside the Thames a short way below Henley Reach, a stretch of the river as safe, secluded and attractive as any from source to sea. The grounds extended right down to the towpath but the fifty yards of lawn fronting the river was out of bounds to students on account of perils presented not by the river, but by young men accustomed to using the towpath. So the river and its traffic had to be regarded from a discreet distance, a distance that lent something more than enchantment to the view. The river seemed to exert an attractive force increasingly difficult to resist as the girls progressed through their first year and entered their second. If a student were to give way to the promptings and break bounds then she was risking expulsion, so why not make an occasion of it by going at night and bathing in the river by moonlight dressed as nature intended? That, in a nutshell, was Molly's argument.

They claimed to have done it before, those two. They said it had been the most exquisite experience they could remember. Harriet believed them. They were adventurous spirits, she was sure, and they had secrets. No two girls in the College were as close friends as they and she was sure they had broken the Rules before. Because they were so close they had covered up for each other. Better than that, they had actually conspired to be favourites of the Plum. It was a privilege really to be invited to share in their escapade. She was slightly mystified why they should have chosen her of all the girls, but there it was.

This and other thoughts occupied her as she lay fully clothed in bed that night waiting for Henley Church faintly to chime the quarter hour past midnight. The Plum had long since made her tour of the building checking that all bolts and catches were fastened. With luck she would be asleep by now, secure in her brass bedstead in the room with the balcony at the front of the house, that balcony from which she liked to quiz the girls through her lorgnette as she basked in the sunshine with her two white cats. After a year at Elfrida, Harriet was less terrified of her than she had been at first, but she was still a formidable personage, a distinctly sour Plum.

Just as she was beginning to fear she had not heard it, the single chime sounded. Minutes later she was in the common room releasing a long breath at having got down the stairs without causing one to creak. Molly and Jane were already at the window easing it upwards with professional stealth.

'You first,' whispered Jane.

Momentarily, as she drew her legs over the sill and felt for a foothold on the lawn outside, the uncomfortable thought crossed Harriet's mind that they might close the window behind her and leave her stranded. But she had misjudged them. Molly, slight and agile, sprang down beside her and together they took Jane's hands and helped her out. They celebrated their liberty with a swift exchange of smiles, and started running across the tennis-lawn. Jane unfurled her bath towel and whirled it like a Dervish in the centre of the court until Molly jerked her away, down through the trees towards the low stone wall that marked the edge of bounds without altogether obstructing the view of the river. They negotiated it easily, giggling now, for they were too far from the house to be heard, and raced down the slope to the row of willows beside the towpath.

CHAPTER TWO

Molly by moonlight—Concerning Harriet's hat—River scene with figures

'It couldn't have been easier, could it?' said Molly, already unfastening buttons.

'Like peeling an orange,' said Jane.

'You say the funniest things, Jane! Peeling an orange! Just when we're about to—' Harriet stopped in mid-sentence.

Molly had stepped out of her dress and was standing naked in front of her. So was Jane. They could not have been wearing anything under their dresses.

'Aren't you ready?' asked Molly, with a slight implication of censure.

'My underclothes. I didn't think to leave

them off.' It was out of the question to ask them to wait while she struggled several minutes more with stockings and stays. 'I'll join you as soon as I'm ready.'

'Very well, then. We probably *would* get cold waiting.'

She watched as they stepped carefully off the bank, Jane markedly taller than Molly. In the water, reflected moonlight faintly underscored the areas of their anatomy nearest the surface. It occurred to Harriet what a silly spectacle they presented. With less enthusiasm she lifted her day-gown over her head.

The conversation that presently carried across the water did little to salve her wounded feelings.

'Is she *still* undressing?'

'It doesn't surprise me. Harriet had a very proper upbringing. She wouldn't dream of coming out without her drawers on. I'm surprised she wasn't wearing a hat.'

This provoked a peal of laughter from Jane. 'The one with the humming-birds—the one she wears to church? Imagine taking to the water in *that,* without a stitch on underneath!'

So *this* was their idea of a companionable dip. Harriet would have put on her dress again and marched straight back to the house if it were not certain to become the principal topic of breakfast conversation next morning. No, she would not give them the chance to say she had taken fright at the last minute. She was going to demonstrate that a proper upbringing was no constraint on a truly adventurous spirit. She started unfastening her tapes with determination.

The river looked another place by night. The ranks of beeches set back on both sides which were such a feature by day made no impression at all, except when a breeze stirred the leaves. Instead the water provided the spectacle, exhibiting a fragmented and elongated moon across its width and so marking the limits of the banks.

Harriet's shape too, was defined against the shimmering moonlight. Naked now, she still had the well-cared-for look of her class, a figure unquestionably cultivated on three good meals a day; perhaps the hips were too rounded for perfection, but her waist was trim and her bosom claimed attention with a sportive bob as she waded towards the centre of the river.

'Here she comes!' Molly announced. 'Get your shoulders under quickly, Harriet. Someone might be watching!'

This suggestion had the intended outcome. Harriet surged into the deeper water with the suddenness of a lifeboat, remembering just in time to keep her hair from getting wet. The Thames was colder than she expected and the mud on the river-bottom unpleasantly soft to the feet, not in the least like the sand of Bognor Regis, where she had bathed from a machine the previous summer. But once the initial shock was over she found the temperature of the water quite tolerable. She pushed forward with her arms and took her feet off the bottom as if she was swimming. She was not really a swimmer, but she enjoyed the sensation of weightlessness in the water. Better than that, she had the delicious satisfaction of defying the Plum in as flagrant a manner as she could imagine. She drew her hands down her body to reaffirm her nakedness.

'Awfully jolly, isn't it?' said Jane, at her side. 'Like water-nymphs. Do you think we could tempt a young man in here and drown him?'

'Don't be so morbid,' called Molly, from closer to the centre of the river. She was able to swim several strokes and she wanted the others to be in no doubt of the fact.

'Let's surprise her,' whispered Jane. Before Harriet had time to consider what was in prospect, her hand was taken and she was tugged towards the centre. She felt the current pressing her from the right.

'I can't swim.'

'I won't let go of you,' Jane promised. 'It doesn't shelve much. We'll approach her from behind and tap her on each shoulder.'

It was the kind of trick Harriet had half-expected the others to play on herself. She allowed Jane to steer her into deeper water. She could touch the mud with her toes, no more. They manoeuvred themselves behind Molly, who was facing downriver. The current carried them effortlessly towards her. Each of them stretched out a hand as they closed on her.

At the contact, she turned, laughing and poked playfully at them. 'I knew what was going on,' she said. Then with a change of expression so sudden that they might have mistaken it for a delayed reaction if she had not at the same instant taken her hand out of the water and pointed behind them, she screamed, not a piercing scream, more of a gasp, but devastating in its timing, that split second after their trick had appeared to fail.

Harriet looked over her shoulder and saw the cause of Molly's alarm.

They were approaching steadily downriver. Three men in a boat, and a dog, keeping watch from the prow.

CHAPTER THREE

Harriet adrift—Advantages of an understanding of Geography—One over the eyot

What happened next need never have occurred if our three bathers had kept their heads. The boat, gliding serenely across the moonlit strip of water, was some forty yards away, its occupants oblivious of the presence of anything remarkable. Its course would bring it, at worst, within fifteen yards of Harriet and her companions. Had they remained where they were and turned modestly towards the Buckinghamshire bank the chance was high that they would not have been noticed.

Instead, they obeyed their first impulse and struck out for the place where they had left their clothes. Jane slipped her hand from Harriet's and glided away with a rapid side-stroke. Harriet, unable to swim and practically out of her depth, might still have been able to follow on tip-toe, and was beginning to, when she was confronted first by the pale, surfacing shape of Molly's rump and, an instant later, the soles of her feet, drawn up in the first position of the breast-stroke. As the legs straightened, the feet made contact with Harriet and pushed her firmly towards the centre of the river.

The current of the Thames is not reckoned to be powerful in the summer months, but it can still be inconvenient to bathers or boats that slip their moorings. Harriet first sank in the deeper water, swallowing enough of it to make her doubt whether she could find the strength to struggle upwards again. Her feet came into contact with something slimy to the touch, possibly water-weed, and she jerked her legs away instinctively, giving herself the impetus to come spluttering to the surface. A gulp of air, and she was under again, but by agitating her arms and legs she avoided touching the bottom. She broke the surface for a second time and succeeded in staying afloat, thanks mainly to the steady pull of the current, which she found she could ride by spreading her arms wide.

It was an extraordinary sensation, strongly reminiscent of dreams she had experienced from time to time which she had always supposed had something to do with being introduced early to *Alice in Wonderland.* Now that she was reasonably confident she could keep her head above the water and would not drown, there was even something pleasurable in being carried along by the river, submitting to its firm, unending pressure. She understood why people said swimming was simply a question of confidence. Being carried by the current, she suspected, was more enjoyable than swimming, which she had always regarded as ungraceful. Like this, she could assume attitudes more natural than ever one could with the breast-stroke or side-stroke. The more relaxed she became, the more buoyant was her body. It was a discovery she was sure Molly and Jane had not made. It brought a new dimension to the night's adventure.

The moment had to arrive when sanity reasserted itself, for whatever agreeable sensations Harriet derived from her predicament, Hurley Weir was only a mile downriver. In the darkness, and at so low an elevation, she was unable to tell how far she had already travelled. She estimated that she must be approaching Medmenham. Near the Abbey the river snaked sharply, before the broad reach leading to Hurley. If she was carried into that reach, there was no way of escaping destruction on the weir's gargantuan teeth.

She had one chance, and the wit to conserve her strength for it.

It was not long in coming. On her left, the sky had been obscured for perhaps a minute by thick foliage along the Buckinghamshire bank. Now there was a break. She knew where she was. One memorable afternoon the Plum had conducted a geography lesson in two rowing boats manned by the gardener and his son. They had rowed the girls half a mile downriver to study the effects of erosion and deposition. From the lawn in front of Medmenham Abbey a party of young men with a banjo had serenaded them with *Paddle Your Own Canoe.* She was quite sure this was the place. Around the next bend, where the river turned almost upon itself, the action of the water had formed three eyots. The smallest and narrowest was to the left. The mainstream of the current passed between it and the two on the right. If Harriet had understood the geography lesson correctly—

and concentration had been difficult that afternoon—water flowing on the inside of a curve is shallower and flows less quickly than on the outside. If she could possibly steer herself leftwards towards the smallest island, there was a chance of getting a foothold on the silt that must have accumulated around its base.

With a determined thrashing of arms and legs she started across the current towards the eyot. She was immediately turned over like a log, but righted herself and tried again at a less ambitious angle to the flow. Several times she started to sink but managed to rear up, and when her strength was all but spent and she submerged again, she felt her knees touch firm mud. She was in three feet of water.

How long she remained kneeling in the shallows waiting for the pumping of her heart to return to normal, Harriet was in no state to estimate. She was not surprised that by the time she remembered the existence of the three men in the boat (to say nothing of the dog) and turned to look for them they were nowhere in sight. If they *had* noticed her in the water they had not demonstrated much concern for her plight. Two, she remembered, had been rowing and would have had their backs to her. The third had sunk downwards somewhat in the cushions at the other end and may well have been asleep. If that was so then the panic in the water must have been unnecessary. Jane and Molly, for all their experience of the world at large, had plunged like porpoises at the first sight of the opposite sex.

Pleasing as that recollection was, it did not alter the fact that Harriet was marooned without her clothes, wet and shivering on a small island in the Thames.

Well, she would look upon it as a test of character. 'A teacher must be equal to each situation, however unpredictable,' Miss Plummer frequently reminded her students, although the Plum's wildest vision of the unpredictable was walking into a classroom and finding no chalk there. Resolutely, Harriet heaved herself on to the island, a narrow strip entirely covered by reeds, waist-high. Some small creature scuttled into the water, putting her nerves to the test at once. Harriet crossed the spine of the eyot with the high, fastidious steps of a wading bird, and entered the water on the other side.

A channel no more than fifteen feet in width separated her from the river bank. Feeling no excessive pressure from the current, she ventured to the level of her thighs and found she could reach the bough of an overhanging willow. She twisted it round her wrist, took a deep breath and set off for the opposite bank with all the strength she had left. At its deepest point the water reached her chin, but she gripped the willow tightly and kept moving until she was clear and safely up the bank.

There, another test of character awaited her. She found as she stood upright that her way was obstructed by an uncountable number of thin metal struts radiating from a common centre. It was like looking into an ornamental bird-cage large enough to house a peacock, but the creature on the other side was not feathered or exotic: it was a policeman, shining his bull's-eye lantern through the fore-wheel of a penny-farthing bicycle.

CHAPTER FOUR

A towpath dialogue—Short digression on diabolical practices—A constable's consideration

'Would you be requirin' assistance, miss?' he gently inquired in the dialect rarely heard by the sheltered community at Elfrida College.

'Oh!' Her hands moved with a speed that would have drawn a cry of admiration from a drill-sergeant. 'It would oblige me if you would point your lantern in some other direction.'

'Certainly, miss. Been swimmin', have you? 'Tis nothin' unusual to drift downstream a little. Where are you from?'

She hesitated, reluctant to throw herself on

his mercy, but recoiling from telling a lie to the law. Candour triumphed. 'I belong to the training college. I was taking a midnight bathe. My clothes are half a mile that way.' She indicated the direction with a small movement of her head.

'Then you'd better put my tunic about you. 'Tis a tidy walk from here.' He set down his bicycle and lamp and began unfastening buttons. 'That's Medmenham Abbey behind me,' he said. 'You'll no doubt have heard of the Hell Fire Club of a hundred years ago. They were a prime set of rogues, they were. We remember 'em in these parts—Sir Francis Dashwood and that John Wilkes and Members of Parliament comin' here regular from Westminster. There, put that round your shoulders, miss. Yes, when I saw you climbin' up that bank I don't mind admittin' the thought crossed my mind that you were the tormented spirit of some poor village girl, taken advantage of by those wicked rascals. Would you permit me to accompany you, miss?'

It seemed a superfluous question when she was wearing his tunic, but he must have asked it out of courtesy. He was a singularly considerate constable, standing in the moonlight in his braces with his bull's-eye pointing discreetly at the ground. And he looked not many years older than she.

'I shall feel the safer for your company,

Officer.'

He left the bicycle on the grass, explaining that he would collect it later when he returned to his vigil. There had been reports that night fishing was going on and he was deputed to investigate.

'I did notice three men in a boat, but I don't believe I saw fishing-rods,' said Harriet. She was feeling more comfortable in the tunic, which she wore like a cloak. It extended past the middle of her thighs.

'What sort of boat was it, miss?'

'Oh, a rowing-boat, a skiff, I believe. Two men were rowing and the third was seated facing them. They had a dog with them. They didn't look like poachers.'

'You can't tell, miss. They might have been trailing nets.'

Even in her moment of greatest alarm this was not a thought which had occurred to Harriet. Imagine becoming entangled in their net! Things could certainly have turned out worse than they had. If the constable's tunic had been only a foot or two longer, or, better still, if he had been wearing a greatcoat, the walk along the river bank might have been quite agreeable. He was a tall young man and he moved with a confident air, one hand gripping his braces and the other pulling aside occasional branches that overhung their route.

It occurred to Harriet that if night fishing was illegal, naked bathing was probably against the law as well. She wondered whether the constable proposed to make an arrest. It seemed to matter less than the reception awaiting her at College. Expulsion was inevitable, for what was 'indecorous or unladylike conduct' if it was not coming back in the small hours dressed only in a policeman's tunic? She would surely become a legend among the students, but she would never become a teacher.

She stole a glance at his face. He still had an accommodating look. Perhaps it was the way his moustache curled at the ends. No, she could see his eyes quite clearly in the moonlight and they twinkled with good humour, like her Papa's. They must be blue, she decided.

'I shall be in fearful trouble.'

'Why is that, miss?' He was genuinely surprised.

'We are not supposed to go out. It was a madcap adventure. I was dared to do it, you see. When Miss Plummer finds out—'

'Miss Plummer?' His accent made the name quite sweet to the ear.

'Our principal.'

'Why should she find out, miss?'

'Aren't you taking me back to the College?'

'You ain't in custody, miss.' He smiled. 'If you got out without that lady knowin' it, I dare say you can get in again. I'll just walk along with you and make sure your clothes are still where you left them. When we get there I'll turn the other way and you can return my tunic and I'll make my way back to Medmenham. I've no mind to disturb your principal's sleep, any more than you have, miss. Besides, I wouldn't know what to say to the lady. After all, I don't even know your name.'

'Thank you.'

They walked the next two hundred yards in silence. Then she put her hand lightly on his sleeve.

'It's Harriet Shaw.'

CHAPTER FIVE

Penny-farthing shocker—Before the Plum—Something rather horrid

'Harriet! Here comes your policeman, riding up the drive on his bicycle.'

'Let me see!' cried Jane, at the landing window before Molly had completed her announcement. 'My word, Harriet, he is a cut above the average. Look at the way he rides—that straight back, like a Prussian. Is it really your policeman? What a perfectly ravishing moustache! Why do you suppose he's here?'

If Harriet had known the answer to that, she would not have turned so pale. Two days after the episode in the river she had begun to hope that she might have got away with it. The Plum had not said a word, nor even looked more disagreeable than usual, although the rest of the College had been buzzing with the story, amended slightly under the influence of good taste and girls' adventure stories. There was not one inmate of Elfrida who had not pictured herself plucked from the roaring weir by Harriet's policeman, wrapped in his enormous cape, carried to safety and dosed with a strong-tasting restorative from a hip-flask.

And now her rescuer, who had given his word not to speak to Miss Plummer about what had happened, was riding up to the front door as coolly as the catsmeat boy.

'He *is* the same one, isn't he?' demanded Jane, pink with excitement.

Harriet admitted that he was.

'Marvellous! Why don't you lean out and wave to him?'

'Let's not forget who we are,' cautioned Molly. 'Besides, it might cause an accident, surprising a bicyclist like that. You're too impulsive, Jane. I don't suppose his visit has anything to do with Harriet. The gardener must have been intemperate again in Henley last night.'

Jane pointed dramatically along the drive. 'And do you suppose that this is the gardener being driven home in a growler?'

Their faces pressed to the window and watched a four-wheeled cab follow the wide curve of the drive and stop below them, almost out of view. Its connection with the policeman was made clear at once. Two bowler hats emerged and approached the helmet, all that was visible from this angle of the hero of Hurley Weir. Words were exchanged, impossible to hear, but suggestive of a prior arrangement. Fully a minute passed before the doorbell rang.

'I believe he is going to tell Miss Plummer everything,' said Harriet, sounding disturbingly like a clairvoyant. 'Those men know all about it and they have come to make sure nothing is left out.'

'Harriet, what an appalling thought!'

Jane had lost her colour completely. 'He doesn't know about us—Molly and me—does he? You didn't tell him there were three of us in the river?'

'I told him I was bathing alone.'

'You wouldn't say anything to the Plum yourself, would you?'

Her fellow-conspirators waited, fingering their necks, for their reprieve.

'No.'

There followed one of the more uncomfortable intervals in Harriet's life. Sensing her ordeal, the others talked of other things, as wardresses do in the condemned cell, but each time a door opened anywhere in the house the conversation faltered.

Crocker, the Plum's personal maid, delivered the summons after forty minutes. 'Begging your pardon, miss, the Principal wishes you to come to her study immediate.'

Sympathy mingled with awe surrounded Harriet as she stepped downstairs. At the Plum's door she drew a deep breath, thought of all the Tudors and Stuarts who had faced the headsman with dignity, and knocked once.

'Enter.'

She had been in the study just once before, on her first day at College, and then it had looked more roomy, possibly because it was not full of large men. The two who had arrived by cab were seated in leather armchairs flanking Miss Plummer's desk. The bowler hats rested catlike on their knees. Harriet's constable was standing rigidly to the right, next to a Chinese screen depicting a stag-hunt.

Her worst intimations were confirmed at once.

'Is this the girl, Constable?' the Plum asked in a voice of doom.

The quickness of his glance showed how ill at ease he was. 'It is, ma'am.'

'You could not be mistaken?'

'No, ma'am.'

'Then it seems that the mistake is mine. I reposed my trust in you, Harriet Shaw, and I am advised that you betrayed it by breaking bounds last Tuesday night. Is this correct?'

'Yes, Miss Plummer.'

Miss Plummer closed her eyes. 'Is it also true that you put your life and the good name of the College at risk by recklessly plunging into the River Thames?'

'Quite true, I am afraid.'

The eyes opened. 'What were you wearing at the time?'

'Nothing, Miss—'

The policeman firmly interjected. 'Nothing liable to cause offence to passers-by, ma'am, if that was what you were thinkin'.'

Whatever Miss Plummer was thinking, she was determined to investigate the matter at source. 'Do you possess a bathing dress, Harriet?'

The person to her right shifted in his chair. 'With respect, ma'am, we haven't time to go into the contents of Miss Shaw's wardrobe. You seem to have established that she was the young lady Constable Hardy came across on Tuesday night and now I propose to put some questions to her. With your permission, I hope.'

The speaker's tone left no doubt that his hope was Miss Plummer's command.

'If that is what you wish. The girl is at your disposal. Harriet, these gentlemen are going to speak to you about something rather horrid that has occurred in our locality. Please answer them truthfully. They are detectives from Scotland Yard, Sergeant Cribb and Constable

Thackeray.'

CHAPTER SIX

Introducing Sergeant Cribb—The hand in the weir—Harriet in custody

Scotland Yard detectives. Harriet knew she had broken the rules, but this was going rather far, even for the Plum. Sergeant Cribb, the one who had spoken, turned in her direction. 'I think you should sit down, miss.'

The other detective stood up and she took his place in the armchair and faced Sergeant Cribb. In profile he reminded her of Portugal, sharp-featured with an imperfect line to the nose. She often saw people as maps, and maps as people. It was a useful faculty she intended to pass on in the classroom, if ever she got into one. His full face was more northern in character, long and somewhat lined by glaciation, with side-whiskers, like Norway. She was not good at estimating men's ages, but she supposed he had reached what her mother called the dangerous time of life. His eyes certainly had the glitter of a man confident in his exchanges with the opposite sex and his clothes showed indications of being chosen with some thought to the impression he would make.

'I want to tell you something at the start, Miss Shaw. You've every right to think that Constable Hardy over there—' he turned a finger at Harriet's policeman without looking at him—'has broken a promise he made to you. And so he has. It's put you in a very difficult position. Constable Hardy isn't going to blame you in the least if you set about him, pummel him all over and lead him round the room by the ends of his moustache. He's mortified with shame, is Hardy.' Sergeant Cribb this time turned to regard the constable, who was staring dolefully in the direction of the wall opposite. 'Now you might be thinking, Miss Shaw, that Hardy lightly disregarded that promise. Not so.' The sergeant moved forward confidentially. 'He's like a cracker on Christmas Day, miss. Torn clean in two. It was his duty as a police officer against his promise to you. Terrible conflict. Duty prevailed.' Sergeant Cribb spread his hands eloquently. 'And that's why we're here.' He immediately countered the callousness of this by holding up a cautionary finger. 'I think you will discover that Hardy ain't the scoundrel you take him for. There were circumstances, miss. Circumstances.' He glanced in Miss Plummer's direction. 'May I speak plain, ma'am?'

Miss Plummer lifted her shoulders a fraction. 'Say whatever you like. A girl who brazenly leaves the protection of this house in the middle of the night to bathe in the river is not likely to be shocked by anything you may tell her.'

'A point I hadn't considered, ma'am. Well, Miss Shaw, there's reason to suppose that at about the time you were taking to the water a rather ugly crime was taking place not far away. It was brought to the attention of the police on Wednesday morning. The lock-keeper at Hurley was crossing the weir bridge at a quarter to seven when he noticed an obstruction caught against the paddles. It looked to him like a sack of rubbish, and he went to fetch his boat-hook to try and work it clear. He was making his way back along the bridge looking for the spot, when it was marked for him in a somewhat unexpected manner. A human hand and arm rose out of the water and stayed there with fingers spread, as rigid as a post. His sack of rubbish was a corpse. The current must have shifted it slightly against the paddles and brought the hand jutting out as if it were alive. Would you like a glass of water, miss? Well, I think *I* would. I've been talking far too much. If it could be arranged, Miss Plummer . . .'

The Principal left the room frowning.

'Now,' said Cribb to Harriet. 'You must be quick, miss. You saw some men, I understand.'

'Men?'

'The men who startled you.'

'Oh,' said Harriet. 'The men in the boat.'

'How many, miss?'

'Three—and a dog.'

'What sort of boat?'

'A long rowing boat of the sort people hire at Henley. Two of them were rowing and the third was sitting facing them. There was a large amount of luggage behind him, enough for a trip of several days, I should imagine.'

'Make a note, Thackeray. Double-sculled skiff. The rowers—did you see their faces, miss?'

'Not at first. They had their backs to me, you see. But they were beginning to draw level and I did glimpse the sides of their faces before I got into difficulties in the water. One was wearing a cap and the other a straw hat. The one in the cap was very like the Gulf of Bothnia.'

'The what, miss?'

'The Gulf of Bothnia, between Sweden and Finland. Studying maps is my favourite pastime and I can remember people best by comparing their outlines with what I have in my atlas. The man in the hat was taller and leaned back a long way, like the Persian Gulf. Are you familiar with its shape?'

'I can't say I am just now, miss. Would *you* remember these men if you saw them again?'

'I think I should if I saw them in their boat. I'm less confident about the third, the man facing them. His outline was difficult to distinguish from the cushions.'

'But you're sure it was a man? It's usually a

lady's privilege to be rowed.'

'It was a man. No lady would recline in quite the attitude this person did.'

'Was it after the manner of Japan, miss?' hazarded Cribb.

Harriet brought her hands together with a small clap. 'You have it exactly!' She was beginning to respect this sergeant from Scotland Yard who could dismiss the Plum so easily and understood the principle of recognizing people as maps. 'And do you actually suspect these men of having something to do with the body at Hurley Weir?'

'Difficult to say, miss. I can't discount it as a possibility. Did you'—Sergeant Cribb tapped his forehead gently with his fingers—'did you say there was a dog, miss?'

'Indeed, yes. A fox terrier. That's a breed I can easily recognize. We kept one at home before Mamma got the French poodle. Rex was so much more dependable than Alphonse.'

'Fox terrier.' As Cribb thoughtfully repeated the information, Miss Plummer returned, followed by Crocker bearing a tray with a jug of water and four glasses. Cribb filled one for himself. 'Most hospitable of you, ma'am. You're sure you won't, Miss Shaw?'

Harriet declined.

'Well, Miss Plummer,' he went on. 'This has been most valuable. If the rest of your young ladies are as sharp-eyed as Miss Shaw, there won't be much that escapes them in their school-rooms. Not like that unfortunate woman entrusted with *my* education. It makes me wince to think of the things we got up to behind our slates.'

The revelations this promised struck no chord with Miss Plummer. 'Do you have the information you came for?'

'As much as I can get at this stage, ma'am. I shan't take up any more of your time. The water was excellent. Sweeter to the taste than river water, I should think, Miss Shaw.'

Harriet nodded, unable to bring herself to smile, knowing that as soon as the policemen left she had to face the cross-examination, summing-up and sentence.

Her apprehension must have communicated itself to Cribb. He paused at the door, already held open by Miss Plummer. 'A word, outside, if you please, ma'am.' When she had made a sound of impatience and complied, he asked, 'What do you propose to do about Miss Shaw?'

'That is a matter I shall have to consider. I do not think it is any concern of the police, if I may say so.'

'On the contrary, Miss Plummer. The girl's a witness. What she saw may be important. I need to know exactly what happens to my witness. You wouldn't be proposing to send her away from here, by any chance?'

Miss Plummer's lips came tightly together, exhibiting a new arrangement of wrinkles. 'The procedure when a student commits a flagrant breach of the rules is to suspend her forthwith, pending a decision which must be confirmed by the governors—almost certainly expulsion in this case.'

Cribb had put up his forefinger before Miss Plummer finished speaking. 'That's my point, ma'am. You suspend my witness and what happens to her?'

'I inform the parents as a matter of course and the girl is collected and taken home within a day or two. In Harriet's case this will not be possible, as Colonel and Mrs Shaw are not in England at present. I shall therefore confine her to her room. A student under suspension must have no communication with other members of the College.'

'How very fortunate!' said Cribb. 'I was just about to say that justice would be served by Miss Shaw being committed to my care for the next few days. It will save you all the trouble of confining her, because that's exactly what I shall be doing.'

Miss Plummer looked doubtful. 'I don't think I could agree to that. I am responsible to her parents.'

'That's a terrible responsibility when the girl is the principle witness in a murder case, ma'am,' said Cribb. 'The newspapers will be on to this by tomorrow, you may depend on that. They'll want to interview the girl and sketch her, full face and profile. You too, I shouldn't wonder.'

'Oh!' gasped Miss Plummer.

'And once the pictures are in the paper,' Cribb continued with a long-suffering sigh, 'it means we'll have to have a squad of constables on duty here protecting Miss Shaw. There's always a possibility of the murderers returning to silence the witness, you understand.'

Miss Plummer closed her eyes and swayed slightly.

'So in all the circumstances it might be wiser if I took Miss Shaw along with me, don't you think?' said Cribb.

Miss Plummer wrung her hands in anguish. 'I really don't know whether such a thing is proper.'

Cribb's eyebrows peaked in surprise. 'Not proper? Not proper to assist a police officer in the execution of his duty?'

'How do I know she will be safe?'

In a confidential tone Cribb said, 'I've guarded the Sovereign herself in my time, ma'am. Have no fears about that. Go back into the room now and tell her you're suspending her and committing her into my custody. She has half an hour to pack her things. We shall leave by the front door'—he drew out his watch—'at half past eleven. Just think of the effect it will have on the other students.'

CHAPTER SEVEN

The Bushman of the Yard—Literary pursuits of the police—Concerning the corpse

That was how Harriet found herself bowling along the Henley road in a growler in the company of three policemen. Her travelling-bag sat importantly on the roof—privileged treatment, because P.C. Hardy's bicycle, which *could* have been strapped up there, was left behind, propped against the gardener's shed. Sergeant Cribb had made a pointed remark about the pace of life in the country and indicated with a jerk of his thumb that he wanted the constable to travel with the rest of the party in the cab. The bicycle had not been mentioned. It said much for P.C. Hardy's judgement, in Harriet's view, that he did not contest the point.

She was seated next to Cribb, with the two constables opposite: a daunting experience considering that Miss Plummer allowed no member of the opposite sex except the Vicar of Henley into the same room with her students. It would have been gross bad manners to stare out of the window for the whole of the journey, however, but unendurably embarrassing to have caught P.C. Hardy's eye (for he seemed determined *not* to look out of the window), so when she shifted her gaze from the beech trees it turned without deviation to Constable Thackeray. And, most unusually when she first examined a face, the image that came to her was not from her atlas but her geography textbook, which had a frontispiece, illustrating the multiformity of facial characteristics throughout the world. There was a striking resemblance between Constable Thackeray and *Bushman, New Guinea.* Harriet had never been quite sure whether 'bush' referred to the man's prodigious growth of whiskers or the sparse vegetation in the background. But Scotland Yard was quite the equal of New Guinea in growth of beard. Thackeray had the same broad forehead, shaggy eyebrows and generously proportioned ears, and if he lacked the finishing touch of a quill through his nostrils, at least he sported a fine brown bowler hat with a curly brim. Harriet decided she would not be intimidated by a set of whiskers. The face behind them was probably quite as jolly in reality as *Esquimau, North America.*

'Have you read it yet?' Sergeant Cribb asked unexpectedly.

After reflection, Thackeray replied, 'Read what, Sarge?'

'*Three Men in a Boat.* Appeared this summer. Popular book. You see it on the bookstalls at every London terminus.'

'I've heard of it.'

'I have, too,' contributed P.C. Hardy.

'What about you, Miss Shaw?' asked Cribb, ignoring such meagre responses. 'Student like yourself must read books by the dozen.'

Harriet shook her head. 'Nothing like that, I'm afraid. Miss Plummer regards books you can buy on railway stations as unsuitable. Somebody came back after the Christmas vacation with *Dr Jekyll and Mr Hyde* and there was the most frightful scene.'

'Pity,' said Cribb. 'I was hoping to have a profitable discussion on the subject. Well-written book, too. I'm surprised not one of you has read it.' He turned his head to look out of the window, as if having taken the cultural pulse of his fellow-travellers, he had decided he would be better employed looking at trees.

Thackeray cleared his throat to speak and, unless Harriet were mistaken, winked at the same time. 'Perhaps you could tell us what it's about Sarge. Just the outline of the story, like. We'd appreciate that.'

Cribb returned a sharp look. 'Three hundred pages, with illustrations? I haven't time for that. You must read it for yourselves. I'll tell you one thing, though. There's a dog in it.'

'So there is!' confirmed Hardy. 'I've seen the picture on the cover—a silhouette with two men rowin' and the third takin' his ease on the cushions smokin' a pipe. The dog is sittin' at the front.'

'In the prow,' said Cribb curtly. 'The author is Mr Jerome K. Jerome.'

'That's right,' said Hardy. 'That's on the cover, too.'

Thackeray, who plainly knew the limit of Sergeant Cribb's tolerance, quickly put in, 'Is it a true story, Sarge?'

Instead of attacking Hardy, Cribb rounded on his assistant. 'That's not a question you should put to me, Thackeray. Only Mr Jerome himself can answer that. If I was so incautious as to say it was true, it wouldn't be admissible evidence, and you as an officer of the law shouldn't place any reliance upon it. However'—the sergeant's tone mellowed a little—'it's a question which indicates that you've applied your mind to recent events, and that's to be welcomed. No doubt you were pondering the significance of the three men in a boat seen by Miss Shaw on Tuesday night.'

'To say nothing of the dog,' added Thackeray.

'That's part of the title!' exclaimed Hardy in some excitement.

Cribb eyed him witheringly. 'What do you suggest I do—arrest Mr Jerome K. Jerome?'

Harriet spoke: 'How can you be sure that there is any connection at all between the three men I saw and the unfortunate man at Hurley Weir?'

'Can't be sure, miss,' said Cribb, 'but there

are certain indications. Circumstantial evidence, we'd say. The doctors tell me that the man at Hurley died from drowning. Now, that's nothing unusual in a corpse taken from the Thames.'

'It nearly happened to me.'

'So I believe, miss. But, as I understand it, you were in the water because you chose to be. You weren't wearing any—that is to say, many clothes. The man in the water was fully dressed down to his boots. It's a wonder the boots stayed on, because they had no proper laces. He was a vagrant, miss, a gentleman of the road, to coin a phrase. We haven't identified him yet. Aged about forty-five, although he looks older—they always do. Good physique. Hands and feet a bit weathered. I'm not distressing you, am I? Not so different, as I say, from scores of other corpses we take from the river every month. Some of 'em get in by accident—drunks falling off the Embankment and the like—and some are suicides and I dare say there's a few that are helped in. They're mostly derelicts and one more wouldn't have brought me here from Scotland Yard except for some uncommon circumstances. You see, he was taken from the water within six hours or seven hours of his death, and there were signs of violence on his body. Bruising round the shoulders: the clear marks of a hand on the nape of his neck, as if somebody had held him face down in the water.'

'But who would want to drown a tramp?' asked Harriet.

'Someone with a grudge, perhaps. Another tramp, maybe. There's a complicated code of conduct among 'em. Or it could be someone from his past—the life he chose to turn his back on. He might have taken to the roads to escape from somebody. We shan't know the answer until we can identify him. One thing's certain: the motive wasn't theft. When he was taken from the water he still had a packet containing almost three hundred pounds in banknotes.'

'A tramp, with *that* money?'

'They aren't all paupers, miss. It isn't only want of funds that can drive a man out of his home. What surprises me isn't that he had the money; it's that his killers left it on him.'

'Did he carry any papers or things that might help you to identify him?'

'Like a set of visiting-cards? No, miss. A knife, some matches and a clay pipe. It won't be easy. That's why we're here from Scotland Yard—Thackeray and me, that is. P.C. Hardy's here because he bumped into you on the night in question. Or did you bump into him? Never mind. What matters is that he was smart enough to put two and two together. When I picked him up at Medmenham this morning he was ready to tell me about his meeting with you and what you said about the three men. It wasn't easy for him, mind. It was breaking a confidence and he didn't do it lightly, but the capital crime was involved, Miss Shaw, the capital crime. I hope you don't blame him in any way.'

'Oh, I don't.' Harriet hazarded a tiny glance at P.C. Hardy and noticed the relief dawning on his face.

'That's good, miss,' Cribb went on, 'because we need your co-operation and I'm proposing to use Hardy on the case.'

'But what else is there that I can do? I've told you all that I saw, and that wasn't much.'

'We'll need you to identify those men, miss. I expect to find 'em before too long.'

Brave words, but Harriet was less confident. 'Surely they will be miles away by now, and in three different directions if they have any sense.' Privately she was doubtful whether they had any connection with the dead tramp.

'I'm not convinced that these particular gentlemen have much sense,' said Cribb. 'They left three hundred pounds on the body, remember. That's shocking carelessness. And, of course, they don't know that the body was picked up so quick, or that you saw them on their boat on Tuesday night. I think there's a good chance that they're still on the river somewhere, paddling innocently along like the three men in Mr Jerome's book. The boat was stacked up as if for a trip of several days, you said.'

'Yes, there was a considerable pile of luggage at the rear of the boat, covered by something—a tarpaulin, I suppose. Oh.' A particularly unpleasant possibility occurred suddenly to Harriet and interrupted her answer.

'What is it, miss?'

'The luggage. You don't suppose it could have been something else under the tarpaulin?'

Cribb shook his head firmly. 'No, miss. All the signs are that he wasn't killed before he was put into the water. There was a struggle. I think the luggage was exactly what you supposed at first—hampers and bags with food and clothes. They're on a trip just like the three men in a boat. They've even brought a dog to make it complete. In the course of their trip they've killed a tramp. It's my job to discover why.'

'You seem so certain that these men are murderers,' said Harriet. 'It worries me. They may be innocent. I should hate to be responsible for their arrest and find that it is all a mistake. There isn't anything to connect them with the tramp except that they were on the river the same night.'

'Not quite true, miss,' said Cribb. 'There's something else I haven't mentioned yet. Before I called at your college this morning I made another call, to the mortuary at Henley. They wheeled the body in for me to look at—

begging your pardon, miss. I saw the bruises the local force identified, mainly round the shoulders and neck, as I mentioned. Then something else took my eye. Some marks on the right leg, the fleshy part of the calf, two small crescents of marks facing each other. The skin was broken, but there couldn't have been much bleeding, so it's no wonder the local lads missed it on a rather hairy leg. A dogbite, miss, made by a dog of medium size, I'd say. Could be a fox terrier.'

CHAPTER EIGHT

A slight hassle at Henley—Transformation scene—All aboard

They called at Henley police station, as Cribb loftily explained, to receive the latest intelligence on the case from the local force. 'Although it's debatable which is the local force. Three counties are involved. The body was found at Hurley and that's in Berkshire. They took it to the nearest mortuary at Henley, which is Oxfordshire. Constable Hardy here, and you, Miss Shaw, come from Buckinghamshire. So which county force do you think should take the case? The three chief constables were about to settle it with pistols when some sharp lad remembered that the Thames itself is under Metropolitan jurisdiction, so they gave the job to Scotland Yard. Convenient for everyone but Thackeray and me.'

The desk sergeant was seated against a backcloth of notices describing the penalties for a range of offences from furious riding to harbouring thieves. Harriet thought him admirably calm for one in such dangerous employment. The unconcern was apparent in his responses to Sergeant Cribb. 'Yes, we combed the riverbank as you asked, right along the Reach as far as Hambleden and we might as well have saved our perishing time. Twenty men diverted from their normal duties! Only Scotland Yard or Drury Lane would dare stage a pantomime like that.'

'You found nothing?' Cribb tersely asked.

'Not as much as a perishing duck. No abandoned boat and nobody who remembered hiring one to three men and a dog. I hear that the Buckinghamshire lads have done no better. Don't know how many men they were using, but it's the devil of a lot of public money to go on a dead tramp.'

'A set of killers,' said Cribb.

'All right. A set of—'

'—who might very likely kill again if nobody stops 'em. I haven't time nor patience to bandy words with you, Sergeant. Are the things ready as I asked?'

The desk sergeant gave a grudging nod.

'In that case,' said Cribb, turning to Harriet, 'I shall be compelled to commit you to this officer's care for a few minutes, Miss Shaw. The constables and I have something to attend to that won't take long, but can't be done in the presence of a lady. I suggest you sit behind the door there. You might be offered a cup of tea if there's enough public money left to pay for it.'

So she sat in the chair Cribb had indicated and listened to the sergeant complaining that if the duty constable hadn't been redeployed to the perishing river bank there would be somebody to make the perishing tea. She got a cup nevertheless and the dissent was presently cut short by the entrance of a butcher whose plaster pig had been removed from outside his shop by two small boys. It took the sergeant eleven minutes by the clock over the door to establish the facts and reassure the butcher that as soon as the perishing station was back to strength an investigation would be put in train.

Then Cribb and his two assistants emerged from the door beside Harriet and swept the desk sergeant and his problems from her mind. They had completely changed their clothes. Instead of sober brown suits, Cribb and Thackeray wore striped blazers and white flannels. To match the stripes Cribb had a red boating-cap with a peak that lay low against his forehead. Thackeray's was more of a fisherman's hat, white and made of some soft material, with a brim that rested snugly over his whiskers.

The most stunning transformation was Constable Hardy's. When Harriet saw him she blushed again for Tuesday night. The blue serge and helmet had lent a reassuring impersonality to that episode which was shattered by his appearance now in a cream-coloured blazer trimmed with red, matching flannels tied with a silk handkerchief, and a straw boater perched nonchalantly on the back of his head. Was this elegant young man, this masher, the policeman she had run into in the dark? It was unendurable.

Between them Thackeray and Hardy carried a large hamper. Cribb had a picnic-basket in his left hand and a white parasol in his right which he now presented to Harriet. 'Compliments of the Chief Inspector of Henley, miss. It belongs to his daughter. You'll look a picture on the river.'

Whether the boating costumes also were on loan from members of the Henley police and their families Harriet did not inquire. Was it possible that the back room contained a property basket filled with boating attire of all sizes for visiting detectives? Was there a similar basket of bowler hats, umbrellas and dark suits at Scotland Yard? She had never heard of such a thing, but she supposed it would be a closely guarded secret. Actually

Thackeray's flannels, now she observed them more closely, ended some inches above his ankles, which looked slightly odd, even for going on the river. But the others could not be faulted.

They set off along the High Street in the direction of the Thames, Cribb accompanying Harriet, and the two constables following with the hamper. She was not in a position to judge whether they *walked* like policemen, but other people in the street appeared entirely unsuspicious and incurious. Boating parties were not worth a second glance in Henley.

On one matter she was unshakably resolved: she would not ask Sergeant Cribb the purpose of this charade. If he did not choose to explain his intentions she did not propose to give him the satisfaction of being asked. She had not known the man long, but he was obviously the sort who gave nothing away unless it suited him, and enjoyed the sensation of power his reticence gave him. He was civil enough, she admitted, and he had got the better of Miss Plummer, which was no mean feat, but that did not give him the right to assume Miss Plummer's authority over her. If she could have been sure he was correct in his suspicions about the three men she had seen, she might have respected him more, but she was not. Sergeant Cribb would need to find something more remarkable than a dogbite before he convinced Harriet Shaw that she had seen a boatful of murderers.

At the landing-stage a brown-skinned man with a peaked cap met them, took the picnic-basket from Cribb and led them to where a skiff was tied up. Harriet's travelling-case was already aboard. She had forgotten its existence in all the excitement at the police station and was astonished to see it lying in the boat behind the seat as if it belonged there. It did not require much in the way of deduction to establish how it had got there, but the planning in all this was beginning to impress her.

As the hamper was taken on board, the stern dipped an inch or two lower in the water. Thackeray deposited himself on the seat at the opposite end and restored equilibrium. Hardy was next aboard, taking the position of stroke. Then Cribb stepped down and handed Harriet to her seat while the boatman held the skiff steady with his boathook.

She had not even put up the parasol when Cribb arrived without warning beside her on the seat, in such inescapable proximity that their hips touched. She gave a small squeak at the contact.

'I didn't mean to alarm you, miss. It's the last seat left on the boat. Shall we draw the rug over your knees, or will you be warm enough?'

'Quite warm enough, thank you.'

CHAPTER NINE

Lunch overboard—Lock-keeper's lament—Three men in a boat

The day was perfect for boating. The Thames stretched ahead like a blue silk ribbon dividing the counties. The skiff cruised through the current at a respectable rate, and if Thackeray's work with the sculls betrayed some inexperience, the splashes did not often carry as far as Harriet and Cribb. Constable Hardy, plainly a practised oarsman, rowed with his eyes fastened on Harriet, obliging her to take an unflagging interest in the scenery along the bank. Sergeant Cribb, who was supposed to be managing the rudder-lines, was deep in *Three Men in a Boat,* a copy of which he had purchased in Henley. For a second reading, it was providing extraordinary amusement.

The agreement was that they would row the mile or so to Marsh Lock and there take lunch. They tied up at one of the posts before the lock gates and Cribb put down his book and began distributing plates with hard-boiled eggs, which proved difficult to control with knife and fork. Two, at least, were lost overboard. The pork-pie was more manageable, but the next course, a Dundee cake, by general consent was consigned to the water and sank like a stone. Thackeray commented that it was a wonder the boat had stayed afloat so long. As compensation a stone jar of beer was provided. Cribb made some remark about the rights of a person in custody and poured Harriet a half-pint glass. It was bitter, but it took away the after-taste of the food.

While Thackeray settled in the bows for a nap and Hardy washed up, Cribb helped Harriet ashore and they approached somebody in shirtsleeves and a white cap who had for some time been eyeing them from a distance.

'Good day to you, lock-keeper,' said Cribb, civilly, but with the air of a man who did not have to do his own rowing. 'Capital for us, this weather, but busy work for you I dare say.'

'It's the job I'm paid to do, sir,' the lock-keeper answered. Something in his tone suggested he was not wholly contented in his work, but Cribb ignored it.

'Interesting occupation, I expect, meeting such a variety of people.'

'I get all sorts, it's true.' The lock-keeper looked Cribb up and down as if he were one of the more remarkable specimens.

'I was wondering whether you might remember a party coming through in a skiff like ours a day or so ago. Three men together.'

This hopeful inquiry elicited a frown.

'People I'd give something to meet,' Cribb explained, putting his hand in his pockets. 'I heard they were somewhere along this stretch. Thought you might have seen 'em through your lock, one way or the other.'

Far from the hoped-for flash of recollection in the lock-keeper's eye, a disconcerting redness was appearing at the edges.

'Name of Harris, I suppose, with George and Mr Jerome K. Jerome, to say nothing of a dog. No, they haven't been through, not today, nor last week, nor the week before. They're people in a book and I spend the greater part of my time now telling folks they don't exist, no more than Oliver Twist nor Alice in blooming Wonderland. I'd like to meet Mr Jerome and tell him all the trouble he's caused in my life. This was a tolerable job before that book of his appeared. I don't get ten minutes to myself now from one day to the next. It's doubled the traffic on the river. Doubled it. They come through here in their hundreds, half of 'em not knowing one end of a boat from the other, all decked up in their flannels and straw hats and asking for glasses of water and things I wouldn't care to mention in present company. I don't know what they think a lock house is. I shan't stand it much longer. My wife's threatening to leave. I can tell you, when she goes, so shall I, and they can go over the blooming weir to Henley for all I care.'

'I wasn't talking about the book,' said Cribb,

keeping his copy tactfully out of sight behind his back. 'I simply wanted to know if you remembered letting three men through your lock. The book has nothing to do with it.'

There was a pause while the lock-keeper considered whether such an unlikely claim could have an iota of truth in it. He looked along the river and said, 'It's novices that cause the trouble. They read the book and before they've finished a couple of chapters they're down at Kingston hiring a skiff. They throw in a tent and some meat pies and away they go just like them three duffers in the book. If they survive the first night at Runnymede, they spend the second in the Crown at Marlow—them that can get in—and next morning they come through here looking for the backwater to Wargrave. "There shouldn't be a lock here," they say. "What's this lock doing in our way? It isn't in the book." "Yes it is," I say. "Marsh Lock. Page 220." The book is generally open on their knees, so they pick it up and frown into it and sure enough they find it mentioned. The reason why they never see it is that the backwater is mentioned *first*, even though it's half a mile upriver from here. And do you think they're grateful when I point it out? Not a bit of it. "Well, if we *must* go through the beastly lock," they say, "you'd better get the gates open or we'll never make Shiplake before dark. When you've done that, be good enough to fetch us some fresh water while we're waiting. Rowing is devilish thirsty work." "So is managing a bloomin' lock," I tell 'em. "You get out and work the paddles for me, and I'll get you your blooming water." That shuts 'em up.'

'I'm sure,' said Cribb. 'But we haven't come to ask for water. Just tell me when you last had three men together through your lock.'

'With a dog,' added Harriet, and realized as she said it that Cribb had not mentioned this because it seemed too much like provocation. She wished she had drunk lemonade instead of beer.

'Three men and a dog,' said the lock-keeper slowly. 'You're asking me, are you?'

'I am indeed,' confirmed Cribb, chinking the coins in his pocket to show good faith.

'Three men and a dog. Three men is quite common,' said the lock-keeper. 'Dogs is not so common. Only your real fanaticals actually go so far as to take a dog along with 'em.'

'But it isn't unknown?'

'Last time were yesterday, towards tea-time. Small white dog, it was, but don't ask me the breed. I don't know a bulldog from a beagle.'

'There were three men, though? Do you remember them?'

'I don't recall things that easy, sir.'

'Sixpence apiece?' offered Cribb.

'For a florin I might remember the name of the boat as well.'

'Done.'

'It were the *Lucrecia.* Neat little skiff built not above a year, I'd say. The wood were light in colour, without many varnishings. Fine set of cushions, too, dark red plush.'

'And the men?'

'You do have that florin with you?'

The exchange took place.

'I reckon the one at stroke weighed all of fifteen stone. Bearded he was, and red-faced. Turned fifty, I'd say, but able to pull a powerful oar just the same. His hair was sandy-coloured and he had bright yellow braces. He were talking plenty, and it didn't seem to matter that the others wasn't listening. The voice matched his build. He'd have passed for a Viking, that one would, if he'd worn a helmet on his head instead of a boater. Sitting at bow was a smaller man. A queer sight they made rowing that skiff. He was dark-complexioned, the small fellow, Jewish if I can spot 'em, and with arms that barely reached the oars. I don't know what difference he was making to the movement of the boat, but he couldn't have got up much of a sweat—begging your pardon, young lady—for he was still wearing his blazer. Oh, and he had pebble-glasses so thick you could hardly see his eyes behind 'em.'

'You've earned your florin already,' said Cribb. 'Do you remember as much about the third man?'

'Most of all, because he was the one that spoke to me as I worked the gates for 'em. A rum cove he was, that one. He didn't talk natural at all. He might have been standing at a pulpit instead of sitting in a boat. "Be good enough to explain, lock-keeper," he said, "why this lock does not appear in our itinerary, which we faithfully compiled from Mr Jerome K. Jerome's celebrated work." I gave him my usual answer and the little man at the bow turned up page 220 and squinted at it. "He's right," he says. "It's here in the book. *We went up the backwater to Wargrave. It is a short cut, leading out of the right-hand bank about half a mile above Marsh Lock.*" "That," says the other, "is of no consequence. It is merely a retrospective reference. If there is a lock here as there appears incontrovertibly to be, then Jerome ought to have mentioned its existence at the appropriate point in the book. The omission is inexcusable." '

'What was his appearance?' Cribb asked.

'For the river on a summer afternoon, very odd, very odd indeed. Pin-stripe suit and grey bowler. He was built on slimmer lines than either of the others, round shoulders and white-faced, with tortoise-shell spectacles and buck teeth. I'd know him again.'

'I can believe you,' said Cribb. 'Did you discover by any chance where they were making for?'

'Haven't I said as much already? They're doing the book, like everyone else. They'll have spent last night on one of the Shiplake islands and today they'll be making for Streatley. They've got two days there. If you're wanting to meet 'em, that's where you'll catch 'em, for sure.'

CHAPTER TEN

Dropping of the pilot—Familiarity in the ranks—How the colour came to Harriet's cheeks

After Marsh Lock the Berkshire bank rises sheerly in a cliff-like formation festooned with ivy and capped with a beech wood. So far Harriet had studied the scenery more from necessity than choice, but momentarily the prospect was so spectacular that she was able to forget Constable Hardy. Then the voice of Sergeant Cribb jolted her out of her reverie.

'You're pulling to port, Constable. I'm trying to steer an even course and you're pulling the blasted thing to port.'

Hardy was quick to apologize. 'I thought we must be goin' by way of Hennerton Backwater. It saves nearly half a mile of rowin'. It's a pleasant way. Plenty of shade.'

Harriet felt obliged to add, 'I seem to remember the lock-keeper mentioning a backwater. To Wargrave, wasn't it? It was the route the characters in the book were supposed to have taken.'

'I can believe that, miss,' said Hardy. 'It's a charmin' little stream. Just right for a small boat, threadin' its way through the rushes and under the trees. If I was writin' a book myself I'd have a chapter on Hennerton Backwater for sure.'

'Well, you're not,' Cribb pointed out. 'You're rowing a boat and you'll take your orders from me.' He gave a tug on the right-hand rudder-line to reinforce the point. 'We shall follow the main course of the river for another mile and then you can put me ashore at Shiplake. I shall pick up a cab at the station and drive to Streatley, where I expect to find the men we're looking for. The rest of you will follow by way of the river, keeping a watch for the suspects in case they're slower than they should be.'

Making it clear from the measured tone of his voice that he was providing information, not criticism, Hardy said, 'It's a good fifteen miles to Streatley.'

'Glory!' said Thackeray from behind him.

'Shan't expect to see you there tonight, then,' conceded Cribb. 'Report to the police station as soon as you arrive tomorrow.'

'Where shall we pass the night?' Thackeray bleakly asked.

'Bottom of the boat. There are cushions to lie on and you can put up the canvas in case it rains. By the time you've rowed a few miles, you won't mind where you sleep.'

Harriet heard this with amazement overflowing into indignation. It was alarming enough to be abandoned to the company of Thackeray and Hardy for the rest of the afternoon, but for Sergeant Cribb blandly to assume that she would spend the night with them at the bottom of a boat was insulting in the extreme. '*They* might not mind, but I most certainly do,' she informed him, dipping the parasol at the same time, so that the others could not see the colour of her cheeks. 'I should like to go back to my college, if you will kindly arrange it.'

'Back to Miss Plummer?' said Cribb.

'Miss Plummer may not hold me in very high regard,' said Harriet with dignity, 'but I am confident that she will offer me a bed for the night when she knows the alternative.'

'I can't let you go back to Miss Plummer, miss. You're still my principal witness and I shall want you to take a look at those men tomorrow. I was about to suggest—before you assumed what you did—that I would book you a room at the Roebuck in Tilehurst. It overlooks the river, so you'll have no trouble finding it. The constables can moor the boat nearby and you'll simply have to step ashore and join 'em again tomorrow morning after breakfast. The Roebuck serves a very good breakfast grill, I'm told. Is that acceptable?'

Cribb had either, as he claimed, planned

this in the first place, or he was a very agile thinker indeed. Since the outcome was satisfactory, she decided to give him the benefit of the doubt. 'But what will the constables have for breakfast?'

'Eggs and bacon,' said Cribb.

'That'll be nice,' said Thackeray, perking up.

'Yes, there's a couple of hard-boiled eggs in the hamper and a slice of pork-pie you can divide between you.'

If Cribb was expecting a chorus of outrage at this, he did not get it. He got a silence that lasted until they reached Shiplake, as though Thackeray and Hardy had agreed to let the remark stand in isolation, parading its meanness. Even at Shiplake they said not a word, and there was a hint of contrition in Cribb's, 'Streatley as soon as you can tomorrow, then,' as he stepped ashore and marched away to look for a cab. Hardy stood in the boat, keeping it against the landing stage with an oar until Cribb's footsteps had receded. Then he doffed his boater ironically in the same direction and pushed powerfully against the oar. The skiff cruised back into the deeper water.

They had not been rowing long when it occurred to Hardy that in Cribb's absence they need not be encumbered with rank. 'My name's Roger,' he announced.

'Ted,' said Thackeray.

'And Miss Shaw's, I learned not long ago, is Harriet,' Hardy volunteered for her.

She blushed, remembering the circumstances.

'That's nice,' said Thackeray. 'You answered the sergeant beautiful, if I may say so, Harriet. He's not an easy man to mix words with.'

'I reckon we got the better of him, between us,' said Hardy. 'By Shiplake he was lookin' a sight less corky than he was at Marsh. He was so quick to step ashore that he left his book behind, did you notice? It's on the seat beside you, Harriet.'

He used her name with a familiarity that disturbed her. The embarrassment would certainly show unless she made a determined effort to overcome it. She reminded herself that he was still a policeman and that his boating costume was just another kind of uniform. She would find it easier to accept if he conducted himself like a policeman, without staring in such a familiar way.

'You're a keen-eyed young fellow, Roger,' said Thackeray. 'I'm sure I didn't notice whether he'd got the book with him. A man of your talents ought to be taking up detective work. Have you never thought of coming to London? There's room at the Yard for anyone who can exercise his optics to good effect.'

'I've no ambition to work for the likes of Sergeant Cribb,' said Hardy.

'Cribb isn't quite so obnoxious when you know him,' Thackeray said for his superior. 'I dare say there's one or two that would run him close here in the Thames Valley. If you're thinking of going into plain clothes I wouldn't let a liverish cove like him put you off.'

'Truth of the matter is that I'm quite content being a country copper,' said Hardy. 'Watchin' out for poachers doesn't have the glamour of stalkin' Jack the Ripper, I know, but it suits me well. I'd rather walk to work through a river mist than a London peasouper, because I know that when that mist clears, Buckinghamshire is the grandest place to pound a beat in the world.'

'Hold on a bit,' said Thackeray. 'You'll have me asking for a transfer.'

'Ah, but it's true. Close your eyes for a moment, Ted. Listen to the birdsong and the water lappin' at the side of the boat and the breeze rustlin' through the beeches. What have you got within five miles of Scotland Yard to compare with it? And that's just the sounds. The sights along the river are a study in themselves, wouldn't you agree, Harriet?'

If it was not calculated to offend, it was an ill-chosen remark, but Harriet took the view that it was blatant provocation. Instead of blushing as she had before, she blanched with fury at the boorishness of this man determined to extract the last ounce of advantage from an incident any gentleman would have banished from his conversation, even if it lingered in his thoughts.

She snapped her parasol shut. 'I may be your prisoner in this rowing-boat, Constable, but that does not give you the right to address me in familiar terms and taunt me with innuendoes. Kindly address me as Miss Shaw if you speak to me again and make certain if you do that you have something civilized to say.' It sounded very like Miss Plummer speaking. Harriet had never reprimanded anyone before, nor realized she could find the words to do it, but Constable Roger Hardy needed to be left in no doubt that he had overstepped the mark. To say that she was disappointed in him was less than the truth. The gallant officer who had lent her his coat on Tuesday night and this buffoon in boating costume were different men. Different men.

The colour had risen to Hardy's cheeks this time. 'I don't see the offence in what I said, Miss Shaw, though I'm sorry if it was there. I was simply invitin' you to confirm that our stretch of the Thames offers finer natural sights than any other. Oh, my Lord!'—Hardy's oars plunged deeply into the water, jerking his arms straight—'I see it all now, miss—I mean—that is to say—I do ask you to forgive me.'

CHAPTER ELEVEN

An extra passenger—Interlude on an island—Pious Jim

There was no need, as it turned out, for Harriet to consider whether she would forgive Constable Hardy, because they had reached Shiplake Lock and the gates were being held open for them. Four or five other small craft were inside and it required total concentration on everyone's part to steer the skiff among them without the rending of wood. Standing up like a gondolier, Hardy paddled them expertly towards the left-hand wall, reached up and fastened the line to a chain. The lock-keeper was already thrusting his back against the beam of the gate behind them to close it. A young man in a yellow blazer was doing the same on the right. When the gates were closed, each man moved to the opposite end and began turning the handles to raise the paddles and fill the lock. Spouts of silver water gushed in, gurgling under the boats as they steadily ascended the gleaming walls.

'How much, lock-keeper?' Thackeray called when the moment came to pay the toll.

'Threepence, sir, but I'll not charge you anything if you'll do me a good turn.'

'What's that?'

'Take my young friend aboard and put him off at Phillimore's Island half a mile upstream.'

Thackeray scrutinized the young man in the yellow blazer. 'Would you mind, Miss Shaw? He'll have to share your seat.'

'I have no objection,' Harriet answered. He looked a clean young man, for all his work on the lock gates. He had a neat little beard the shape of Tasmania at the base of his chin.

'I'll hop in, then,' he said. 'Much obliged to you, young lady. Bustard's the name, spelt with a "u", like the bird. Just as far as Phillimore's, if you'd be so kind, gentlemen. I'm in camp there for the night with a friend of mine, Jim Hackett.'

Harriet drew her skirt across to make room for Mr Bustard and introduced her companions, taking care to prefix 'Mr' to their names.

'Going far?' he inquired.

'We're hoping to reach Reading by this evening,' answered Thackeray. Hardy had lapsed into silence now.

'Not a pretty place to stop,' said Mr Bustard. 'Gasworks and factories. You'd be better off on an island, like us.'

'We intend to pull up as far as Tilehurst,' Thackeray explained. 'Miss Shaw has a room at the Roebuck.'

'You'll be in clover there, my dear,' said Mr Bustard. 'Better than a night under canvas, what? Somebody has a care for your comfort, I can see. If you bear to the right of the island, gentlemen, you'll find I'm moored under a willow. Jim Hackett should be boiling a kettle for tea. That's what I went to Shiplake for.' He tapped his blazer pocket. 'Can't survive without my Indian brew. I cadged a lift on a steam-launch that had taken a mooring on the island. Filthy way to travel—I'm not in favour of steam at all—but beggars can't be choosers, what?' He turned to smile at Harriet and displayed an immaculate set of white teeth. 'This is my ideal—a seat beside a pretty girl and two strapping fellows to do the rowing for us.'

The ends of Hardy's mouth had turned down in a perfect miniature of the central arch of Henley Bridge. And the ends of his moustache curled in precisely the opposite direction. Harriet could not suppress a smile. To avoid embarrassment she turned it on Mr Bustard. 'How long have you been on the island?' she asked.

'Since yesterday. We're doing the Thames by easy stages. Don't know how far we'll get in a fortnight, but the exercise does you good, what?'

Thackeray said, 'I can think of better ways of getting it. I've got a blister the size of half a crown on each hand.'

'Then it's ten to one you're not one of the labouring class,' said Mr Bustard. 'Delicate skin, unused to manual work. Don't tell me.

I'll guess. Shopbroker's clerk. No, I don't see you at a desk. Behind a counter, possibly. Grocer. Yes. I'd buy a dozen eggs from you. I'll go for grocer. Am I right?'

'How did you guess?' said Thackeray, with the resource born of long experience.

'Training,' said Mr Bustard proudly. 'I'm a tallyman myself. You need to be quick on the uptake in my profession.'

'I'm sure,' Thackeray agreed. 'I don't suppose you miss a thing. Come to mention it, I was wondering if you might have noticed a party on the river a few hours ahead of us. Some people we were hoping to come across. Three men in a skiff like this, with a dog.'

'Three men in a boat? You wouldn't be pulling my leg, by any chance, because I wouldn't buy any more eggs from you if you were?' Mr Bustard winked at Harriet.

'No, I'm serious,' said Mr Thackeray.

Mr Bustard trailed his hand thoughtfully in the water. 'Would one be built like Dr Grace, the cricketer—bearded, with a large size in belts?'

'That's right!' said Thackeray.

'And are his companions smaller men, with spectacles?'

'Absolutely correct!' said Harriet, clapping her hands.

'Small white dog?'

'The very same!' said Thackeray.

'Haven't seen 'em,' said Mr Bustard.

There was a pause. Thackeray was the first to say, 'But how the devil did you know—'

'Jim Hackett met 'em this morning when I was cooking breakfast and told me about 'em. Straight out of Jerome K. Jerome, I said. We had a laugh about it. You must meet Jim. You've time for a cup of tea on the island, haven't you?'

As duty obviously required that they meet Jim Hackett, they made the skiff fast beside the one already under the willow, and stepped ashore. They found him squatting beside a small fire not far from the bank, cooking a sausage on the end of a toasting-fork. He got quickly to his feet, putting fork and sausage guiltily behind his back, which looked quaint, because he was built like a barge-horse, with massive shoulders and three inches of height to spare over Thackeray.

'What's this, Jim?' said Mr Bustard. 'This ain't supper-time, you know.'

'How right you are, Percy,' said Jim Hackett. ' "Be sure your sin will find you out." Numbers Chapter 32, Verse 23.'

'He's very knowledgeable about the Good Book,' explained Mr Bustard. 'Never mind Jim. You can eat it cold at the proper time. Has the kettle boiled? That's the question. We've got visitors, as you can see. Miss Shaw, this is Jim Hackett. I wouldn't shake his hand—it's thick with sausage-grease. This is Mr Thackeray, Jim, who is escorting Miss

Shaw and her young man, Mr Hardy, up to Tilehurst. They rowed me up from the lock.'

'Kettle just boiled,' said Jim Hackett, picking it up and thrusting it into the fire. Harriet was relieved not to shake his hand. Besides being very large, it was calloused and, from the slowness of his movement with the kettle, insensitive to heat.

'Do you prepare all your meals like this?' she asked.

'Lord, no, my dear,' said Mr Bustard. 'When we have the chance we buy our creature comforts from riverside inns such as the one you're making for it. It's boiling, Jim. We got a very good veal and ham pie from the George and Dragon at Wargrave on Tuesday evening. Very welcome, veal and ham.'

'Dog and Badger,' said Jim Hackett, removing the kettle from the flames.

'Eh?'

'Dog and Badger, not George and Dragon.'

'If you insist, Jim, old boy, if you insist.'

'There's a Dog and Badger at Medmenham,' said Hardy. 'It's my local pub.'

'It was a spanking pie, wherever it came from,' said Mr Bustard. 'Milk and sugar, Miss Shaw?'

'I believe you spoke this morning to some people we were looking for,' Thackeray said to Jim Hackett. 'Three men in a boat—not to mention a dog.'

'That's right. Helped push them out. Was

they mates of yours?'

'Not exactly,' said Thackeray, who must have seen a glint of menace in Jim Hackett's eye. 'We was told they was ahead of us on the river and we want to find them if we can.'

'They wasn't your sort. Swells, they was. Threw me a tanner piece after I gave 'em a shove.'

'I wonder if we're talking about the same three,' said Thackeray artfully. 'Was one of them a large, bearded cove? Not large by your standard, but just as tall as I am and a sight heavier?'

'One of 'em, yes.'

'And the others?' chipped in Constable Hardy.

'Half-pints. Dressed and talked like they owned the river, but couldn't even push their own bleeding boat out.'

'Language, Jim,' protested Mr Bustard.

'God, I'm sorry, lady,' Jim Hackett told Harriet. ' "Every idle word that men shall speak, they shall give account thereof in the day of judgement." St Matthew Chapter 12, Verse 36.'

'He should have gone into the Church,' said Mr Bustard.

'Did these men say where they were going, by any chance?' Thackeray asked.

'Streatley,' said Jim Hackett. 'They was making for Streatley.'

'They didn't mention where they came

from?'

'They'd been three days on the river. Spent the first night at Runnymede and the second in the Crown at Marlow.'

Later in the afternoon, when they set off again, with Thackeray ostentatiously pushing the skiff away from the bank without assistance, Harriet opened *Three Men in a Boat.* If Jim Hackett's memory of the movements of the suspects was reliable, they were scrupulously faithful to the itinerary of George, Harris and Mr Jerome K. Jerome.

CHAPTER TWELVE

Night thoughts in the Roebuck—Murder and Mr Jerome—Nude with fern

That night, as the rain trickled down the eaves into the guttering of the Roebuck, Harriet returned to *Three Men in a Boat.* Once or twice she laughed until the bed shook. Men stood so much on their dignity; it was comical to think of them out of their element doing ridiculous things. She would have laughed even more if she had not been reading for a serious purpose. She wanted to decide for herself whether there was anything in the book suggestive of murder, as Sergeant Cribb apparently supposed. The more she read, the more difficult it was to conceive of it as a manual for assistance. George, Harris and J making their inexpert way up the Thames with the dog Montmorency were anything but sinister.

The place-names were there, of course—Hurley Weir, Medmenham Abbey, the Backwater to Wargrave and the islands at Shiplake—so recent events impinged a little on her thoughts, even if they seemed remote from the book. The three mysterious men whose arrival on the scene had created such havoc among the bathers on Tuesday night were not so alarming in retrospect, not now she had got to know Mr Jerome's good-humoured trio. To think of them as brutal murderers, callously killing a helpless old tramp and then continuing upriver as if nothing had happened, was difficult in the extreme. Obviously Sergeant Cribb thought otherwise. He had fastened on them as his suspects from the beginning, and the lock-keeper's information that they were following the route in the book had not discouraged him; it had sent him haring off to Streatley to make an arrest.

Tomorrow he would want her to identify them. She shrank from the business, not because she doubted her ability to recognize them, but because of the significance Cribb put upon it. He made no bones about it; identification was tantamount to guilt. If they did not admit it at once he would beat them with a truncheon, or whatever policemen did to extract confessions. He was not a man for refinements; that was obvious from the way he treated his subordinates.

If she had witnessed the murder itself, seen the tramp held under the water until the last bubble of breath had risen to the surface, she would not have hesitated to identify the killers. But all she had seen was three men and a dog in a boat moving serenely towards Hurley, unaware of the confusion in the water. Suppose they were not the murderers; suppose somebody else had killed the unfortunate tramp further up the river. Suppose her testimony sent three innocent men to the gallows. It would always be on her conscience.

Too ridiculous: she was getting morbid. This was not the time to lose a sense of proportion. She returned to her book, to Chapter 16, describing, topically enough, the stretch between Reading and Streatley. Her eyes drifted down the page without the fullest concentration until she came to that '*something black floating in the water*' that George noticed and drew back from '*with a cry and a blanched face*': the dead body of a woman.

Harriet drew the sheet closer round her and read, with wide eyes, how the corpse was consigned without fuss to some men on the bank and how the three in the boat paddled on to Streatley and there lunched at the Bull, their appetites seemingly unimpaired by the experience. She shuddered and closed the book, putting it face down on the table beside the bed. It was not, after all, wholly unsuggestive of sudden death.

She pulled the sheet aside, got out of bed and for a second time checked that the door was bolted from the inside. She took a hairbrush from her travelling-case and sat at the dressing-table, tugging at her hair with short, agitated strokes. For a moment, just for a moment, she wished she were in the boat with the two constables. As company they left something to be desired—more than that, in Hardy's case—but at least she had the measure of them now. Better the devil you know than the devil you don't, as Jim Hackett might have said in the circumstances, probably adding chapter and verse as well.

She tossed her head to shake such silly notions out of it, and wielded the brush more vigorously still.

Of course, it was out of the question to pass the night with Thackeray and Hardy. Goodness, her reputation was in ruins already after Tuesday's episode. It was enough to face Mamma and Papa with *that* when they got back to England. She had been over the scene in her mind a dozen times. Mamma would collapse sobbing into a chair and Papa would pace the drawing room invoking the Almighty and saying he should take a whip to her, but going straight to the whisky instead. Mortifying. To confess after that that she had spent a night sleeping in a boat with two policemen would drive Papa beyond the brink. She could not do it.

Besides, the conditions down there must be insufferable. The canvas was up, admittedly, but it could be counted on to leak, and a night on damp boards was enough to give you rheumatism for life if you did not die of pneumonia within a week. No wonder the constables had spent the entire evening in the public bar.

Not that she pitied them much. Thackeray she had a spark of compassion for—he had not been unkind, and he was rather large to fit into a small boat. She would have preferred to think of Cribb suffering down there, but he was doubtless in a hotel bed himself, the wily man.

Hardy was another matter. It would do that young man no harm at all to suffer some discomfort. His boating clothes would be hideously crumpled by morning and she would leave him in no doubt that she noticed the fact. He might even be a shade more endurable with wrinkles in his trousers. Perhaps it would improve his manner. He had not been so objectionable in uniform; he had behaved quite differently, in fact.

Harriet's brushing became slower, and the

strokes carried to the ends of her hair.

She recollected Tuesday evening. Not the three men in their boat, nor the dangerous time in the water, but the meeting with Constable Hardy. Up to now she had thought of it exclusively from her own point of view.

How must it have seemed to him as he stood shining his bull's-eye lamp through the spokes of his bicycle wheel?

She put down her brush and flicked her now gleaming hair over her shoulders. Then she got up and went to the curtains. Through the rain she thought she could just make out the shape of the skiff with its canvas awning. She closed the curtain carefully, collected the candle from the bedside table and deposited it on the dressing-table to the left of the mirror. From a flower arrangement on the mantelpiece she selected a fern and placed it beside the candle.

She took three steps back from the dressing-table and unfastened the bows at the front of her nightdress so that it parted at the bodice. Watching her movements in the mirror, she guided the garment over her shoulders and allowed it to fall to her feet. Without looking down, she stepped over it and advanced slowly towards the mirror, stooping slightly, as she had when she had climbed the river bank, feeling the movement of her bosom, then straightening as the light caught the bloom of her skin. Her hand reached forward for the fern and held it close to her eyes, so that she could study her reflection through the fronds—the best she could improvise for bicycle spokes. What she saw was neither vulgar, nor offensive, but rather elegant. She thought she might understand the effect it could have on an impressionable young man.

Harriet put down the fern and smiled shyly at her image in the glass before extinguishing the light. She picked up her nightdress, drew it quickly over her head and climbed into bed. She slept well.

CHAPTER THIRTEEN

Thackeray runs out of steam—Hooray for the G.W.R.—A proposition for Harriet

In the morning they pulled up to Streatley, an eight mile row which the constables accomplished in a little over two and a half hours without stops, except for the locks at Mapledurham and Whitchurch, and without much conversation either. Harriet could only suppose that the previous night's sleeping arrangements were responsible, but she deemed it tactful not to inquire, nor did she comment on the breakfast provided by the Roebuck. By the time the bridge connecting Streatley and Goring came into sight she was actually looking forward to Sergeant Cribb rejoining the party.

This proved to be premature, for when they had tied up and found the police station, they were told Cribb had left the town two hours before. 'The gentlemen he was taking an interest in made an unexpectedly early start,' explained the constable on duty. 'He was obliged to board a passenger steamer to pursue them. His instructions are that you are to make the best speed you can and keep your eyes skinned for a sight of the *Lucrecia.*'

'Make the best speed we can!' said Thackeray, wiping his forehead with his soft hat. 'What does he think we are—blooming galley-slaves? Till yesterday I'd never touched an oar in my life—save for a day in Southend—and I reckon we've covered more than twenty miles since Henley. I've got stilts for legs and arms six inches longer than they were, and they're the only parts of me with any feeling left at all. The rest is numb. Make the best speed you can! That's a fine blooming message to leave as you step aboard a steamer, ain't it?'

'We could try drawing the boat with a tow-rope,' Harriet suggested. 'I could take a turn at that. It would give you a change from rowing.'

'A tow from a steam-launch would be more like it,' said Thackeray.

'It happened in *Three Men in a Boat*,' said Harriet. 'They met some friends who pulled them all the way from Reading to within a mile of Streatley.'

'A fat lot of good that is to us,' said Thackeray.

'Now, Ted, that ain't no way to speak to a young lady,' Hardy unexpectedly put in. 'We know you're sufferin', and we're grateful for all the work you've done with the oars, but you've no cause to take it out on Miss Shaw. Matter of fact, she's given me an idea. Do I understand from what you said, miss, that you've read the book now?'

'Yes, I read most of it last night and finished it this morning,' Harriet answered, surprised at Hardy's intervention, and curious where it was leading.

'I can see you wasn't idlin' away your time in the Roebuck, miss,' said Hardy with a glance at Thackeray. 'I wonder if by any chance you remember where the three men in the story made for after they left Streatley.'

'I do. They passed the next night under canvas, in a backwater at Culham.'

'Culham?' vacantly repeated the constable on duty, looking up for the Occurrence Book.

'It might as well be Timbuctoo,' said Thackeray unhelpfully.

'I believe they stopped on the way at a place nearby called Clifton Hampden,' Harriet added. 'The Barley Mow inn came in for special comment, I remember.'

'Very good, miss,' said Hardy, venturing a

smile. 'I think we can take it from what we heard about *our* three men that they'll spend this evening at the Barley Mow too. They sounded most particular about copyin' what happened in the book.' He turned to Thackeray. 'At least we'll get a drink when we get to Clifton Hampden.'

'You'll need one,' said the constable on duty. 'It's fourteen miles from here.'

'Jerusalem!' said Thackeray.

'No, Clifton Hampden.'

Thackeray muttered something inaudible.

'But don't you see?' said Hardy. 'Now we know where we're goin', we needn't go by river at all. We can take a train. If we cross the river to Goring we can catch a slow to Oxford. It'll put us off at Culham Station and we can walk up the road to Clifton Hampden. We might be there before Cribb.'

A moment's silence followed this audacious suggestion.

'Do you think that's wise?' asked Harriet, turning to Thackeray.

'It may not be wise, miss, but it's good enough for me. "Make the best speed you can," he said, and that's what we'll do. There's no better way of making speed than on the Great Western Railway.'

They returned to the boat, crossed the river and found a mooring. Hardy produced a mallet and drove spikes into the bank to secure the boat fore and aft, taking the initiative quite naturally now that his plan was being acted upon. Watching the two men, Harriet understood why Thackeray had never been promoted to sergeant. Subordinate positions undoubtedly suited some people. Hardy, on the other hand, had a personality better fitted for responsibility. There were grounds for supposing that if he were promoted he might lose some of his more objectionable characteristics and even develop into a passable young man.

'We'll take the travellin'-case,' he told Thackeray. 'Miss Harriet will want her things with her at Clifton.'

'That's very considerate,' said Harriet, 'but won't it be awfully heavy to carry? You remarked just now that there is a mile to walk at the other end.'

'No trouble, miss. We'll manage between us. Take the other end, Ted. Hello, that's a familiar blazer out there.'

The others followed the direction of his eyes and saw a skiff steering towards the Goring bank with obvious respect for the foaming water on the weir side. The crew were Mr Bustard still in his blazer, and Jim Hackett in braces. An old sensation of revulsion afflicted Harriet at the sight of them. She supposed the yellow blazer reminded her of her angry mood the previous afternoon, when Hardy had made his tactless remarks and she had rebuked him by taking extra notice of Mr

Bustard. It was a cheap thing to have done, and she would have preferred to forget it.

She was not allowed to.

'It's your friend, Bustard,' Hardy pointed out in an unconvincing attempt to be casual. 'Aren't you goin' to wave to him?'

The fury rose in Harriet like a head of steam. 'Yes, I am,' she said on the impulse. 'Certainly I am.' She stood up in the boat, took off her hat and brandished it like a battle standard. 'Mr Bustard! Mr Bustard! Don't pass us by!'

It was the more infuriating that Hardy took no notice as the skiff changed course and headed towards them. He simply carried on moving the case out of the boat and on to the towpath.

'What a capital surprise!' called Mr Bustard when they came parallel, an oar's length away. 'What do you think of that, Jim? If it isn't the Lady of the Lock herself, the delectable Miss Shaw, with her two sturdy watermen in attendance. Where are you going, Miss Shaw? Not abandoning the trip, I trust. There's nothing wrong, is there?'

Everything was wrong that could be, but Harriet answered, 'No, we have decided to continue our journey by train, that is all.'

'On a day like this? It's criminal to go by train. Look at those hills ahead. Beautiful country!'

'Mr Thackeray and Mr Hardy have done

enough rowing,' said Harriet.

'So that's it. Watermen not so sturdy after all, what? I say, I have a suggestion, my dear. Come aboard with us. Allow me to repay your kindness yesterday. Then if the others go by train they can wait for you further up the river.'

'I couldn't do that,' said Harriet.

'Why not, for goodness' sake?'

'It wouldn't be proper, going on a boat with two gentlemen I hardly know at all.'

'Not so, my dear. Two's quite safe. I wouldn't recommend an outing with one gentleman, but two's a most acceptable arrangement. Besides, I'm a married man, as Jim will testify. He used to work for my father-in-law, a very upright gent. You don't see me doing anything my pa-in-law wouldn't approve of, do you, Jim?'

'Christ, no,' said Jim emphatically.

Harriet was still dubious. 'It's much too far. We have to get to Clifton Hampden.'

'We can make it to Clifton by tonight. What do you say, Jim? Jim can row all day. I might take a rest now and then, but he carries on. Part of his philosophy, you see.'

On cue Jim Hackett quoted his authority, 'Psalm 104, Verse 23: "Man goeth forth to his work, and to his labour until the evening." '

'So it's agreed,' said Mr Bustard. 'We'll come alongside and you can step aboard.'

Harriet stole a glance at Hardy. He was

back on board, putting up the hoops that supported the cover. He appeared to be totally absorbed in the task.

'Could you really take me as far as Clifton?' Harriet asked. 'It's fourteen miles, I'm told.'

'No trouble at all. Stand by to come aboard.'

Hardy's voice, thick and close at hand, muttered, 'Put one foot into that boat, Harriet Shaw, and I'll hump you over my shoulder and carry you to Goring Station myself.'

She was in no doubt that he meant it. There was nothing she could do. Tears of humiliation blurred her vision.

'She has to come with us. We're responsible, you see,' Hardy explained to Mr Bustard, pushing his foot firmly against the skiff as it came alongside. 'Decent of you to offer.'

On the train, twenty minutes later, Harriet's indignity flared into anger. 'I strongly resent the way you spoke to me.'

'I could have lifted you off Bustard's boat without so much as a word, but you wouldn't have thanked me for that,' Hardy quietly answered.

'You seem to presume that you have the right to order my actions.'

'I do, miss, up to a point.'

'Take care what you say, Constable.'

'I shall,' said Hardy.

'I intend to speak to Sergeant Cribb about you. I shall tell him that you threatened me with physical violence.'

'And I shall tell him what you were proposin' to do, miss.'

'It was nothing criminal. I have the right to accept a perfectly proper invitation from a gentleman, do I not?'

'Not while I'm responsible for you,' said Hardy.

'You are not my chaperone.'

Here Thackeray judged it right to intervene. 'It was for your own good, miss. I don't think those two are quite what they may appear.'

'Neither are you, come to that,' said Harriet, glancing contemptuously at his ill-fitting flannels. 'But at least they know how to speak to a lady.'

No more was said until Culham. Having had the last word, Harriet should have felt better for the exchange, but Hardy's inexcusable behaviour still rankled. If he had not taunted her into waving to Mr Bustard, the incident need not have happened.

CHAPTER FOURTEEN

Hardy buys a German—Three men in the Barley Mow—Touching on Jack the Ripper

They managed to agree on one thing by the time they reached Culham: they needed a meal. At the ticket barrier Hardy asked if tea was served anywhere locally. 'I can think of three places,' said the ticket collector after some reflection. 'The first is in Culham, but that's closed down. The second I wouldn't recommend and the third is the Railway Hotel across the road.'

It was an attenuated meal, owing partly to Thackeray's repeated requests for more tea-cakes and partly to a general understanding that it would not be prudent to get to Clifton Hampden before Sergeant Cribb. There was not much conversation, but Hardy did find the good grace to congratulate Harriet on pouring a perfect cup of tea, an observation she acknowledged with a nod. It would want more than *that* to reinstate him.

Towards six o'clock the waitress signalled that tea was officially over by laying the tables for dinner in a good imitation of a rifle volley. After a short consultation, Hardy approached her and asked for the bill. 'You serve a good dinner, too, by the looks of it,' he told her, indicating a table spread with various kinds of cold meat. 'That large sausage at the back—is that the sort they call a polony?'

'I couldn't tell you, sir. Germans is what we call them in the kitchen.'

'Do you have another one like it? I'd like to take one with me.'

'You'll have to ask the waiter, sir. Germans are supposed to be for cold dinner, you see.'

'Is he available, then?'

'Just coming across the road from the station, sir. He comes on at six.'

It was the ticket collector. He had exchanged his railway livery for a black tie and tails. 'Can I be of assistance, sir?'

'Yes,' said Hardy. 'That—er—German on the table—'

'The polony, sir?'

'Polony. I'd like to buy it, or another like it.'

So when the party started along the road to Clifton Hampden, Hardy's polony, wrapped in cheesecloth, perched on Harriet's travelling-case.

'That was a good thought,' Thackeray remarked. 'You never know when you might need something to eat.'

'Oh, it's not for eatin',' said Hardy. 'I've got something else in mind for this.'

The sunlight of early evening on the brickwork of the village produced a roseate glow of the intensity only a pavement artist would dare reproduce. The church stood high in the background and the river was to the right. When they were midway across the narrow, six-arched bridge to the Berkshire bank, Hardy asked Thackeray to put down the case, and drew him into a bay. He pointed to a moored skiff with the hoops up and the covers gathered along the top. As they moved on, they were able to see the name *Lucrecia* on the side. When they drew level, a dog barked twice. Smiles were exchanged. They had saved themselves fourteen miles of rowing.

The Barley Mow lay ahead, a timbered structure of genuine antiquity with whitewashed walls and a thatched roof.

'Before we go in,' said Hardy, 'I don't think Cribb will thank us if we walk straight up to him and say "Here we are, Sarge".'

'Which of us do you suppose would be so stupid as to do that?' Thackeray asked. He was still frowning as they entered and took their places at a corner table.

Cribb was sitting in an armchair facing the door, staring into his beer with the preoccupied air of an angler waiting for a strike. The only others present were three seated round a table against the window adjacent to the door. Without question they were the crew of the *Lucrecia,* a bearded man of Viking proportions telling a story in painstaking detail of his not too attentive companions, a short, squat man with glasses so thick that all you could see from the side was concentric rings, and another in a pinstripe suit, hunched over a glass of sherbet.

Hardy dipped his head under the beams to cross the floor to the bar, through the doorway opposite. Thackeray escorted Harriet to a table screened from the other group by a short projecting wall, but still visible to Cribb.

The narrative in the corner finished as Hardy ordered his two beers and a cider, so his conversation with the landlord was heard by everyone in the room.

'Come by the river, have you, sir?'

'Over the bridge, actually. The village is charmin' from the river, but we wanted to see it at close quarters.'

'I hope it didn't disappoint you.'

'Quite the reverse. It's as pretty a spot as any of us have seen. We'd like to stay the night. Do you have three rooms—or a single and a double?'

'Whichever you like. Have you got luggage?'

'One case only. It's all in one for ease of travellin'. We'll take three single rooms, then.'

'2, 3 and 4,' said the landlord. 'The gentleman in the parlour is in number 1. The party in the corner are going on to Culham. They're following the route of the—

'Don't tell me—*Three Men in a Boat*!' said Hardy, loudly enough to be heard at the end of the room.

The Viking turned in his chair. The others also moved their heads for a better view, and a low shaft of sunlight flashed on two pairs of spectacles. At the other table, Harriet's hand caught Thackeray's and held it.

'Did somebody make a reference to the celebrated book by Mr Jerome K. Jerome?' asked the man in pinstripes. As he spoke, his top lip rolled upwards to reveal a row of large, uneven teeth.

'Merely a quip,' said Hardy, appearing with his tray of drinks. '*Three Men in a Boat* d'you see?'

If the man in the pinstripes did see, he was not amused. 'Are you familiar with the work, then?'

'I've heard of it, of course,' said Hardy, 'but I wouldn't pretend to have read it.'

'Just as well, sir,' commented the landlord, following him in to pursue the conversation. 'These gentlemen know it better than a bishop knows his Bible. What does Mr Jerome say about the Barley Mow, gentlemen?'

'Come, come. That's no test at all,' said the large man. 'It is well known that some of the book was written in this very house last summer. I'm sure you like to hear it repeated, Landlord, but anyone with the slightest knowledge of *Three Men in a Boat* must remember the complimentary things Jerome says about your inn. If you want to put our knowledge to the test, do us the credit of devising a more difficult question than that.'

The landlord coloured and found something needing attention in the taproom.

'I've got one for you,' said Cribb, apparently deciding that the conversation ought to be encouraged. 'Where did the three men put up in Marlow?'

'Easy!' said the man with the thick spectacles. 'The Crown. We were there on Tuesday night.' He spoke in bursts and with an excess of enthusiasm, as if every phrase ought to be punctuated with an exclamation mark.

'Splendid!' said Cribb, catching the habit. 'What is it—a pilgrimage you and your friends are making?'

The large man looked at each of the others and back at Cribb. 'In a manner of speaking it is. We're each of us admirers of Mr Jerome's work. From your question, sir, I take it that you share our enthusiasm.'

'It's a book I greatly enjoyed, but never finished,' said Cribb. 'I left my copy somewhere and haven't picked up another since. My name's Cribb, by the way. I'm travelling the lazy man's way—by passenger steamer.'

'Humberstone,' announced the large man. 'And my co-pilgrims are Mr Gold'—he extended a hand towards the owner of the thick spectacles '—and Mr Lucifer.' The lip lifted to diplay the teeth again in something between a smile and a snarl.

'So you stayed at the Crown on Tuesday,' Cribb repeated. 'You must have passed through Hurley the day the body was picked up from the water.'

'Body?' said Gold. 'We heard nothing about a body.'

'Well we wouldn't have, unless we asked,' said Humberstone with a glare. 'It isn't the sort of thing people mention to strangers, like the weather.'

'A suicide, I suppose?' said Gold, shrugging off the rebuke.

'Only a tramp,' contributed the landlord, appearing again. 'Probably drank too much and fell in. Carrying quite a lot of money, he was. Didn't you see it in the newspaper?'

Lucifer shook his head. 'One of our reasons for embarking upon this little excursion was to escape from newspapers and their dismal tidings. You cannot open *The Times* these days without reading of death and disaster. Thank Heaven for men like Mr Jerome, who afford us a brief respite from such things.'

'I'll drink to that,' said Cribb, lifting his glass. 'It's a wonderful things to get out of the City for a bit and take a boat up the river, even if it's only in your imagination. Are you gentlemen in business together?'

'We work for a prominent life insurance company, the Providential,' said Humberstone. 'As you may imagine, there isn't much occasion for jollity in the claims department, so Mr Lucifer here occasionally reads us items from periodicals he buys at the station bookstall in the morning. One of these is *Home Chimes,* in which he found the first instalment of *Three Men in a Boat.* Gold and I were surprised to hear belly laughs coming from his corner of the office, particularly as his job is answering letters from the recently bereaved. We insisted that he read the chapter aloud. We read it every day for a week, until the next issue of *Home Chimes* appeared. It was such a wonderful pick-me-up that we got through our work in half the time, and the claims department was soon known as the jolliest office in the Providential. Naturally we all bought a copy of the book as soon as it appeared and read it from cover to cover again. It followed quite without question that we arranged to take our holiday together on the Thames. We know every incident by heart, and consequently everything along the route has its interest, you see. By the way, Lucifer, one shouldn't suggest that death and disaster are totally absent from the book.'

'Ah!' said Gold. 'The dog in the water at Windsor.'

'No, I think Humberstone must be referring to the woman in the water at Pangbourne,' said Lucifer. 'That unfortunate creature of sin who put an end to her troubles by drowning herself—like your tramp, I presume, Landlord. Are bodies often recovered from the river in these parts?'

'Occasionally, sir, occasionally. It's more common the other side of Teddington, I believe, in the tidal river. The closer you get to London, the more unfortunates there are, you see. Women mostly, that have taken to a life of sin and come to regret it. I believe they jump off the bridges. I'd do the same if I was in their position, come to think of it, with that there Jack the Ripper stalking the streets murdering and mutilating those he finds.'

'The Ripper?' repeated Gold. 'Hasn't been

heard of for months. Gone into retirement, in my opinion.'

'He obviously favours the winter for its dark nights and fog,' said Lucifer. 'I have no doubt we shall hear of him again before the end of the year.'

'If the police were any good at their job, they'd have caught him long ago,' said Humberstone. 'He leaves them enough clues. They even found the knife after one of the murders. A great long-bladed thing it was, with a wooden handle, and the blood still on it.'

Across the room Thackeray said confidentially to Harriet, 'I think you ought to step outside for a bit, miss. This sort of conversation ain't suitable for one of the fair sex.'

She had to make an effort to compose herself before replying. Thackeray's suggestion had been kindly intended, no doubt, but what presumptions it made! 'From what I have heard of Jack the Ripper's doings,' she said, 'my sex has more reason to be informed about him than yours. *You* may step outside if you like, but I shall remain.'

'Some say he took his own life after the murder in Miller's Court,' Cribb was saying. 'He spent at least an hour dissecting the unfortunate woman. It was the ultimate in his style of killing. There was nothing more dreadful he could do.'

'Yes, I am familiar with the theory,' said

Lucifer, speaking with disquieting authority on this subject. 'A man of his description is said to have drowned himself in the Thames a few days later. A very convenient occurrence, for it reassured the public that London was safe again and stopped the accusations of police ineptitude. My own belief is that Jack slaked his thirst for blood last winter, but it will be as irresistible as ever when the nights get long again. Would anyone care for another beer?'

'The conversation seems to have taken a morbid turn,' said Humberstone, pushing his glass towards Lucifer. 'Whatever got us round to this subject?'

Cribb helpfully recapitulated. '*Three Men in a Boat* and a body in the river.'

'Who would have thought there was any connection at all between Jerome and the unspeakable Jack?' said Humberstone.

'It takes all sorts to make a world, eh?' said Gold. 'Take any night last summer in London. There was Jerome under one roof writing a comic masterpiece and Jack under another brooding on murder and mutilation. Lord knows what was going on under all the other roofs.'

'Safest not to inquire,' said Cribb. 'Mind, I don't suppose it's generally known that *Three Men in a Boat* is read aloud in a certain life insurance office, but if it hurts nobody, I don't see that there's anything offensive in it. Doing the river trip yourselves is a stunning idea, if I might say so, gentlemen. Are you following Jerome to the letter?'

'So far as we are able,' answered Lucifer. 'He is disconcertingly ambiguous at times. In Chapter 18 you will find that the three sleep under canvas in the backwater at Culham. Next morning, two or three pages on, they wake up three miles downriver, for they proceed to pass through Clifton Lock.'

'Perhaps Jerome had a drink too many in the Barley Mow,' suggested Cribb. 'But do you propose spending the night at Culham?'

'Most certainly. Like the characters in the book, we want to be in Oxford as early as we can tomorrow. We shall have to leave here in half an hour.'

'I don't suppose you have a dog like the one in the book,' said Cribb.

'Oh, but we do. We borrowed one for the excursion from a friend of Gold's. It answers to the name of Towser, which is a poor substitute for Montmorency, but we have problems enough persuading the beast that we are well-intentioned, without altering its name. The skiff, so far as we can ascertain, is exactly similar to the one in the book. And we are visiting the same places, but we are not so slavish in our length of stay. You will remember that Jerome's immortal trio spent two days at Streatley. One only was enough for us.'

'Why was that?'

'We saw all that there was to see in one morning. A pretty place, but not one to linger in.'

'Marlow's got more to offer,' added Gold. 'I'd have spent another night in Marlow gladly.'

'It's very comfortable at the Crown, I gather,' said Cribb, seizing on this.

'Oh yes. Comfortable, indeed.'

'I'm trying to think which hotel the Crown is,' Cribb went on. 'Is it the one near the bridge?'

'Tolerably near, yes,' Gold cautiously replied.

'With a good view of the river, from the best rooms, of course?'

'I don't quite recall.' Gold hesitated, taking off his spectacles and replacing them as if that might improve his memory. 'We had rooms at the back, you see, so you wouldn't see the river from there.'

'If it's the Crown at Marlow you're talking about,' said the landlord, 'you wouldn't see the river wherever your room was. It's at the top of the High Street.'

CHAPTER FIFTEEN

A reluctant promenader—Introduction of forensic science—Towser makes his mark

'If we're going to take a walk by the river before sunset we'd best be movin',' said Hardy, his eyes transmitting something of mysterious significance.

Thackeray, baffled, put down his glass.

'My word, yes,' Harriet piped up. 'We mustn't leave it any later.'

With copious nodding and touching of hats they took leave of the others in the parlour and stepped outside.

Thackeray immediately rounded on Hardy. 'What's this about? Haven't we done enough walking? If you want to promenade along the towpath with Miss Shaw, then ask her straight out, but understand that I'm not playing the part of blooming chaperone. I'm in no condition to walk anywhere except up them stairs to a proper bed.'

'Hold on, Ted,' said Hardy. 'You'll get to that bed in good time, but there's things to do before that. I hope we all understood what was going on in there just now.'

'Of course we did,' retorted Thackeray. 'Cribb was drawing them out as the beer loosened their tongues. You can't tell me *nothing* about his methods, young Hardy. I was working with him when you was running about in short trousers.'

'Please moderate your voices, gentlemen, or they'll be coming out to see what's going on,' warned Harriet. 'Let's walk at least a short way from the windows. Then perhaps one of you will enlighten me as to the significance of the conversation we just overheard.'

They started towards the river, Thackeray kicking petulantly at stones along the path, Harriet striving to recollect Miss Plummer's advice on the management of difficult pupils.

'First will you tell us if you recognized them, miss?' asked Hardy. 'Can you positively say they were the three you saw from the river the other night?'

Positively: this was what they would ask in court when she was there to testify. This was the reason why she was here. 'I cannot be positive without seeing them in profile. The largest, Mr Humberstone, certainly had the same sort of hat, and there was something of the Persian Gulf about him, but I did not get a view of the others from where we were seated. That isn't much help, I'm afraid.'

'No matter, miss. Cribb caught them out famously, anyway. Their game is up. Did you notice the mistake they made over the Crown at Marlow? Couldn't see the river from the back! They've never been near the Crown, and that's plain.'

'It might have been a slip of the tongue,' said Harriet. 'I don't see how anything so trivial as that condemns them. What does it matter where they put up in Marlow?'

'It matters because they claimed to be there on Tuesday, the night the tramp was murdered. If they *did* stay at the Crown, they've got an alibi. Marlow is two miles downriver from Hurley.'

'Couldn't they have rowed up from Marlow after dark?'

'No, miss. There are two locks in that stretch of the river, Temple and Hurley. Locks are closed at sundown. *They* might have got to Hurley, but their boat couldn't. That's if they did put up at Marlow. If they were lyin', as seems to be the case, they could have rowed beyond Hurley on Tuesday, murdered the tramp that night and carried on upriver in the morning.'

'But why should three respectable employees of an insurance company take it into their heads to murder a wretched vagrant?'

'That's the biggest mystery of all, miss. Sergeant Cribb is doin' his best to unravel it at this moment. First he needs absolute proof of their guilt. He was hopin' you would identify them, but you say you can't.'

'Not yet. If I see them in their boat, I shall try to be sure. The light is very poor in the Barley Mow.'

'Quite so, miss. You've got to be convinced. Proof positive. And I think I've got the means of obtainin' it.'

'What's that?' demanded Thackeray.

'This.' Hardy took the wrapped polony from under his arm and held it between them in his two hands like an oblation.

'That sausage?'

'We shall shortly put it to the service of Scotland Yard,' Hardy went on, 'in accordance with the principles of forensic science.'

'Good Lord!'

'We are not so backward in the country as you might suppose, Ted. When you come up against a crime as sinister as this one, you have to bring the latest methods of detection to bear on it.'

'Sausages?' squeaked Thackeray.

'Murder on the river,' continued Hardy, undistracted by the outburst, 'produces its own special problems for the detective. On solid ground the scene of a crime tells some sort of story if you go over it carefully. Footprints, marks of entry, bloodstains, strands of cloth, hairs. On the river, nothing. You're lucky if the body is recovered. Happily for us the corpse in this case had certain marks of great significance.'

'Bruising round the neck and shoulders,' said Thackeray. 'We know all this.'

'And something else.'

'The dogbite, you mean?'

'Exactly. Now suppose you and I could obtain proof that the dog on Humberstone's boat was the same animal that sank its teeth into the dead man's leg.'

'Strike a light!' said Thackeray. 'Teethmarks—the sausage—that's bloody smart, young Roger. Forgive my language, miss, but you've got to give praise when it's due. Don't you think it's bloody smart too?'

'That is not the expression I would choose,' Harriet answered, 'but the idea had not occurred to me, I confess. Do you think it will work?' To admit that Hardy's plan had set her heart pounding with possibilities was inconceivable. Yet if he actually managed to obtain teethmarks on the polony that matched those on the dead man's leg, the guilt of the three would surely be proved beyond doubt. The matter would no longer hinge on her ability to identify them. She would be absolved of that awful responsibility.

'We can but try,' said Hardy. 'Let's introduce ourselves to Towser.'

They walked down to the *Lucrecia* without subterfuge. The direct approach was always the best with dogs, Thackeray announced, mentioning that before he joined the C.I.D. his duties had included rounding up strays for the dog-pound. It did cross Harriet's mind that Hardy had taken a little more than his share of the limelight. Fortified by Thackeray's experience, Harriet and Hardy passed no comment on the intermittent barking as their footsteps sounded on the gravel.

Towser stood on one of the rowing thwarts with his forepaws on the side, a small fox terrier mainly white in colour, with brown patches on the head and tail. From his collar a leather lead hung slackly, its other end attached to the rowlock. He had given up barking now that they were near. He was growling instead, a low, reverberating sound like a boiler with the vent open.

'Leave this to me,' said Thackeray, taking the polony from Hardy with all the authority of the only canine expert in the party. 'Keep a reasonable distance from him. That's just right. You're downwind of him there. I want him to get a good scent of the sausage before I offer it to him.'

Their vantage point was ten yards from the bank. Thackeray approached the snarling Towser with gladiatorial confidence, keeping the polony wrapped and tucked out of sight under his left arm.

The skiff was moored at the bow and lay at a narrow angle to the bank, held steady by the current. To reach the dog he would need to board by the bow.

He approached indirectly, in the long, sweeping curve of an experienced tracker, covertly removing the cheesecloth from the polony as he drew level with the bank. Two yards more and he would have been aboard, but the unexpected intervened. He had underestimated the length of the lead trailing from Towser's collar. The terrier bounded on to the bank just ahead of him, stretching the lead taut against his shins. The impetus of his movement lifted the end of the lead over the rowlock, and the dog was free.

Ignoring Thackeray and the polony it rushed at Hardy, baying with predatory passion, and sank its teeth into his leg.

CHAPTER SIXTEEN

Ace of trumps with iodine—The polony comes in useful—Hardy gets his marching orders

'Beautiful!' declared Sergeant Cribb, a man not often given to aesthetic pronouncements.

A perfect set of teethmarks was displayed on Hardy's left calf, uncovered for inspection in his room at the Barley Mow. He lay face down on the bed moaning faintly as Harriet dabbed the wound with iodine.

'Believe me, Constable, I'd never have asked you to do such a thing,' Cribb went on. 'Quite beyond the call of duty. I don't know who it was that thought of this, but it's the ace of trumps. Exhibit number one! There's a commendation in this for someone.'

'It was Constable Hardy's own idea to

purchase the sausage,' said Harriet generously.

'Good thinking,' said Cribb. 'Give the dog a scent of meat and then show it your leg.'

'It wasn't quite like that,' said Harriet. 'Constable Thackeray was holding the polony and—'

'Thackeray, eh?' said Cribb. 'I thought this had the stamp of Scotland Yard on it. Stout work, Thackeray! I should have known that if there was a dust with a dog you'd be in the thick of it. And when the evidence was firm, so to speak, you disconnected Towser from Hardy and secured the beast to the boat again?'

'*That's* right, Sarge.'

Thackeray's emphasis sought to convey that Cribb's assumptions were not correct in every respect, but it was lost on the sergeant. 'Capital work! The suspects won't have any notion of the evidence we've secured. They're paddling blissfully up to Culham at this minute to spend the night in the backwater, quite unaware of what was going on while they were drinking. I forgot to ask if you recognized them, Miss Shaw.'

That question again. Harriet had hoped it had been forgotten in the excitement over Hardy's leg. 'They could well be the men I saw on Tuesday night, but I am not ready to swear to it yet. My view was partially obstructed downstairs and the conditions were altogether different, as you must appreciate.'

Cribb nodded tolerantly. 'We'll see if we can get you a better view of them on the river tomorrow. Actually, you must have come quite close to it today. You can't have been too far behind them. A nifty piece of rowing, gentlemen.'

In the short pause that followed, Hardy did not stir a muscle, even when Harriet in her unease tipped some iodine directly on to his perforated skin. 'We—er—came by train, Sarge,' Thackeray confessed. 'We left the boat at Goring.'

'If you remember, you left a message there asking us to make the best speed we could,' Harriet quickly added in support, 'but up to then we followed their route most faithfully. We established conclusively that they spent last night on an island at Shiplake.'

'You did?' said Cribb, still absorbing the information that they were without a boat.

Rapidly, Harriet moved on to a breathless account of the meeting with Mr Bustard and Jim Hackett, on the principle that if she bombarded him with detail something sooner or later would make an impact. It turned out to be Jim Hackett's habit of quoting from the Bible.

'Do you remember any of the texts?' Cribb asked.

'"Be sure your sin will find you out" was one, and there was another about giving account for idle words on the day of judgement.'

'I remember a third,' said Thackeray enthusiastically. '"Man goeth forth to his work, and to his labour until the evening." Psalm 104. Thirty-five verses. I learnt it at school.'

'I wonder if Jim Hackett did,' said Cribb. 'Did he have much else to say?'

'Very little,' answered Thackeray. 'He corrected Bustard once, I remember, a question over where they'd bought a veal and ham pie. Bustard said it was the George and Dragon at Wargrave, but Hackett insisted it was the Dog and Badger. The way he said it made me think he was talking about the contents of the pie. Which reminds me, would anybody like a slice of polony before we all retire? It wasn't touched by Towser, I promise you. I'll use my pocket-knife, if nobody objects.'

'Just what I could do with,' said Cribb, his spirits quite restored. 'How about you, Miss Shaw?'

'I would rather not,' said Harriet. She was about to add that she had eaten very well at the Railway Hotel, but stopped herself in time. 'The smell of the iodine is too strong for me, I'm afraid.'

'A piece for our intrepid hero, then?' said Cribb, clapping his hand on Hardy's inert thigh. 'Got to pull yourself together, man. You're lying there as though you're settled for the night.'

Hardy came swiftly to life, rolling on to his side. 'Pull myself together? What for, Sergeant?'

Cribb consulted his watch. 'For a train journey. In just over an hour you're going to be at Culham Station to catch the 11:15 to London. It's a slow, the landlord tells me, so you can change at Twyford Junction and with luck you'll get a connection to Henley before morning. I want you at the mortuary at seven, when the keeper gets there, to compare your dogbite with the tramp's. We know his name now, by the way. Another vagrant identified him yesterday. He's called Walters, known among the tramps as "Choppy". It's still a mystery why anyone should want to kill him. He kept to himself, but he wasn't disliked. Stayed mostly in the Thames Valley, but always on the move. Anyway, when you've had a look at Choppy's bite, arrange for drawings to be made of it. And yours, of course. After that, take a cab to Marlow, locate the Crown at the top of the High Street, and check the register for Humberstone, Lucifer and Gold. Then make your way to Oxford and wait for me at the central police station in St Aldate's. Any questions?'

'How am I to get to Culham Station from here, Sergeant?'

'You walk, Constable.'

'My leg is injured.'

'I'm aware of that. A stiff walk should do it good. Roll down your trouser leg and have a slice of polony. I can't send anyone else, can I? You're exhibit number one! The sooner you're cheerfully on your way, the sooner the rest of us can get to bed.'

CHAPTER SEVENTEEN

Intervention of the elements—Lock-keepers, abusive and obliging—Oxford, and an untimely end

Harriet was surprised on waking to find it as late as ten past seven. Cribb had warned her before retiring that an early start was essential in the morning to catch up with Humberstone and his companions at Culham. He had learned from the landlord that a steam launch left Clifton Hampden at 7.15 a.m. for the convenience of people from the village employed in Oxford. And already it was 7.10. Nobody had called her. A disquieting thought darted into her mind: having despatched Hardy to Henley last night, had Cribb abandoned her this morning? She flung aside the bedclothes, ran to the curtains and swept them apart. There was no sign of Cribb, nor a steam launch. There was no sign of anything. A dense river mist hung in the air.

So it happened shortly after eight o'clock that Cribb, Thackeray and Harriet took to the water not in a steam launch, but an ancient skiff with broken rowlocks, the only vessel anyone would commit to their use in such conditions.

'Visibility's improving every minute,' Cribb said with conviction. 'This is probably quite local. It'll be perfectly clear before we get to Culham. Steer us close to the bank, Miss Shaw, and we'll know exactly where we are.'

Harriet clung grimly to the tiller-ropes, sensing that an emergency which brought Cribb to the oars called for exceptional efforts on everyone's part, but steering was hardly the word for the small influence she had on the direction of the boat. Twice in the first minute she went too close to the bank and the oars struck solid ground. Soon after, they found themselves somewhere in midstream without anything to steer by except the flow of the current.

'No matter,' Cribb encouragingly said. 'Somewhere ahead is Clifton Lock. We need to move across for that. If we stayed on the Berkshire side we'd find ourselves running into the weir.'

Five minutes after, his confidence was noticeably on the wane. 'No need to be quite so energetic with the oars, Thackeray. This ain't the boat-race, you know.' He had got to the point shortly afterwards of saying, 'This is madness—' when the prow struck something solid and the rowers were pitched off their seats. They had found the lock gate.

They had to disembark to rouse the lock-keeper, and then endure a torrent of abuse about lunatics who put to the water in conditions like that, until Cribb coolly reminded the fellow that he was a public servant and it was no business of his to question the sanity of people considerate enough to keep him in employment. As if to reinforce the point, the mist miraculously lifted as the gates parted to let them out of the lock. In sunshine they got down to the serious business of rowing to Culham in the shortest time they could.

It was after nine when they went through Culham Lock. The keeper there was agreeably civil, but he had discouraging news. There had not been a suspicion of mist at Culham that morning. He was not surprised to hear about the mist at Clifton Hampden. It was quite usual in September for pockets of the stuff to hamper navigation along the river for an hour or so in the mornings. His lock had been open since six. Yes, three men answering Cribb's description had gone through shortly before he had closed the night before. They had asked the way to the backwater at the end of Culham Cut, where they had proposed passing the night.

Cribb decided not to explore the backwater,

assuming instead that the three had already left for Oxford. They would be able to confirm this at the next lock, which was Abingdon.

'Will you arrest them when we catch up with them?' Thackeray inquired.

'I want Miss Shaw to identify 'em first,' said Cribb.

This, they discovered at Abingdon, was likely to take longer than they had earlier supposed. The three had been the first through the lock that morning, at seven o'clock. They could well be in Oxford already.

It was a party exercised in more ways than one that covered the last miles to Oxford, learning at each lock how far behind the *Lucrecia* they were. The suspects seemed not to have stopped even once along the way. As the distance from Culham to Oxford was nine miles, and none of them had looked like athletes, the question arose whether the quarry had been alerted to the chase. Nobody said a word, but Cribb's face became increasingly pink with the exertion of rowing at a rate he obdurately refused to slacken. It made fretful the business of waiting in locks for other craft to enter before the gates were closed, but it compelled him to take rests. While Thackeray put his head between his knees like a beaten blue, Cribb paddled the boat as close as possible to the upriver gates and stood with hands impatiently on hips watching the slow ascent as the water coursed in.

Beyond Iffley Lock the tangle of currents formed by the confluence of the Thames and Cherwell sapped what remained of Cribb's strength. He dismally acknowledged that they might as well ship oars and tow the skiff from the path. Thackeray was deputed to take the first turn.

'We'll follow the main stream,' Cribb instructed. 'They could have gone up a backwater if they wanted to, I know, but Jerome seems to have kept to the names, so I don't propose to waste time looking anywhere else unless I'm persuaded otherwise.'

Harriet thought she divined a note of desperation in this. It was confirmed when Cribb tetchily ordered her to stop admiring the college barges moored beside Christ Church Meadow and look for the *Lucrecia.* 'You're not on a pleasure cruise, you know.'

'I'm well aware of that,' she answered, ready to take him on. 'Has it not occurred to you that they might as well have left their boat on that side as this? Not everyone is obliged to use the towing path.'

Cribb was either too surprised, or too tired, to reply.

At Folly Bridge, he shouted to Thackeray to halt so that they could make inquiries at the boatyard. The facetious remarks they had got from just about every lock-keeper along the river when putting their question about three men in a boat had caused Cribb to modify it a little. 'Do you happen to have seen a double-sculled skiff with three passengers aboard and a fox terrier?' he asked.

He could have saved his breath. 'Only on my bookshelf at home,' said the boatman with a grin.

'Could they have passed here earlier without you noticing?'

'Why not? I only started work at ten this morning, didn't I?'

They decided to go on as far as Osney Lock, in hope of finding the *Lucrecia* moored beside the bank. Cribb took the towing rope and hauled them slowly past the gasworks and under the railway bridge. The best of Oxford is not to be seen from the Thames.

Shortly after the bridge, the river divides. A backwater leads away through the fields to the left.

'Moses!' said Thackeray. 'What's going on over there?'

A cluster of people had formed round a spot on the towpath, not unlike the crowd round a pavement artist, except that they were standing on gravel. A figure was on his knees working at something, even so. Too many on the outskirts were moving about, trying for a better view, for anything more to be made out from the river.

Cribb signalled to Thackeray to take charge of the boat and went to see what was happening. 'Is something wrong, do you think?' asked Harriet.

'Let's go and see, miss.' Thackeray steered the boat into the backwater and moored it. They went ashore and approached the cause of all the interest.

The kneeling man was still at work. He was moving the arms rhythmically on and off the chest of a motionless man, stretched on his back on the path. Somebody else was gripping the ankles.

'Resuscitation?' asked Cribb, who had forced his way to the front.

'Yes, mate,' someone replied. 'It's doing no good. They've been at this for twenty minutes. Poor blighter's dead as mutton.'

CHAPTER EIGHTEEN

A nice class of corpse—Cribb makes a discovery—Help from a scout

Harriet, still on the fringe of what was going on, heard a murmur and made out someone standing up. Several men around her removed their hats. A voice intoned, ' "So teach us to number our days that we may apply our hearts unto wisdom." The ninetieth Psalm, Verse 12.'

It could not be anyone else but Jim Hackett.

As people replaced their hats and dispersed

in all directions in case someone should ask them to assist with whatever happened next, Harriet was enabled to move to the front. Jim Hackett it was who had worked unavailingly to persuade air into the dead man's lungs. Mr Bustard had held the ankles.

Cribb had not met Bustard and Hackett, so Thackeray made the introductions, taking care not to mention rank. They shook hands across the corpse like football captains before a match.

'Where did you find the poor fellow?' Cribb asked.

'Out there,' said Bustard, indicating the water with his thumb. 'Floating face downwards. Jim picked him out of the river and we brought him here and tried resuscitation. Jim had lessons in life-saving, you know.'

'But raising the dead wasn't included, eh?' said Cribb, adding, before Jim could supply a text, 'This one must have joined the majority before you hooked him out of the water. Does anyone know who he is?'

'If his clothes are anything to go by, he's out of the top drawer, or was,' contributed Thackeray. 'It looks as if he's wearing a Norfolk jacket under that waterproof. Perhaps there's something in the pockets.'

'I don't approve of pilfering from the dead,' said Bustard in a scandalized voice.

'For identification,' said Thackeray, red-faced. 'I was thinking that he might carry a pocket book.'

They examined the jacket and found the pockets empty. So were the pockets of the waistcoat and trousers.

'He didn't want to be recognized,' decided Bustard. 'Suicide probably.'

'Nice class of person, too,' insisted Thackeray, examining the lining of the jacket.

They looked down at the pale face marbled with lines of mud. Thackeray was right: the features matched the tailoring. It was a fine Roman nose with narrow nostrils and a black moustache beneath it. The lips were thin, but neatly formed, the teeth well cared for. He could not have been much over thirty-five.

'We ought to tell the law,' said Hackett.

'By now, somebody has,' Cribb cryptically remarked, bending to rearrange some hair that was plastered over the dead man's forehead. 'You're a lifesaver, then, Mr Hackett. Which resuscitation drill do you favour, the Silvester or the Marshall Hall?'

'Silvester.'

'As taught by the Royal Humane Society,' said Cribb. 'Clear the throat, attend to the tongue, place a support under the back, loosen the garments and begin working the arms in the approved manner. You did all that?'

'Of course he did,' said Bustard. 'I was holding the ankles. That's my blazer underneath him.'

'You had no cause to hold him by the neck?'

'Lord, no! This was life-saving, old sport, not strangulation.'

'So I understood,' said Cribb, stooping to make a closer examination. 'I only asked because of these marks. It looks to me as if someone gripped him from behind. They must have used a lot of force to leave the marks of their fingers on his neck.' He pulled aside the loosened collar so that everyone could see the set of marks, purple on the white flesh. 'Perhaps you grabbed him by the neck to take him from the water, Mr Hackett?'

'No, guvnor. I took hold of his clothes first and then I held him under the arms, like.'

Cribb stepped over the body to examine the left side of the neck. A similar formation of bruises was displayed there. 'If this was suicide, I'm the Archbishop of Canterbury.'

'A very God-fearing man,' commented Jim Hackett.

'Are you quite well, miss?' Thackeray asked Harriet.

The colour must have drained from her face. 'I think so. The shock. I am not used to such things.' In truth the sight of death frightened her less than she would have supposed. The real horror that gripped her was Cribb's discovery—the marks on the neck, marks similar to those on the murdered tramp at Hurley. Cribb was not saying so yet, but he might as well have blown a whistle and shouted to everyone within earshot that this was murder, a second brutal and callous murder within an hour of his three suspects reaching Oxford. If she had done what he had asked her to do, identified Humberstone, Gold and Lucifer as the three she saw the night the tramp was killed, this second man need not have died. She had shirked her responsibility, put off the moment when she had to be definite, and this was the consequence.

'It's a good thing Jim's got a sharp eye,' said Bustard. 'I'd never have spotted a body in the water on my own. Wouldn't have noticed a confounded whale swimming by this morning. I was still thinking about the college barges. Handsome things! The carving on them—magnificent!'

'Impossible to ignore,' said Cribb, although Harriet remembered him advocating the impossible ten minutes before. 'Is that why you were on the river—to see the barges?'

'The barges and any other delightful objects visible in Oxford early in the morning,' said Bustard, glancing Harriet's way. 'We like to be about before the river gets too cluttered, don't we, Jim? We were going up to Osney to see the mill. We started from Folly Bridge.'

'Is that rowing boat yours?'

'Hired for the morning, yes. One's supposed to see Oxford from a punt, I believe, but I've never trusted the things.'

'You had a skiff like ours when I saw you

last,' said Thackeray.

'In Goring, yes. Now for my confession,' said Bustard. 'We abandoned it at Benson two hours after we saw you. Jim was game to carry on, but I was feeling the effects of too much sun. We had some tea and caught the four o'clock bus to Oxford. We're putting up at the Gentle Bulldog by Folly Bridge. B. and B. for seven and six. Very comfortable.'

'That's worth knowing,' said Thackeray.

'We were up early to look at the barges,' said Bustard. 'Then we decided to come this way. When we got to those vile gasometers we nearly changed our minds, but the stretch ahead looks altogether more salubrious.'

'Apart from what you find in the water,' said Cribb. 'Hello, the bluebottles are buzzing this way. I thought it wouldn't be long.'

A uniformed constable of the Oxford City Police came heavily along the towpath with two men in attendance who must have fetched him. 'Stand aside, if you please,' he said breathlessly as he arrived. 'Is this the body?'

'It's the only one I've noticed,' said Cribb.

'Did you discover it?'

'No, but—'

'Better get on your way, then. We don't want every Tom, Dick and Harry crowding round it. Who's the man that took it from the water?'

'Jim Hackett,' Bustard loftily announced, with a hand towards his companion.

'Hackett,' repeated the policeman, taking out his notebook and pencilling the name carefully inside. 'What's the nature of your employment, Mr Hackett?'

Hackett frowned.

'Your job,' Cribb explained.

'Oh. Removals.'

'Nobody can get a piano up a staircase like Jim Hackett,' said Bustard.

'Who is your employer?' asked the constable.

'Morgan and Morgan, Islington,' Bustard replied for Hackett. 'Before that he worked in my father-in-law's business. That's how we met.'

'Business?' said the constable. 'From the look of his hands, I'd say Mr Hackett was a labouring man.'

'That's right!' said Bustard. 'Every inch of him is muscle.'

'That's convenient,' said the constable. 'I shall want some help to carry the body back to the ambulance. And what's your name, sir?'

'Bustard with a "u". Tallyman, of Notting Hill Gate, taking my vacation on the river with Mr Hackett. We hired a rowing boat from the man at Folly Bridge this morning, thinking of exploring the City from the river, and Jim noticed this. He's eagle-eyed, is Jim.'

'I shall require you both to accompany me to the station to make a statement. The rest of you,' the constable added, raising his voice, 'had better move along quick unless you've got something useful to impart. Pull the man's waterproof over his face, would you, mate, and that'll put a stop to the peepshow.'

Thackeray was about to drape the ends of the coat over the head and shoulders when a voice to his right said, 'Stop a moment! I know the face.' A thin, silver-haired man, shabby in appearance, came forward, looping spectacles over his ears. He crouched by the body and peered with earnest concentration at the features. 'I'm sure of it. This is Mr Bonner-Hill, a Fellow of Merton College. Whatever made him do such a thing?'

'A don?' The constable scrutinized his informant, plainly doubtful whether a person with frayed cuffs and no collar was any authority on members of the University. 'Are you quite sure of that?'

'Sure? Of course I'm sure. I scouted for him for six months before I lost my job last April, didn't I? Henry Bonner-Hill, Tonbridge School and Merton. He's a terrible loss. A very sharp dresser, he was, always wanting a clean shirt and a fresh crease in his trousers. Strewth! Look at them shoes! What a state! He wouldn't like that, being seen dead with his shoes in a state like that. I'll give 'em a polish for him.' He pulled a handkerchief from his pocket.

'No, you won't!' the constable said. 'That mud is evidence. Leave him just as he is. I'm not taking a rap from the coroner just because Mr Bonner-what's-his-name wouldn't like to be seen in the mortuary with muddy shoes.'

CHAPTER NINETEEN

The late Mr Bonner-Hill—Over the friar's balsam—Concerning the murderess

'This is exceedingly distressing,' the Warden of Merton told Sergeant Cribb. 'A grievous loss. Bonner-Hill was one of the youngest of our Fellows, not much above thirty years of age. I remember him perfectly as an undergraduate. Even then he was a discriminating dresser. Hand-made shirts, you know, and a different cravat at every meal. He was better turned out than most members of the Senior Common Room. Yes, he made his mark in the College when we were at a low ebb sartorially. So many academics neglect their dress lamentably, Sergeant. I recall remarking to the Estates Bursar that it was only a matter of time before Bonner-Hill took his place at High Table, and I was right. He was a little longer earning a respectable degree than I expected, but he got there, he got there. If he was not the most inspiring tutor in medieval history in the University, he was indubitably the best-dressed.'

'Under his waterproof he was in a Norfolk jacket with matching trousers,' Cribb confirmed. 'It seems he was fishing.'

'He always dressed to fit the occasion,' reflected the Warden, pausing to look at Cribb's blazer. 'His angling had become quite a passion of late. There was a time when we had nothing but theatrical gossip from him at table. In recent weeks it was all hooks and worms. Not so conducive to the digestion. Fernandez, one of the other Fellows, must take the blame for introducing him to the pastime. They used to get up early on Saturday mornings to look for a pike, of all things. I presume he went alone this morning. Fernandez has not been out of College.'

'The time of death was estimated as between half past nine and ten o'clock, sir.'

'On a Saturday? Ungodly!'

'A punt was found later, moored in Bulstake Stream, the backwater just beyond the second railway bridge. His fishing tackle was in it, and an umbrella inscribed with his name.'

'A sensible precaution,' said the Warden. 'One is dreadfully exposed to the elements in a punt.'

'Did Mr Bonner-Hill have any other fishing companions, sir?'

'Not to my knowledge. Not from Merton. Two anglers in the College is more than enough, I assure you.'

'Only one now,' Cribb pointed out. 'He was

a bachelor, I take it, as he was living in College.'

'Not so, Sergeant, I am afraid. He leaves a widow, although one ought to add that they have been estranged of late. That is why he moved back into rooms in Merton a year ago. Someone must break the news to Mrs Bonner-Hill, although where she lives now I, er . . . The matrimonial home was a villa in North Oxford—one of those ghastly mock-gothic structures in red brick, I was told. There was quite a stampede in that direction after the celibacy rule for Fellows was lifted in seventy-seven. Things are settling down again now, as I predicted they would at the time. It was a very outmoded rule—a relic of popery, I suspect—and got the younger dons into some embarrassing extra-mural entanglements, not to go into the intra-mural consequences. Bonner-Hill joined us a year or two after the rule was lifted and he was married and moved out within a year. Mrs Bonner-Hill was one of the prettiest women in Oxford, but she wasn't right for him. An actress—and I don't imply anything to her discredit in that—she is moderately well known in the dramatic world—but her experiences on the boards had ill-prepared her for marriage to a medieval historian.'

'Are there children?' Cribb asked.

'No. That may have contributed to their estrangement. She was isolated in North

Oxford—told me so herself at the Vice-Chancellor's garden party—and missed the theatre dreadfully. She tried to persuade him to let her continue with her acting after marriage, but it was out of the question.'

'Why was that, sir?'

'It would have made his life insufferable in the Senior Common Room. People fasten on to such things. They did, as a matter of fact, shortly after he moved back into rooms here last Michaelmas and she went back on the stage. Some precocious undergraduate recognized her in *Forget Me Not* at a repertory theatre in Henley. She was using another name, but he was fairly sure of her identity and a few sharp questions at the stage door confirmed it. Next time Bonner-Hill appeared for a lecture he found a bunch of forget-me-nots stuffed into the water glass. Every undergraduate in the front row was wearing one in his button-hole. You may imagine his difficulty after that in introducing a lecture on feudalism.'

'Even so,' said Cribb, 'I would have thought a man could live a thing like that down.'

'Admittedly, but Bonner-Hill's temperament was not well-suited to living things down. He took himself seriously, cultivated refinement in conduct and appearance and hated to be ridiculed. The episode upset him profoundly, the more so, I think, because it was rumoured about the same time that the lady had formed an alliance with an actor. No reference was made to it in Merton—not in his presence, anyway—but he seemed to sense that we all knew about it—and of course we did, for news travels fast in Oxford—and for a week or more he declined to join in any conversation at table.'

'Was he unpopular among the Fellows?'

'He was on tolerably good terms with everyone. Fernandez was his closest confidant, but even he found himself cold-shouldered at the time. More recently, however, they were on close terms again.'

'I should like to meet Mr Fernandez. Bonner-Hill had no enemies in the College, you think?'

'I am sure of it.'

'He *was* murdered, sir.'

'Then you must look outside Merton, Sergeant. First let us see if Fernandez is in his rooms.'

He answered their knock after a delay so long that they were on the point of going away. He had a towel draped over his head and his moustache was glistening with damp. 'It's you, Warden! My word, I do apologize. I had my head over a basin. I was inhaling friar's balsam, the only remedy I ever found effective for a sore throat.'

'I'm sorry to hear you are indisposed, Fernandez.'

'The crisis is past, Warden, I am confident

of that.'

'Are you well enough to spare us a few moments? This is Sergeant Cribb of the police—'

'Police?' Fernandez repeated the word with distaste.

'Investigating the death of poor Bonner-Hill,' the Warden went on.

Fernandez nodded. 'Rest his soul, yes. Do come in, gentlemen.'

Cribb turned to the Warden. 'I don't think I need detain you any longer, sir. Mr Fernandez can tell me everything else, I'm sure. I'd like to see Mr Bonner-Hill's rooms before I go, but I'll speak to the porter about that. Thank you for your time, sir.'

Fernandez, with the towel still draped over his head like a Bedouin, led Cribb into a sitting room with a window overlooking the Fellows' Quadrangle. One wall was lined to the ceiling with books. The others presented an odd juxtaposition of religious paintings, antique maps and photographs of actresses. Cribb crossed to the window and looked out. 'Finish your inhaling, sir. It's got to be done while the stuff is still hot.'

'I am fully cognizant of that, thank you. I have inhaled sufficiently for now.' From the tone Fernandez used, he must have detected patronage in Cribb's offer. Unexceptional in height, but broadly built, with hands like a stevedore's, he was not the sort to provoke.

‘Pray enlighten me as to how I can be of assistance to the police.’

Cribb had picked up a tiny twist of scarlet feathers from the window-sill. ‘Fly-fishing. Is that a pastime of yours, sir?’

‘Pastime?’ Fernandez screwed his face into the expression it had formed when the Warden had mentioned police. ‘I do not indulge in pastimes, Sergeant. Fly-fishing is a sport. Yes, as you so cleverly deduce, I have taken a few fish with the fly in times past. Of late I have favoured live bait. I fish for pike, although what this has to do with poor—’

‘Pike, sir? The large ones? Are there many to be had in Oxford?’

‘Sufficient for good sport. The record catch from one of the backwaters weighed twenty-nine pounds. That is no small fish, Sergeant. I nurse a small ambition to take a pike that weighs thirty pounds or more. For some two years I have devoted most of my Saturdays to this quest. I have several times seen one not far from here, a very large one, but it would not take the strike. They are devious adversaries.’

‘I understand Mr Bonner-Hill used to accompany you in your hunt for pike.’

Fernandez held up a finger dramatically. ‘Now I see the drift of your interrogation! Ah, the subtlety of the detective police! We have got to Bonner-Hill. Yes, Sergeant, he joined my Saturday expeditions two months ago. He was a novice with the rod, but prepared to learn.'

'He was on the river this morning.'

'The morning is a favourable time,' said Fernandez. 'I should have been with him myself but for this abominable laryngitis.'

'After his body was taken from the water we found his punt in Bulstake Stream. His fishing tackle was still aboard.'

'Had he caught anything? I suppose not. Trolling is an art not easily acquired. Bonner-Hill scarcely knew one end of the rod from the other, for all his enthusiasm. Would you care for a sherry?'

'He was murdered, sir,' said Cribb, determined not to be deflected. 'Why should anyone choose to murder Mr Bonner-Hill?'

Fernandez held open his hands. 'It is enough for me to fathom the behaviour of a simple fish. I suggest you put your question to somebody who professes to know something about the intricacies of the human mind. In Oxford there are experts upon everything.'

'You saw a powerful lot of Mr Bonner-Hill, though,' Cribb said in justification.

'No, Sergeant. Kindly do not jump to conclusions. I saw more of Bonner-Hill than others in Merton, but I did not see a powerful lot of him, as you so graphically assert. I am a man with many responsibilities, which often take me away from Oxford for days on end. I frequently visit the Royal Geographical

Society in London. I am a member, you understand, and I have the honour to serve on more than one of the committees. If a meeting lasts until the evening I stay overnight at my club, the Oxford and Cambridge. It would be quite misleading to suggest that Bonner-Hill and I were often in each other's company. When it was possible, we went fishing together on Saturday mornings, and that was the extent of it.'

'Did he talk to you about his troubles, sir?'

'Troubles?'

'Matrimonial. I understand he left his wife a year ago and moved back into Merton. Have you met Mrs Bonner-Hill?'

'The murderess? I've met her, yes.'

'Did you say "murderess"?'

Fernandez smiled. 'A frivolous remark, Sergeant. It was Bonner-Hill's term for her—only, of course, in a jesting sense. She is an actress, you know—very good in romantic comedy. At some point in her career she was persuaded to try a more demanding role. The local newspaper commented that if she and the actor playing Macbeth had murdered Duncan with a modicum of their success in murdering Shakespeare the play could have stopped at Act One and so prevented further suffering. Uncharitable, but amusing. I saw her in something of Pinero's at Windsor not long ago and thought her quite enchanting.'

'Why did Bonner-Hill leave her?'

'There you go again, Sergeant, inviting me to speculate on the mysteries of the human mind. I decline the invitation for the reason I gave you before.'

'I thought he might have told you.'

Fernandez tossed his head so vigorously that the towel fell off. 'You think he might have told me why he left his wife? How in Heaven's name do you suppose a subject like that arises between two gentlemen on a fishing expedition?'

'If you tell me it didn't arise I must believe you, sir, but my experience is that confidences are frequently exchanged in circumstances like that. The early morning. Nobody about. Two of you sitting in a punt in a quiet backwater waiting for the fish to bite. I'm no angler myself, but I've done observation duties in the police that aren't so different from that and I've invariably found that if I have a fellow officer with me, we'll talk, and before long he's telling me about the arguments he has with his wife and I'm telling tales about my days in the army. The most reticent of men become talkative when there's no-one else about and three or four hours to pass.' Cribb gave a short laugh. 'Perhaps you did all the talking, sir. Poured out so many confidences that Bonner-Hill couldn't get a word in edgeways.'

Fernandez crossed the room to within a yard of Cribb, his eyes alarmingly red-lidded. 'What are you saying? What are you implying about me?'

Cribb put up a placatory hand. 'One moment, sir. I don't think I'm implying anything. I'm simply trying to assist your recollection of those fishing expeditions in case Bonner-Hill told you something that might be pertinent to my inquiries. When did you last speak to him? There's a straightforward question for you!'

Fernandez continued to gaze inhospitably at Cribb for several seconds more before replying. 'Last night, after dinner.'

'Did he mention his plan to go out fishing this morning?'

'He did. I had to tell him I wouldn't be joining him. My laryngitis put it out of the question.'

'Of course. Did anyone else in Merton know he would be going out alone? Did he mention it at dinner?'

'I told you,' Fernandez said. 'It was after dinner that we spoke.'

'To your knowledge had he ever been out before on his own looking for that pike?'

'To my knowledge, no.'

'Well, there's a curious thing,' said Cribb. 'The first time the poor man decides to do a bit of fishing on his own he gets murdered. The only other person in Oxford who knows he is going out alone is yourself, but you're confined to your rooms with laryngitis. It looks as though this murder wasn't planned at all.

Whoever killed Mr Bonner-Hill might as well have put an end to anybody else unfortunate enough to have been about at that particular time. A tramp. A university don. It's all the same. This is murder for the sake of killing. I've come across some nasty things in my time, Mr Fernandez, but this really makes me shudder.'

CHAPTER TWENTY

Manhunt—Murderers in straw hats—How Harriet was reduced to tears

The search for the three wanted men, Humberstone, Gold and Lucifer, was given the highest priority. At the Chief Constable's orders every fit man in the City force was deployed. Those who had done night duty were recalled after four hours, and the police reserve were used for house to house inquiries. Hotels, public houses, shops, parks, music halls, the college precincts, even houses of accommodation were visited and Cribb's meticulous description of the three recited, followed by the grim injunction, 'If you should recognize these men, do not approach them yourself. Call a policeman. They are wanted for questioning in connection with a serious charge.'

Despite the thoroughness of the description and search, nothing of importance was found until late in the afternoon, when a check was made of the skiffs lashed together near Magdalen Bridge in the Cherwell and one was found to be the *Lucrecia.* The covers were taken off and the luggage removed for examination. The two wicker baskets and one carpet bag contained between them three pairs of pyjamas, two towels, three blankets, toothbrushes, combs, leather boots, a map of the Thames, a set of playing-cards and two bottles of cider. 'What did you expect?' asked the sergeant who had found the boat. 'A signed confession?'

Cribb had come back from Merton convinced that Bonner-Hill had been murdered in the same fashion as Walters, the tramp at Hurley. 'He must have met his murderers early in the morning,' he told Thackeray and Harriet in a room at Oxford police station. 'It was a quiet backwater, with nobody about. They approached him in their boat and got him aboard on some pretext. Then one of them must have pinioned his arms, while another gripped him round the neck, applying pressure to the artery until he lost consciousness. It wasn't strangulation: that would have been too obvious. Even so, some marks were left around the neck and shoulders. Once he was insensible, they heaved him over the side and held his face under for long enough to fill his breathing passages with water. Verdict: drowning. So many bodies are taken from the Thames that there was every chance of the coroner finding a verdict of death by misadventure or suicide. The possibility of murder wouldn't arise unless there was something suspicious. Our set of murderers didn't reckon on the marks appearing on the victims' necks after death.'

Thackeray's mouth shaped as if to whistle, but drew in breath instead. 'Killing two men in cold blood like that! The calculation in it—it's horrible. Most murders you can understand, even if you don't altogether agree with the outcome. Jealous husbands, neglected wives, sons and daughters wanting to inherit—murder's a family thing, as often as not. But killing strangers as a way to pass the time on a river trip isn't nice, not nice at all.'

'It's beyond understanding,' said Harriet, still tortured by the knowledge that she might have averted Bonner-Hill's death. 'Where is the reason in it? It's quite insane.'

'I can't agree with that, miss,' said Cribb. 'There's a good intelligence behind all this. It may be inspired by the Devil, but it's coolly planned, I'm sure of that. Here we are at the end of a summer when young men in hundreds have taken to the river, paddling gaily up to Oxford like the three in Mr Jerome's book. It's high ton—the thing to do. Good sport, good exercise, good fun. A world away from sudden death. Who would believe in a party of assassins in a skiff? Murderers in straw hats? It's preposterous—and that's why they've done it. Three men in a boat, not to mention the dog, doing the journey in the book lock by lock, pausing only to commit jolly little murders at intervals along the way.'

'For amusement, Sarge?' said Thackeray, his face a study.

'Well, it wasn't for gain, or they'd have taken the money the tramp was carrying. Can you think of any other reason? I wondered first of all whether the first murder—of Choppy Walters—was to try out the method. If you think of it callously, as they would, a tramp is a perfect subject for trying out your skills as a murderer. Nobody notices a vagrant, or misses him when he isn't seen any more. If that's what the first murder was about, a dress rehearsal, so to speak, it suggests that the second was the real performance. In other words, they'd been planning Bonner-Hill's destruction from the start. A neat idea—until you recollect that Bonner-Hill wouldn't have been alone in the backwater without Fernandez getting laryngitis, and that's a circumstance they couldn't have planned for.'

'So they happened to see Bonner-Hill alone in his punt and decided to kill him, just like that,' said Thackeray, still struggling to accept the truth of what he was saying.

'Just like that.'

'And they're quite liable to do it again. Glory, Sarge, we've got to stop them this time!'

For Harriet, the last two words were twists of a dagger. She covered her face with her hands.

CHAPTER TWENTY-ONE

The Widow at Windsor—A Providential insurance—The failings of a Fellow

Later that afternoon a small group assembled in the City Mortuary for the formal identification of Bonner-Hill's remains. Out of respect for Mrs Bonner-Hill, who was coming from an address in Windsor, Cribb had exchanged his boating costume for a borrowed suit. Harriet, her eyes still red from crying, was wrapped in a black shawl. The attendant made the understandable error of supposing her the freshly bereaved widow and was murmuring condolences until Cribb explained that she was there in case Mrs Bonner-Hill needed support from one of her own sex. With that made clear, the attendant's conversation switched to horse-racing and the entry for the Cesarewitch. A movement outside the door caused him just as suddenly to revert to: ' . . . and so young, and with his whole career ahead of him. He would surely have risen in the

University were it not for this. Ah! This must be . . .' The voice trailed respectfully away.

'Mrs Bonner-Hill' announced the man who had pushed open the door.

The young widow was heavily veiled and in deep mourning.

'This is Sergeant Cribb of the police,' explained the attendant. 'And Miss Shaw. Sometimes, on occasions such as this, it is helpful if another lady . . .' He left his sentence unfinished from forbearance, not forgetfulness. Predictably in Oxford, he was a very polished mortuary attendant.

'Jacob Goldstein, manager of the Playhouse at Windsor,' said Mrs Bonner-Hill's companion, so young that for a moment it was not clear whether he was referring to somebody else, but as he said no more the inference was that he had introduced himself. Dark-complexioned, with a handsome, sensitive face, he wore a lightweight black overcoat. The quality of the cloth suggested that the Playhouse did not run at a loss.

'Shall we go through to the . . . ?' the attendant suggested.

'That is why we are here,' said Goldstein. 'Are you prepared, my dear?'

Mrs Bonner-Hill made a small sound of acquiescence from under her veil. They filed into a room without windows. It was cold and smelt of carbolic. The body was on a wooden trolley covered by a grey sheet. First, the attendant drew Mrs Bonner-Hill to a table at the side of the room. 'His clothes,' he whispered, turning over the jacket to reveal the lining. 'Are you able to state with certainty . . .?'

She nodded.

'Was there anything in the pockets?' Cribb inquired.

'A small amount of money and a handkerchief,' confided the attendant. 'The practice is to deliver all such things to the executors. The recently bereaved are thus spared the . . .'

'Shall we do what we came to do?' asked Goldstein, moving towards the trolley. His eagerness to get the formalities over must have been to spare Mrs Bonner-Hill unnecessary distress, but Harriet could not exclude the thought that there was probably a 7.30 performance at Windsor that evening.

'As you wish. Madam, if you would kindly stand just here . . .'

Harriet, too, stepped forward, ready to justify her presence.

'You won't see much through your veil, Melanie,' Goldstein gently pointed out.

Mrs Bonner-Hill lifted it and revealed a face of unarguable beauty, the more winsome for its tiny indications of strain, the slightly pursed lips, damp eyelashes and just perceptible creasing of the forehead. Her eyes were large and blue and her hair, clustered in natural curls, was so fair that against the veil it could have been white.

'If you're ready . . .' said the attendant, taking hold of the edge of the sheet. He peeled it back.

Harriet, poised to cope with an hysterical woman, need not have bothered. The hysterics happened, but their force was directed elsewhere. 'Dead!' cried Mrs Bonner-Hill as if she had not expected it. 'My Harry dead! Oh Jacob, what shall I do?' She clutched Goldstein determinedly round the waist and pressed her face sobbing against his chest. 'Widowed, at twenty-six! What will become of me?'

Cribb motioned to the attendant to replace the sheet. They steered the distracted widow into the ante-room and found a chair for her, but she still clung to Goldstein. Harriet decided that Mrs Bonner-Hill's suffering was so extreme that nobody could censure her for forwardness in regard to Mr Goldstein. Circumstances could provide exceptions to polite convention. It was unfortunate that he was not a few years older, an uncle, say, or a friend of her father's, but she could not be blamed. Her grief might have appeared just a little histrionic, and she was, indeed, an actress, but this was quite outside the repertoire of romantic comedy.

Cribb leaned confidentially towards the attendant. 'I believe you make a good, strong cup of tea in these places.'

In ten minutes Mrs Bonner-Hill had recovered sufficiently to relax her hold on Goldstein and accept the cup which was offered. The theatre manager took out his watch and glanced discreetly at it.

'Your husband owned a property in North Oxford, I understand,' Cribb said to Mrs Bonner-Hill. Conversation was difficult in these circumstances, but he was not the sort to be inhibited. 'It's a consolation to have somewhere to live. Will you go there for the next few days? There are formalities to attend to, of course. It would be difficult from—where are you residing at present?—Windsor.'

She glanced in Goldstein's direction. 'I had not thought of that.'

'You could put up at a hotel, of course,' Cribb went on. 'It might be less distressing for you than your former home.'

'I suppose it might.'

'This young lady, Miss Shaw, is in Oxford for the weekend. I'm arranging for her to take a room in a small hotel in St Aldate's. It occurs to me that you might care to join her there. You could take your meals together. At times like this, a little company is a great support.'

'I am not ungrateful, but—'

Goldstein broke in. 'Sergeant Cribb is speaking good sense, my dear. I shall not be able to stay overnight and it would be too distressing for you to pass the night in that house in Banbury Road. If Miss Shaw has no objection to the plan, I think you should do as the sergeant suggests.'

'I shall be pleased to help in any way I can,' Harriet offered.

'Things should be completed in a day or two,' said Cribb. 'Once the funeral is over and his affairs are tidied up, you'll be able to resume your normal life, get back on the stage. Good to have something to occupy the mind. Has Mrs Bonner-Hill performed in your theatre, Mr Goldstein?'

Goldstein's cheeks went slightly pinker. 'Yes. In several different productions.'

'That's how you met, I expect,' Cribb went on staunchly. 'Looked after your cast as if they were your own family. I've a great admiration for the way you theatricals stick together. This lady won't be short of parts when she returns to the boards, I'll wager. Are you in anything at the moment, ma'am?'

'No.' Mrs Bonner-Hill's hand sought Goldstein's and held it. 'I am between plays.'

'Ah. Shows how wrong it is to jump to conclusions. Seeing Mr Goldstein here, I supposed you were in the current production at Windsor.'

'We are playing *Lear*,' said Goldstein acidly. 'Mrs Bonner-Hill is a comedy actress. I happened to be visiting Melanie when the constable called this afternoon and broke the news to her. I could do no less than accompany her to this place. We are old friends.' He added, with emphasis, 'I met poor Bonner-Hill more than once.'

'Really?' said Cribb. 'I thought he disapproved of the theatre.'

'Oh no,' interjected Mrs Bonner-Hill. 'He liked it well enough. He disapproved of my continuing on the stage after we were married, that is all.' She dabbed her eyes with a lace handkerchief.

'Disapproved? He forbade you. Issued threats!' said Goldstein. 'He would have terminated your career the day he married you if he had got his way. I don't like speaking ill of the dead, but it doesn't show much concern for the theatre to marry one of its most talented young actresses and order her never to go on to a stage again. Like pulling the wings off a butterfly.'

'We had misunderstandings,' explained Mrs Bonner-Hill unnecessarily. 'About a year ago I returned to the stage and Harry moved back into his rooms in Merton. It was a civilized arrangement, with no bitterness on either side. By then we had come to accept that our careers were more important to us than an unfruitful marriage. He sent me money regularly.'

'You will notice the lack of it, then,' said Cribb.

'There is the insurance,' said Mrs Bonner-Hill, her eyes wider and bluer at this consoling thought. 'His life was insured for five thousand pounds. That should be enough to support me whether I return to the stage or not.'

'Insurance?' said Cribb. 'Which company insured him, ma'am?'

'The Providential. He made the arrangements a week after we were married. It depressed me somewhat at the time, thinking about death so soon after the wedding, but Harry was quite unshakeable. His own papa had died young and left his family unprovided for. They were not penniless, but they lived in reduced circumstances. Harry went to Tonbridge as a scholarship boy. It was only when he got to Oxford that he had any money to spend on himself. An uncle made him an allowance in recognition of his scholastic achievements. I think the reason why he was so particular about his appearance at Oxford was that he had been compelled to wear old clothes at Tonbridge. Other boys can be very cruel, I believe.'

'Utterly heartless,' Goldstein confirmed, and added, moved by some personal recollection, 'Little monsters.'

'Your husband was happier in Oxford, then?' suggested Cribb.

'Yes, indeed! He took to the academic life like a duck to water. Oh dear!' Mrs Bonner-Hill bit her lip like a schoolgirl who had given a wrong answer. A large tear rolled down her left cheek. She wiped it away. 'Forgive me.

Such a foolish thing to say.'

'Don't concern yourself on our account, ma'am,' said Cribb. 'If it distresses you to talk about your late husband . . .' He was catching the mortuary attendant's habit.

'Not at all,' said Mrs Bonner-Hill. 'I want to help you if I possibly can. We must find the person responsible for this terrible thing. I have been trying to think of anyone who might have harboured a grudge against Harry, but I am at a loss. You see, I have not seen so much of him in the past twelve months. His colleagues in Merton could give you a better idea of his comings and goings.'

'Mr Fernandez?' said Cribb. 'I spoke to him earlier.'

'That man! Don't rely on anything he tells you. A most unwholesome person. It is too embarrassing to go into now. He is not a gentleman, I am afraid.'

'Do I gather that there was an incident, ma'am?' Cribb asked.

'The lady prefers not to speak about it,' cautioned Goldstein. 'I think this has gone far enough.'

'You're wanting to get back in time for *King Lear,* sir?'

'That is immaterial. Melanie should not be forced to submit to more interrogation.'

'I wasn't forcing her, sir. She just expressed her willingness to help. If she prefers not to speak about her experience with Mr

Fernandez . . .'

But Melanie had evidently decided it was better if the truth were out. 'One afternoon at Merton before Harry and I were married, he was standing in the corridor outside Harry's rooms as I came out alone. I knew him as one of the Fellows, so I smiled—just a polite smile of recognition, you understand—and prepared to pass him. Imagine my astonishment when he stepped in front of me without a word, pressing me physically against the wall. I was too shocked to cry out and I could not move, he was so close to me. I thought he was attempting to kiss me and I tried to move my head aside. Then—I am a married woman now, but it makes me shudder still—I became conscious of the presence of his left hand inside my blouse.'

'Deplorable!' said Goldstein.

'It was only there for a second and then he withdrew it, released me and was gone. I was too mortified with shame to go back to Harry, so I rearranged my clothes and walked twice round the Fellows' Quad.'

'What self-possession!' said Goldstein.

'It was more than a year before I mentioned the matter to Harry and by then he was my husband. To make things worse, he expressed no particular surprise when I told him, and actually tried to fabricate excuses for Mr Fernandez by saying that he had a weakness—a blind spot, he called it—where ladies were concerned. It was fairly common knowledge in the Senior Common Room. He dismissed it, just like that! And then went on to tell me how unfortunate it was when a man had things he was ashamed of, because sooner or later they became known to his colleagues. Do you see what he did? He turned the whole thing upside down to make me feel that if I went back to the stage it would be betraying him. That started our first serious argument. I should never have spoken to him about it.'

'He was already friendly with Fernandez, I expect,' said Cribb.

'Of course he was—and determined that my experience should not spoil the friendship. Harry was a fine man in many respects, and a dutiful husband, but he brushed aside my feelings in this matter. He insisted that we both behaved towards Mr Fernandez as if nothing had happened. In fact, he took to inviting him to dinner, to show me that he possessed qualities I had not appreciated before. I admit that after several such evenings I started to revise my opinion of our visitor. I began to wonder whether I had exaggerated the incident in the passage. Mr Fernandez has a very charming manner and he could not be faulted at our dinner parties. Harry was delighted, and I was greatly reassured—to my cost.'

'There was another incident?'

'Worse than the first. I would rather not

speak about it now.'

'It made no difference to your husband's friendship with him?'

'Harry did not find out. I had no encouragement to tell him. It was a chance encounter that led to something more. I tried to forget about it, but John Fernandez is not easily put down. He has often pestered me since. These days I find such approaches more tiresome than frightening, but he is still an odious man. After Harry and I had gone our own ways he exerted more and more of an influence over him. This is the result.'

'You blame Fernandez for your husband's death?'

'Most certainly. Harry had no interest in fishing until John Fernandez introduced him to it. He used to laugh at the man for getting up so early on Saturday mornings. I did not know until this morning that he had come so much under his influence that he was doing the very thing he used to hold in contempt. Find your murderer by all means, Sergeant, and hang him, but I shall always know who really was responsible for Harry's death.'

CHAPTER TWENTY-TWO

In which Thackeray acts on information received—A boarding party—And a party of quite another sort

A rowing boat drifted slowly with the current, the oarsman holding his blades clear of the water as his passenger, Constable Thackeray, trained a pair of binoculars on four small squares of light, the windows of a houseboat just distinguishable against the dark mass of Christ Church Meadow. The sun had set more than an hour before. The sky was overcast and the river had the solid look of tar macadam.

'Are you sure?' Thackeray asked, putting down the binoculars.

'Sure as a dose of salts,' affirmed his companion, a small rotund person of the type generally found where there are boats and water. Through the darkness his cheeks gleamed like the last two apples in a barrel. He had walked into Oxford Police Station at half past eight. Hearing his story, the desk sergeant had brought him in to Thackeray, in charge of the search during Cribb's absence at the mortuary.

It had been difficult to tell whether he genuinely had information. Searches on the scale of this one could be relied upon to excite certain members of the public into concocting totally spurious accounts of things they thought the police would like to hear. Cribb's way of testing his informants was to put a few sharp questions to them. Thackeray, not equal to that, had muttered imprecations of appalling violence instead. 'Honest to God I saw them,' the boatman had insisted. 'One like a blooming great bear, one cove with a large head and thick glasses and a thin one with glasses. And a dog.'

The dog had settled it. Thackeray had swiftly formed a posse of six regular constables and two special and marched them down St Aldate's to Folly Bridge, where they had commandeered two skiffs. With the boatman showing the way in his rowing boat and the skiffs respectfully astern, this small flotilla had moved downstream past the spectral college barges until they had drawn level with the houseboat.

Everyone now waited in midstream for Thackeray's signal. He held the glasses to his eyes again. If this proved to be a mistake, if the occupant of the houseboat turned out to be some Oxford worthy preparing to retire for the night, it would not be easy explaining what nine constables were doing aboard his floating home. It would not be easy explaining it to the constables. Or Cribb.

'I can't hear the dog,' he said, wanting reassurance.

'It wouldn't bark all the time, guv.'

'I can't see anything through the window either.'

'It was a dog, not a blooming horse,' said the boatman.

When he had reached the inescapable conclusion that there was nothing to be salvaged from the adventure by giving up at this stage, Thackeray told the boatman to move alongside the houseboat. As they approached, he was able to see that it was actually a barge some thirty feet in length, with a broad deck on which the 'house' was constructed, in fact a diminutive version of the Ark, except that the roof was flat, forming an upper deck with a wrought iron balustrade around it.

The strains of a concertina from within the boat lifted Thackeray's confidence as they came alongside. If there was music, the chance was good that more than one person was aboard. The spectre of the irate houseboat owner in his nightshirt ceased troubling him.

Standing in the rowing boat, Thackeray was unable to see through the lighted windows, which was a pity, because there was nothing for it now but to interrupt whatever was going on inside. He signalled to the waiting constables to approach, and then he clambered aboard with ponderous care. With good fortune the concertina would drown any sounds he made on the deck. He could do without Towser announcing his arrival.

The door of the cabin was ahead of him, ornately gilt-panelled. To its right a set of iron stairs painted white led to the upper deck. On an impulse he climbed them and stood aloft, beckoning to his support party to come aboard. With five hefty constables posted at the cabin door, he crouched and passed his hands speculatively over the surface of the deck.

In a moment he located a metal ring about four inches in diameter, inset level with the deck. By stroking his fingertips outwards from the ring, he traced the outline of a trapdoor to the room below.

He sat back on his haunches and rubbed the side of his beard, mentally invoking all the benign influences that ever favoured policemen. He drew a long breath and pulled up the trapdoor.

His first sensation was of dazzling light. Cigar smoke was billowing from the hatchway. The smoke thinned, his eyes adjusted to the light and he looked into the amazed and upturned face of a blonde woman in a black corset standing motionless on a red carpet. To state that she was motionless is not quite accurate, for parts of her were quivering, but all conscious movement had stopped, as if she were petrified by the interruption. The position of her arms suggested she had been performing a dance—and out of sight the concertina continued playing—but what kind of dance was performed in stays Thackeray did not know.

If it were not for the cigar smoke, he would have muttered an apology, put down the hatch, called off his constables and disappeared into the night. The way young women amused themselves on houseboats was no part of his present inquiry. The smoke reminded him that although the prospect through the hatch was enough to occupy one pair of eyes, there were parts of the cabin obscured from view.

The concertina stopped. 'What is it?' asked a man's voice.

The dancer unfroze sufficiently to point above her head and whisper, 'Look!'

A suggestion that could only be helpful, Thackeray decided. Anyone curious enough to take it up would be obliged to stand where they could be seen. It saved him risking an accident by dipping his head and shoulders through the hatchway.

Yet the accident nearly happened when he lurched forward in surprise as two more young women appeared in view, one, like the first, in a corset, white in colour with purple trimmings, the other pulling on a silk gown with such unconcern that it was starkly clear she, at least, could not be faulted for wearing stays.

'Lawks! It's another fellow dropping in on us,' said the one in the gown.

'Well give him a hand, Meg. He can't be worse than mine,' said the other. As she tossed back her head to laugh at her own wit, fumes of gin wafted upwards.

'Permit me to see for myself,' said a voice, a thin, clinical voice that Thackeray recognized. The three women were hustled aside by Mr Lucifer. He was wrapped in a gown like Meg's. 'What the Devil . . . ? It's the blighter with the beard we saw in the Barley Mow.'

'Follows you around, does he?' said one of the women. 'A regular peeping Tom! Have you had your eyeful, darling?'

Insults could not touch Edward Thackeray. He was enjoying one of the grander moments of his police career. Almost single-handed, he had caught the three most wanted men in Oxfordshire.

He did not have long to savour it. Without a word, Humberstone, the biggest of the three, arrived beneath the hatch, reached up, caught Thackeray by the collar and jerked him head-first into the cabin.

His shoulder hit the carpet and saved him from concussion but his body crashed painfully through a small table. He lay among the splintered wood in an enclosure of legs without a skirt or trouser among them. Somewhere nearby a dog was barking.

He propped himself up on an elbow. Nothing was going to deflect him from his proper duty. 'Gentlemen, I am a police officer.

A warrant has been issued for your arrest and I am here to take you into custody.' He fainted.

CHAPTER TWENTY-THREE

Humberstone at bay—Pinning in on Towser—Cribb learns about insurance

'What are they going to say about this at the Providential?' Cribb asked.

'About what in particular?' Humberstone replied, managing to preserve his loftiness of manner while wearing a silk kimono. He was sitting handcuffed in the charge room at Oxford Police Station facing Cribb across a table. A uniformed constable sat nearby, notebook in hand.

'Why, about three respectable members of its Claims Department visiting a houseboat named, I understand, the *Xanadu,* and being round there in the company of three ladies of very uncertain reputation.'

'I can think of no reason why the Providential should hear about it. Is this a threat of some kind? I don't care for your tone, Sergeant. You may not approve of the ladies on the *Xanadu,* but there is nothing unlawful in what we were doing.'

'I grant you that,' said Cribb, 'but assaulting

a police officer isn't lawful. We regard that very seriously in the Force. Constable Thackeray is going to get an uncommon nasty bruise on his shoulder as the result of your attentions.'

'I merely pulled the man down through the hatch. How could I have known he was a policeman? It's a sorry state of affairs if a gentleman can't challenge a fellow who intrudes upon his privacy. If your constable wanted to be treated in a civil fashion, he should have knocked on the door and introduced himself, instead of peering through the skylight.'

'Are you suggesting that Thackeray didn't tell you he was a police officer?'

'Not until I had him on the floor. He was too busy goggling at the girls, old boy. It's lucky for him I had the dog locked in the galley, or he might have had some more injuries to complain of. Policeman! If he told you he announced himself before I had him helpless on the floor, the bounder's lying.'

Cribb sniffed. 'And I suppose the two officers who attempted to apprehend you as you bolted through the door are just imagining they were hurled into the river—or perhaps you didn't notice they were wearing uniforms?'

'There's no need to be sarcastic with me, Sergeant. The events aboard that houseboat were very confused, believe me. Between the dog barking and the women screaming and your policeman jabbering something about a warrant, it's not surprising that we made for the door. And with Gold and Lucifer pushing at my back I may have met your officers with something of an impact. I'm sixteen stone in weight and once I'm moving it isn't easy to stop. I'm sorry about the wet uniforms and the man with the broken nose. I'm sorry about Constable Thackeray's shoulder. But if you burst in upon people as he did, unexpected things are liable to happen. Now perhaps you'll tell me what it was all about.'

For a man in Humberstone's situation, it was a polished performance, Cribb had to concede. Anyone who could fell three policemen trying to arrest him and put it down to circumstances beyond his control was a cool customer. It was already past midnight. Here he was, figuratively squaring up like a prizefighter, ready to trade punches by the hour. It would be unwise to mix it with him when there were two others to come. Best take him quietly through the evidence and then try conclusions with Gold and Lucifer.

'When I saw you last, Mr Humberstone—it was in the Barley Mow, if you remember—there was talk of a dead man, a tramp, down the river a bit, at Hurley.'

'You mentioned it,' said Humberstone with caution. 'I didn't attach much importance to it. You didn't tell us you were a detective, or I might have taken more interest. It's a queer thing when you think about it that a member of the public can be locked away for impersonating a policeman, when there's policemen all over England masquerading as members of the public.'

'The tramp was murdered,' Cribb went on, refusing to be drawn. 'Someone took him on a boat and very likely got him drunk. They pushed him over the side and held him down until his lungs filled with water. We found the marks of someone's hands on his neck and shoulders. There were other marks, Mr Humberstone. There must have been a struggle aboard the boat before they got him into the water. We found a dogbite on his leg.'

'My word!' said Humberstone in an exaggerated squeak. 'I begin to understand how Scotland Yard works. You suspect Towser. I hope you will allow him to get in touch with his solicitor.'

'Today a second body was found, here in Oxford. The victim was a don from Merton College, Mr Bonner-Hill. The state of his body indicates that he was murdered in the same manner as the tramp.'

'Don't say it, Sergeant! You found Towser's teethmarks again. A tramp and a don! That animal makes no distinctions at all. He'll bite anyone who comes his way.'

Cribb was disinclined to smile. 'No, Mr Humberstone. This time there were no teethmarks. I happen to know that you and your friends were on the river at about the time the murder was committed—that's the connection.'

Humberstone sat back in his chair and rested the handcuffs on the table's edge. 'At this point, you would like me to deny emphatically that we were anywhere near the scene of the murder at the time it happened. You then ask me how I can possibly know when and where the crime took place when you haven't told me. Checkmate.'

'This ain't a game, sir. But since we're talking about the when and the where of it, where were you when the first murder was committed at Hurley?'

'If you want an answer to that, you had better remind me when it happened,' said Humberstone, cocking his head provokingly.

'On Tuesday night.'

'An age ago.'

'In the Barley Mow you said you put up at the Crown in Marlow, just as the characters in the book did. No, I'm doing you an injustice. Mr Gold said that. You were silent on the matter.'

Humberstone nodded. For the first time in the interview, a look of caution flickered across his face. 'Gold is usually very authoritative on matters of detail.'

'He wasn't too convincing on the location of the Crown,' said Cribb. 'Didn't seem to know whether it was beside the river or at the top of the High Street. Are you sure you stayed there, sir?'

'That's a question you should address to Sammy Gold, not me.'

'It doesn't matter, sir. I've got a man checking the register of guests.'

'Then you'll get your answer.'

Cribb changed tack. 'Did you know Mr Bonner-Hill, by any chance?'

'What makes you think that I should?' said Humberstone, smiling again.

'Be so good as to answer my question,' said Cribb more firmly.

'No, I did not know Bonner-Hill. When you mentioned the name just now, it was the first time I had ever heard of it.'

'You're sure of that, Mr Humberstone?'

'Do you doubt me, Sergeant?'

'I'm a little puzzled, sir. I thought you might have come across the name. It's not a very common one. I met his widow this afternoon. She told me his life was insured with the Providential.'

'Ah.' Humberstone leaned forward, propping his elbows on the table and his chin on his hands. 'You supposed that the name ought to be on the tip of my tongue, together with the million and a half others who insure with the Providential. If you suppose we spend our time reciting the names of our policy holders, you have a very mistaken impression of what goes on in a City insurance office,

Sergeant. For one thing, policy holders' names are kept confidential and for another, my companions and I are employed in the Claims Department. Bonner-Hill's name would not be drawn to our attention until a claim is lodged. From what you tell me, we can expect to deal with it when we return to the office a week on Monday.'

'Possibly,' said Cribb. 'For the present, you're returning to the cells.'

CHAPTER TWENTY-FOUR

Mr Lucifer's cautionary tale—The perils of poker—The demon and the dance

Lucifer, when he appeared in a dressing-gown before Cribb, was in no mood for verbal sparring. A muscle at the side of his mouth was in spasm, providing fulsome views of his teeth, and his eyebrows were rearing up like dogs on chains.

'No, I shall not sit down. I have not been so humiliated in all my life. A cell for common criminals! You shall hear more of this, my man. I propose to use every process of the law that is open to me to see that innocent members of the public are protected from such vile experiences as this.' He stepped towards the desk and glared at his inquisitor. 'I remember you, by thunder! You're the person who was sitting in the Barley Mow the other evening. You didn't tell us you were a policeman then.'

'No,' said Cribb. 'I didn't mention it. I suppose I could have put on my helmet and whistled *If you want to know the time, ask a p'liceman,* but it's not encouraged when you're on plain clothes duty. Shall we begin, sir? It's getting late and I hope to get some sleep tonight. I've been talking to Mr Humberstone. He told me a little about the way things work in your insurance office. Have you always worked with the Providential, sir?'

'Am I obliged to answer these questions?'

'Not at all, sir. If you're innocent it might help to convince me of the fact, but if you're guilty you can only make things worse for yourself by speaking up. I should definitely not say a word if you have anything to hide.'

The look Lucifer returned showed no gratitude for this advice, but he was unable to ignore its implications. He said, 'I joined the Providential after I left school in 1870.'

'And when did you join the Claims Department?'

'That was six years ago. Humberstone and I were transferred together from Fire and Accident. Gold was already working there.'

'And you soon became friends?'

'We shared the same office,' said Lucifer, not only answering the questions, but beginning to be expansive. 'One learns in the first place to tolerate people. Later, a kind of understanding develops. Only in the last six months has it grown into anything resembling a friendship.'

'This trip on the river, sir. Who suggested it?'

'I am not at all certain. The notion arose from our interest in *Three Men in a Boat,* as I believe we mentioned at Clifton Hampden. I recollect that we were saying that not one of us had got out of London all the summer and perhaps we had become a trifle jaded. We were staring at each other across our desks, each of us, I suppose, hoping he did not look so jaded as the others, when someone—it was Gold, now I call it to mind—said, "Let's go up the river." To tell the truth, I don't believe he meant it. He was quoting the words of George in Chapter One. It was intended as a droll remark, nothing more. Humberstone took it literally, said, "Yes, by Jove, let's do the trip they did in the book!"—and we all agreed it was a first-class suggestion.'

'It was Gold who sowed the seed, then,' said Cribb.

Lucifer's mouth twitched again. 'I'm not sure what you are implying.'

'No matter, sir. The three of you embarked on the trip on Monday. I presume you set out from Kingston.'

'That is so. We followed the itinerary in the

book. We camped at Picnic Point that night and rowed up to Marlow on Tuesday.'

'And put up at the Crown?' Cribb mildly suggested.

Lucifer hesitated.

'That was what Mr Gold said in the Barley Mow,' pressed Cribb.

'He must have been mistaken,' said Lucifer. 'It is a pardonable error. We certainly *proposed* spending the night at the Crown. We had it firmly fixed in our minds that the characters in the book stayed there, so it was not surprising that Gold should have committed a slip of the tongue. When Marlow is mentioned, any person familiar with the book thinks of the Crown. It is as simple as that.'

'Was it full when you got there?'

'We did not actually get to the Crown. It was late when we reached Marlow, and we were tired. It's a pull of nearly twenty miles from Runnymede to Marlow. We took rooms at a private lodging house, the first we could find.'

'Would you remember the address, sir?'

'I'm quite certain I wouldn't,' answered Lucifer. 'I might be able to find the place again if I was in Marlow, but I'm not even confident of that. It was dusk, you see. Is this salient to your inquiry?'

Cribb ignored the question. 'These, er, ladies you were visiting on the houseboat today. Had you made their acquaintance before this evening?'

Lucifer coughed behind his handcuffs. 'This afternoon, to be precise. We were taking a constitutional through Christ Church Meadow. They were having a picnic on the grass. We raised our hats and smiled, and they invited us to join them. It seemed a jolly thing to do in the sunshine of a September afternoon. The thought crossed my mind that they might be some of the blue-stockinged invaders of the University one hears so much about these days. I believe there are quaint little villas here and there in Oxford with exalted names like Lady Margaret Hall purporting to provide young ladies with a university education, so it was not impossible that these three picnickers had anticipated the beginning of term by a few days. When the conversation started, I modified my theory somewhat. Don't misunderstand me—there was nothing indelicate in what they said. The accents, you know—definitely not University. Yet they were very agreeable company. After the picnic we promenaded along the footpath with them, looking at the barges. Presently one of the young ladies, the one called Moll, pointed out their houseboat and suggested we might like to go aboard. We had really proposed spending the afternoon touring the colleges, but Humberstone and Gold agreed with me that it would be discourteous to refuse the invitation, and anyway one college was very like another and we could safely leave out one or two from our itinerary in the interests of discovering what it was like aboard a houseboat. They took us to a small rowing boat nearby, and we went out in two parties.'

'What time was that?' Cribb asked.

'Oh, early in the afternoon. Before two o'clock, I should say.'

'I had every copper in Oxford looking for you and there you were sitting in a blooming houseboat. What happened after that?'

'They showed us over the boat. It was comfortably furnished, but, of course, rooms are at a premium aboard a vessel of that sort, so the sitting room served a secondary purpose as their bedroom, which might have given rise to embarrassment if they had not been so splendidly unconcerned about the matter. They suggested a game of cards. Humberstone and Gold enjoy a hand of poker and offered to teach the game to two of the girls, Moll and Meg, while I went on the upper deck with Towser to take a look at the view. I rather disapprove of cards. There was a canvas chair up there and I suppose I fell asleep in the sun, because when I next looked at my watch it was gone five o'clock. I rejoined the others and found them eating oysters. The game of poker had ended in victory for the ladies, who must have learned the rudiments of the game with remarkable speed. Gold had lost seven shillings and Humberstone nearly ten, so when somebody suggested we ought to have a champagne to accompany the oysters, I felt obliged to row ashore and bring back a magnum of Mumm's and a bottle of gin from a public house near Folly Bridge. That was a mistake, I now realize.'

'How was that, sir?'

'The girls were manifestly unused to strong drink. I am a teetotaller myself and I should have realized the danger. During my absence they had produced a concertina from somewhere and Humberstone, who is quite virtuoso, was playing it. Towser was locked in the galley, whining mournfully. After one glass of champagne the young lady called Meg pulled me out of my chair and pinioned me with her arms in such a way that I was obliged to perform a dance with her. It was a most distracting experience, I assure you.'

'I believe you,' said Cribb.

'I think that possibly my companions were a little shamed at having lost at poker to novices. They rather enjoyed the spectacle of me, the friend who had declined to play cards, suffering indignities of my own. Within a short time, however, Gold was prised from his seat by the other two young ladies and compelled to join in a waltz. It started as a waltz and ended in a gallop, for Humberstone, wretched fellow, increased the tempo of the music until our heads were spinning. I confess that we ended by collapsing in a heap on one of the beds. For a short time I was unable to focus my eyes with any certainty, but, oddly enough, the ladies seemed not at all distressed. On the contrary, they exhibited such exuberance that the thought crossed my mind that the gyrations of the dance must have generated some mysterious force, on the principle of the electric dynamo. Before I could draw breath, my jacket and waistcoat were removed and I had the greatest difficulty in dissuading Meg from parting me from my shirt as well. My colleague Gold, I discovered at this point, is susceptible to tickling. He was laughing uncontrollably as his partner grappled with him, which encouraged the ladies to believe we were enjoying the experience,'

'You were not?' said Cribb.

By way of response, Mr Lucifer straightened his back, drew in a sharp breath through his nostrils and looked at the ceiling.

'You protested, then?'

'I am afraid not. The possibility of an effective protest was undermined by Gold being so convulsed with laughter. Fortunately, that particular crisis passed eventually with the ladies getting out of breath and asking for another drink. By this time my nerves were in such an agitated state that I decided to set aside my temperance principles to the extent of half a glass of champagne. I must own that my memory of the next two hours is somewhat patchy. Certain things I can still see quite vividly—'

'I can imagine, sir. Constable Thackeray saw plenty when he opened the trapdoor. Two women in their under-garments and a third wearing only a dressing gown.'

Lucifer nodded thoughtfully. 'It must have come as a shock to an outsider. I am afraid that we failed those young ladies. As gentlemen, we should never have introduced them to the influence of the grape. It is a demon, Officer, and I hope for your sake that it never holds you in its thrall. And to think that by going out to purchase gin and champagne, I was the Devil's agent! If only we had adhered to our original plan of spending the afternoon visiting the colleges! It grieves me to think of the blushes of Meg and her friends when they are sufficiently sober to remember this evening and the shameful encouragement they got from three respectable employees of the Providential Assurance Company.'

The man was either a simpleton or a humbug. 'They were ladies of the town, sir. Common prostitutes.'

Lucifer's jaw dropped. 'Good God! In Oxford?'

'By your own account they took seventeen shillings from your friends at poker and the price of two bottles of drink from you. How much else did they collect from you? Speak up, Mr Lucifer.'

His face performed contortions again.

'How much to take off their clothes?' Cribb asked.

'A shilling a garment from each of us,' Lucifer managed to say.

Cribb whistled. 'Just as well you're going to spend the rest of the night here. You can't have much left for a hotel. Take him down, Constable, and bring up Mr Gold.'

CHAPTER TWENTY-FIVE

The cocoa treatment—Russian Gold—Fried kidneys and Great Tom

A steaming mug of cocoa was waiting on the table when Gold arrived, an indication if he had known it that he was to get a different style of interview from his fellows.

'Unlock the handcuffs, Constable,' ordered Cribb. 'I don't expect any unpleasantness. My word, sir, you *have* been in the wars.'

The right-hand lens of Gold's spectacles had shattered. The fragments of glass were held in the frame, quite uselessly, for the spaces between the cracks were frosted over. There was also an ugly bruise above his eyebrow. 'No complaints, Officer,' he quickly said. 'My own fault entirely. Should never have panicked on the houseboat. Got too close to Humberstone, you know, and found his elbow in my eye.'

'Try the cocoa, sir. If you'd like cold milk to take the heat off, say the word. I wouldn't like to burn your tongue as well. I thought you might have got cold, sitting in the cells in a bathrobe. I'm Sergeant Cribb from Scotland Yard, making inquiries into the death of a man at Hurley last Tuesday night. I met you briefly at the Barley Mow the other evening.'

'So you did!' said Gold. 'I say, I'm sorry I didn't recognize you at once, Sergeant. I thought I knew the voice, but I can't see too famously like this. I blame nobody, mind. The death of a man, you say. That tramp, I take it. Somebody mentioned him at Clifton Hampden.'

'That's right, sir. And since we spoke, there's been another death. A don from Merton College was picked out of the water here in Oxford this morning.'

'You don't say!'

'They were both murdered, sir.'

'By Jove!'

'You and your friends have been arrested on suspicion of murdering them both.'

'I say, that's a bit thick. I've never heard of either of them.'

'I didn't mention their names,' said Cribb.

'So you didn't.' Mr Gold put the mug of cocoa to his lips and said, 'Lord! I've done it! Burnt my tongue.'

'Vicious stuff, hot cocoa, if you ain't used to

it,' said Cribb, pouring milk into the mug. 'You don't mind personal questions, do you, sir? What's your name in full?'

Gold dabbed his mouth with a handkerchief and said, 'Samuel Isaac Gold.'

'And your father's name?'

'Leonard Gold. What's my father got to do with it?'

'Nothing, I hope. Born in England, was he?'

Gold frowned. 'You want to know if I'm Jewish, is that it?'

'I'm asking where your father came from, Mr Gold.'

Gold spread out his hands. 'So he came from Russia. Does that make me a murderer?'

'Russia. What was his name in Russia?'

'What's this about? I told you my father's name. Gold is my name. If you want to call me Jewish, I won't stop you, but leave my father out of it. It's the same all over the world. If there's trouble, blame the Jews. Jack the Ripper is a Jew, did you know? That's what they say in Whitechapel. Who am I to argue, with a name like Sammy Gold?'

'Your father didn't change his name when he came to England?'

'What is it to you if he did?' Gold bitterly replied. 'He was a good man and he died ten years ago. The name on his stone is Leonard Gold.'

'As you say, sir.' Cribb steered the conversation into calmer waters. 'I was speaking to Mr Humberstone not long ago. He paid you a compliment, sir. Said you were a great authority on matters of detail, or something of the sort. We were talking about last Tuesday, the night you stayed in Marlow. The Crown, wasn't it?'

'The Crown,' Gold repeated flatly.

'You don't sound quite so positive as you were in the Barley Mow, sir. It *was* the Crown where you stayed, was it? Big hotel at the top of the High Street. Mentioned in *Three Men in a Boat.*'

'As you say. Chapter Twelve. The way Jerome puts it, you'd think it was beside the bridge.' Gold took off his spectacles and started polishing the good lens with his handkerchief. 'I have a confession, Sergeant. A Jew with a confession—what do you say to that? We didn't stay at the Crown.'

'What made you say that you did?'

He shrugged his shoulders. 'Conceit. We *meant* to stay there. Wanted to do the whole journey according to the book. That was the purpose of our holiday. When you mentioned the Crown, I couldn't bring myself to admit that we hadn't even seen it.'

Cribb indicated with a nod that the explanation was plausible. 'What prevented you from staying there?'

'The truth of it is that we found a cosy little inn beside the river and by the end of the evening we were in no condition to walk up the hill to the Crown.'

'Where did you put up?'

'Under canvas on our boat.'

'That's odd,' said Cribb. 'Mr Lucifer told me that you stayed at a private lodging house. He didn't mention an inn.'

'Lucifer wouldn't,' Gold said with a grin. 'He likes to think of himself as a teetotaller, but he lapses, you see, he lapses. I don't suppose he remembers, but he lapses. I don't suppose he remembers anything about Tuesday night, the state he was in. Yet to hear him talk, you'd think a drop never passed his lips. Did you question him about this evening? I'd like to have heard his account of that.'

'Never mind this evening,' said Cribb. 'Tell me about this morning. You were on the river very early, weren't you?'

'All night, to be accurate. We slept in the boat, in the backwater above Culham Lock. We were under way before seven this morning. Had breakfast in Oxford. Fried kidneys. Delicious.'

'What time was this?'

'Between half past eight and nine. We heard Great Tom striking as we finished off the toast. What time was your murder?'

'The doctor who examined the body estimated that death took place shortly after half past nine. Which hotel served you with breakfast?'

Mr Gold opened his palms again. 'Pity

about that. We almost had an alibi, didn't we? It was the Hotel Humberstone, Sergeant. We cooked the kidneys over an open fire on the edge of Christ Church Meadow.'

CHAPTER TWENTY-SIX

To Merton for Matins—An encounter in Mob Quad—The absurdity of Henry Bonner-Hill

As the oldest of Oxford's colleges, Merton had suffered from the improving zeal of twenty generations of architects. The buildings surrounding its four quadrangles presented an agglomeration of styles that had managed to conserve a sense of dignity until an early Victorian named Blore redesigned the main gate and the street front, and the notorious Butterfield eclipsed that with his grotesque block at the corner of Merton Grove. Happily, the chapel, conceived on the scale of a cathedral, dominated everything. The choir, dating from the thirteenth century, was in the Decorated style; the tower was Perpendicular. The rough stone on the west wall showed the intended outline of the nave, which had never been built.

So it was in the choir that Harriet sat with Melanie Bonner-Hill for Morning Service. The term not having started, the congregation was sparse. Across the aisle in the front pew was a white-haired, bearded man Mrs Bonner-Hill pointed out as the Warden. Behind him, at a higher level, were three others—'The Fellows,' she explained in a whisper. 'Hear no evil, speak no evil, see no evil.'

'Which one is Mr Fernandez?' Harriet inquired.

'The third one in, with the glossy hair and moustache.'

Once they had overcome the first awkwardness of their situation, Harriet and Melanie had found no difficulty in making conversation. By the end of dinner the evening before in their hotel, the colour had returned to the widow's cheeks and Harriet had felt herself buoyed up by the company of one of her own sex. Three days afloat with policemen had been more of an ordeal than she ever would have supposed. It had been a tonic to talk of nothing else but the theatre and Miss Terry's gowns and Mrs Langtry's conquests. By the time the *crêpes Suzette* arrived, Harriet had quite forgotten Sergeant Cribb; she had almost forgotten Constable Hardy. And Melanie Bonner-Hill, judging by the sparkle of her conversation, had forgotten she was a widow.

Sunday morning breakfast had been more subdued, but the friendship had blossomed when Melanie had asked Harriet to accompany her to Merton Chapel for Matins. 'The Warden invited me yesterday, out of respect for Harry, I presume. It's an honour, I'm sure, but I'm dreading it, the one woman among all those men. Would you come with me? I'm sure the Warden wouldn't mind, and it would be such a support. I can point out all the notables, Harriet. Oh, they're a dreadfully dull old lot! You'll see exactly what I mean.'

Certainly the Chaplain fitted the description. His voice was pitched on a monotone. When he introduced a note of topicality to the proceedings by prefacing the Collect of the Day with, 'In this we also commend the spirit of our brother, Bonner-Hill, so tragically taken from us only yesterday', the words passed generally unnoticed. So, happily, did the text of his sermon: 'Deliver me out of the mire and let me not sink.'

When it was over and they stepped into the sunshine of Mob Quad, a group was waiting to offer its condolences to Melanie. The Warden quite properly made the first approach. Harriet used the opportunity to take two steps backwards—two steps which took her within a yard of Mr Fernandez. As she had hoped, he needed no bidding to start a conversation. Lifting his top hat, he asked, 'Are you also from the theatre, ma'am?'

She turned to face him, and found the interest in his expression flattering, so flattering that she was quite relieved to notice that there was something just a little invidious in his smile. 'I am afraid not. I happen to be staying at the same hotel as Mrs Bonner-Hill. I am a visitor to Oxford.'

'How kind of you, in that case, to have escorted the poor lady to chapel.'

'Not at all, sir. I could not do less. You are a colleague of her late husband's, I expect?'

'Yes indeed. Knew him well. Better than, er, never mind. And what have you seen of Oxford on your visit?'

The river and the mortuary, Harriet wryly thought, but answered, 'Very little, sir. The college barges are beautiful. Like wedding cakes.'

'So they are, my dear, so they are. A pretty notion. I didn't catch your name . . .'

'Harriet Shaw. I am a student teacher. My college is farther down the river, the other side of Henley.'

'A teacher. And what do you propose to teach?'

She smiled. ' "Who" would be a better question. I am training to teach elementary school, so I have to get a grounding in all the subjects.'

'Quite properly.' Fernandez nodded with high seriousness. 'But I expect you favour one subject more than the others.'

'Geography is my favourite, Mr . . . ?'

'I do apologize, John Fernandez. Geography? That really is remarkable. I am a modern historian myself, but geography is my secret passion. I tell you, if it were ever recognized in Oxford as a subject worthy of proper study, I should abandon history overnight. I say, wouldn't it be grand to—'

Whatever Fernandez might have suggested was cut short by a tall, nervous man on his left. 'The Warden's moving, Fernandez. Are you going to speak next, or shall I?'

'Very well.' Fernandez doffed his hat to Harriet and moved to Melanie's side.

The tall man inclined his head to confer with Harriet. 'Flescher, ma'am. Principal of Postmasters. I wouldn't take Jack Fernandez too seriously, if you'll accept a word of advice.'

'It wasn't a serious conversation.'

'That's all right, then. We understand him in Merton, but we make allowances, you see.'

'I'm not sure whether I do.'

'It doesn't matter, then. Ah, Mrs Bonner-Hill is free.'

Melanie was, but John Fernandez was not. Another of the Fellows was in solemn conversation with him and they were walking slowly away across the quad.

'Aren't they quaint?' Melanie said when she had received all their condolences, and she had started back along Merton Street with Harriet. 'I was near to giggling at one point. I suddenly thought of the Vice-Chancellor's Ball last year—it was exactly the same ritual as they lined up to write their names on my card. I was terribly tempted to say to Mr Flescher—he's the thin one who came last—that all I had left was the polka. Is that very wicked? He was so flustered anyway that I don't think he would have noticed. Harry used to call him Goose-Flescher. Poor Harry—he was so scornful of them when I first knew him. The idea of becoming like them was unthinkable. I am afraid they must have worn him down in the last months. Murder is an unnecessary end, but to be murdered because you got up early to go fishing is absurd, don't you agree?'

'If you put it like that, yes.' Actually, Melanie had put it like that once or twice the night before as well. The circumstances of her husband's death seemed to distress her more than the fact. Yet the circumstances *were* important. The absence of sentiment in what she said made Harriet blink at times, but the sharpness of the observations was helping her question certain assumptions concerning Bonner-Hill's death. 'Didn't he have any interest in fishing when you were married?'

A ripple of laughter came from under the black veil. 'My dear, we had other ways to occupy ourselves. We didn't get up till noon. I'm used to theatre hours, you see. I never retire until after midnight. No, he only started his fishing after I left him and he went back to Merton.'

'Do they all go in for fishing?'

'Heavens, no! Only Fernandez, and he's been an enthusiast for years. I despise the man for reasons we needn't go in to, but I am bound to admit that he was the only possible companion for Harry in the College. Just think of the rest! If Harry was to have a friend in Merton, he had to affect an interest in fish. Isn't it monstrous?'

'I suppose if he were without a friend ...'

'My dear, I wouldn't have blamed him for going after other women. But fish!' Melanie pulled a face. 'I thought he was doing it to humour Fernandez until they told me he was out *alone* yesterday morning. I couldn't believe it!'

Harriet was beginning to pity Harry herself. 'A lot of men go in for angling, Melanie. I noticed scores as we rowed up from Henley. It doesn't seem to have prevented Mr Fernandez from taking an interest in other things. He spoke to me this morning—'

'Oh, did he? I noticed him standing conspicuously near. He wasn't unpleasant, I hope?'

'On the contrary, he—'

'Don't be taken in by his honeyed phrases, my dear. The man is dangerous. He has no more concern for women as individuals than he has for fish. If he hooks you, the best you can hope for is that he'll throw you back. Did he try to arrange—'

'Nothing was arranged,' Harriet quickly answered. Here, she sensed, was a threat to the friendship she had kindled with Melanie.

For whatever the odium was that surrounded John Fernandez, she was determined not to ignore the interest he had shown in her. Not from girlish notions of romance, but because she had been drawn into the investigation of the river murders. There still gnawed at her conscience the knowledge that Bonner-Hill need not have been killed if she had identified the three men in the boat in time. Sergeant Cribb had them prisoner now, but there remained the question of a motive, and without that he could not provide a case for a prosecution. Cribb had not speculated much on the case, but Harriet had heard him build one theory only to knock it down again. The murder of the tramp, he had postulated, could have been a rehearsal for the murder of Bonner-Hill, a testing of the method. The theory had foundered on the fact that no-one but Fernandez could have known Bonner-Hill was going out that Saturday morning. And Fernandez could not be implicated because he had been nursing his sore throat in Merton College.

Harriet had accepted all this, accepted that the murders must have been done on a whim, without motive. Then Melanie's statement had transformed her thinking. 'To be murdered because you got up early to go fishing is absurd.'

Of course it was absurd!

Nobody could have anticipated that

Bonner-Hill would go fishing alone. The whim was not the murderer's, but his. The intended victim had been John Fernandez.

CHAPTER TWENTY-SEVEN

Cribb lights a cigar—The world says 'murder'—All that glistens

Sergeant Cribb was not at Morning Service that Sunday. He was sitting in the Chief Inspector's chair at Oxford Police Station making a series of telephone calls. Sergeants at Scotland Yard did not qualify for telephone sets of their own, so he took unaccustomed pleasure in calling up the duty officers at Windsor, Marlow, Great Scotland Yard and the headquarters of the City of London Police at Old Jewry, and giving each of them a small task, as he put it, 'to expedite certain inquiries we are at present engaged upon in the City of Oxford'. When Thackeray returned from exercising Towser along the High, he received a sharp rebuke for 'presuming to bring that savage animal into the same room as a telephone set'.

At ten o'clock, the questioning resumed in earnest, couched with more craft than the previous evening. 'These friends of yours, Mr Humberstone—James Lucifer and Samuel

Gold—you trust them, do you?'

The handcuffs had been taken off Humberstone; the fetters were in the mind by now. 'I think so.'

'You'd trust them to give a truthful character of yourself if I asked them?'

'What are you trying to do, Sergeant—set us against each other?'

'Answer my question, please. Can I accept what Mr Lucifer has been telling me about you?'

'I can't say. I don't know what he's told you.'

'Nothing to be concerned about, sir,' said Cribb. He turned to Thackeray. 'You didn't hear Mr Lucifer say anything untoward about this gentleman, did you, Thackeray?'

Thackeray considered the question. He could be relied upon to pause long enough over any question to shake the confidence of a man in Humberstone's position. 'I can't recollect anything, Sarge.'

'There you are, Mr Humberstone. So you worked with Lucifer in Fire and Accident, is that correct?'

Humberstone nodded.

'And you both joined Mr Gold in the Claims Department six years ago?'

'Yes, but the circumstances of our employment have no bearing on this business.'

'Oh,' Cribb's eyebrows jumped half an inch. 'Are you suggesting I should ask about your domestic circumstances?'

'Nothing of the sort. I was merely pointing out—'

'Because that's what I was coming to,' continued Cribb. 'The City of London Police will be making the necessary inquiries at the Providential.'

'God in Heaven! I'm finished!'

'I'm not,' Cribb drily said. 'One of the things I haven't asked you is where you live.'

'Does that mean you propose sending a policeman to my house as well as my place of work?' demanded Humberstone, beginning to vibrate with anger.

'I hope that won't be necessary. If you don't want to tell me the address just now, I'm sure the desk sergeant must have taken it as he booked you in last night. I can look in his book.'

'Don't trouble yourself,' said Humberstone, heavily. 'Orchard Walk, Beckenham.'

'Sounds nice, sir. And your colleagues Mr Gold and Mr Lucifer—do they live in the same neighbourhood?'

'I share the house with Lucifer. Gold lives in Bethnal Green.'

'A married man, perhaps?' Cribb ventured.

'No, he lives with his two sisters.'

'Ah. A family. I expect they keep together more than we do, being immigrants. The Golds came originally from Russia, he was telling me.'

Humberstone said nothing, seeming to

regard Gold's origins as unworthy of comment.

'I expect the family changed their name. A lot of these foreigners do,' Cribb went on. 'If it was Russian, it was probably unpronounceable. Although I dare say the name of Humberstone would be difficult for a Russian,' he continued, trying too obviously for a response and getting none. 'Let's talk about Mr Lucifer, since you know him better. Blue-ribboner, I believe.'

'Blue-ribboner?' At least the expression had made Humberstone vocal again.

'Teetotaller. Wears the blue ribbon.'

'He tries,' said Humberstone. 'From time to time he lapses.'

'Don't we all? He's a very proper gentleman. I'd almost say an innocent. I'm not even sure whether he realizes yet what sort of houseboat the *Xanadu* is. He was saying that he felt responsible for the actions of the ladies—should never have introduced 'em to strong drink. Is he the innocent, or am I, for listening to him?'

'I thought you had an interest in guilt, not innocence,' said Humberstone with a glare. 'I begin to think you might be losing your confidence, Sergeant. If you're reduced to proving that Gold is a Russian and Lucifer a secret man of pleasure, that sounds to me like desperation. Are you going to bully them into a confession?'

Cribb made a sweeping gesture with his

arm. 'Get him back to his cell, Thackeray. He's wasting my time.'

'Or getting too near the truth?' Humberstone called over his shoulder, as he was bundled away.

When Thackeray returned, Cribb was lighting one of the Chief Inspector's cigars.

'It's a long time since I saw you smoking, Sarge.'

'There are times when it's appropriate, Thackeray.'

'It's not your birthday?'

'Lord, no. I take no account of them. I'm lighting up because I see the way to nail our three insurance gents.'

'That's good! Mr Humberstone seemed to think you was running out of steam. He said some very uncharitable things about you as I was returning him to his cell. I was so put out that I missed my footing on the steps and brushed against him with my arm. He fell downstairs and cracked his head on the door of his cell, I'm afraid.'

'No serious injury, I hope?'

'No, Sarge. My shoulder's slightly tender, but that'll wear off. I don't think we'll have any trouble with Gold and Lucifer. Do you want to see them?'

'All in good time. Well, Thackeray. You've heard the evidence. What's the case against 'em?'

Thackeray ran his tongue over his lips and

fingered the side of his beard, as he usually did when Cribb invited him to theorize about a case. Whether the purpose of these sessions was to instruct him or to impress him with the sharpness of Cribb's deductive powers, he was never clear, but he found them embarrassing in the extreme. He cleared his throat. 'Concerning the tramp's death, Sarge, they was seen in the vicinity by Miss Shaw on the night of the murder. They claimed to be in Marlow, but their stories are all different. First it was the Crown they stayed in, then a lodging house and then the blooming boat. They must be lying.'

'Good. Why did they murder the tramp?'

'Because they are a set of cold-blooded killers without a twinge of pity among the lot of 'em. They murdered him for the pleasure it gave 'em. They did for poor old Bonner-Hill for the same reason. I suppose working in an insurance office could make you lose your respect for life, when you're dealing in death all day long.'

'It's a thought. What's the evidence against them?'

'Well, P.C. Hardy's fetching that, isn't he? If the dogbite on his leg matches the bite on the tramp's, we've got 'em. They'll swing for Choppy Walters, and we don't need to go in to Bonner-Hill's murder.'

Cribb shook his head. 'That's shirking it, Thackeray. I'm still inclined to think the murder of Walters was a try-out. They wanted to be sure of the method before they used it on Bonner-Hill.'

Thackeray looked sceptical. 'But why did they want to murder Bonner-Hill?'

'His life was insured for five thousand pounds.'

'And with the Providential. I realize that, Sarge. But Humberstone said they have a million and a half people insured with them, so it isn't such a coincidence after all.'

Cribb drew on his cigar until it glowed quite menacingly. 'Thackeray, you're disappointing me. What happens now that Bonner-Hill is dead?'

'A claim is made for the money,' said Thackeray. 'I suppose one of the three men we've arrested would have to deal with it if we hadn't copped 'em.'

'That's better. And who gets the five thousand?'

'Mrs Bonner-Hill. You don't think there's any connection between—'

'What's the name of the fancy-man she brought with her from Windsor?'

'That theatre bloke? Goldstein, wasn't it? I still don't see—'

'Haven't you heard of immigrants shortening their names to make them sound English?'

Thackeray's eyes narrowed as his mouth formed the shape of the word 'Gold'.

'I've yet to prove it,' said Cribb, 'but let's suppose that Goldstein and Gold are related—cousins, perhaps. We know that Mrs Bonner-Hill was determined to get back on the stage and that Goldstein is a theatre manager. It's like the game of Consequences. Melanie Bonner-Hill met Jacob Goldstein at the Windsor Playhouse. She said to him, "My husband's life is insured for five thousand pounds." He said to her, "My cousin Sammy Gold can help us." And the consequence was Bonner-Hill's death.'

'And the world said, "Murder",' added Thackeray.

'Just so. Of course, the world was supposed to say "Accident"—and a good share of the money was to go to Humberstone, Lucifer and Gold. Mrs Bonner-Hill would be free to marry Goldstein, and there's a house in Oxford to dispose of, and presumably a legacy coming her way from her husband's will.' Cribb leaned back in his chair and knocked ash from the cigar into an umbrella-stand. 'I expect you're going to ask me how the murderers knew Bonner-Hill would be out on the river alone yesterday morning. How could they possibly have known that Fernandez would be indisposed with laryngitis?'

'It's a fair question,' said Thackeray, with enough conviction to suggest that he might actually have asked it.

'And I haven't got the answer yet,' said

Cribb. 'A few ideas, but nothing that fits all the facts. Don't worry—it'll come. Let's have another talk with Gold.'

If there was a family resemblance between Sammy Gold and the suave manager of the Playhouse, it was difficult to spot this morning. His left eye was black and swollen behind the broken spectacles, and he had not shaved.

'Wouldn't they let you use a razor?' Cribb asked.

'I tried, but I couldn't judge the distance with one good eye,' said Gold. He put forward a restraining hand. 'I don't blame anyone. I want no trouble, Officer.'

'That's good,' said Cribb, 'because I want cooperation this morning, Mr Gold. There's a small matter that I must get clear at the start, and that's your family name.'

'I told you last night. It's Gold. I don't want to be known by anything else.'

'I'm sure you don't, but answer me this: was your father known by another name in Russia?'

'Leonard Gold was my father's name. He did nothing to be ashamed of. He was an honest man all of his life. A tailor by trade. Smile, if you like. A Jewish tailor. What else would you have expected him to have been, eh? He made this blazer I'm wearing and it's lasted eleven years. Eleven years. You can look at the name on the label if you like, Leonard Gold. That was good enough for him. It's good enough for me.'

'Did he have any brothers?'

Gold smiled and shook his head emphatically. 'No, Officer, you won't get it from me that way. My Uncle Solly and my Uncle Joe are Golds like me.'

'And so are your two sisters in Bethnal Green, I suppose,' said Cribb, playing his ace. 'I wonder if they're as sensitive on the matter as you are. It's a pity I've got to send a constable round there on a Sunday morning to talk to them, with all the neighbours looking from behind their curtains. I have to make a telephone call to Bethnal Green Police Station to arrange it. It's a lot of trouble to go to for a simple piece of information.'

Cribb's penny-dreadful picture of Sunday morning in Bethnal Green did the trick. 'All right,' said Gold. 'It's an infringement of my liberty, but I want no trouble for my sisters. The name we had in Russia was Goldberg.'

'Gold*berg*?' repeated Thackeray.

Cribb took the cigar from his mouth and stubbed it out with enough force to have pushed it through the desk.

CHAPTER TWENTY-EIGHT

Harriet goes to the station—Interesting story from Hardy—Dynamite and the Polecat

Harriet had decided to talk to Sergeant Cribb about her theory. She had thought it over from every point of view and she was now convinced that the unfortunate Bonner-Hill had been murdered in error. On reflection, she had decided not to talk to Melanie about it. It was tragic enough to learn that your husband had been murdered, without having it suggested he had been murdered by mistake.

The theory was soundly based, otherwise Harriet would not have contemplated going to Cribb. From her observations he was not the sort to welcome other people's help unless he asked for it. He liked to take the credit for himself. Yet it was her duty, if she had information, to give it to the police. And his to take account of it.

It was clear to her that Bonner-Hill had been murdered because he happened to be at the spot where Fernandez fished on Saturday mornings. Only lately had the two of them taken to going out together on these expeditions. All the signs were that this was a murder which had been planned for many weeks, before Bonner-Hill ever joined

Fernandez. Humberstone, Lucifer and Gold had rowed up from Kingston like the characters in *Three Men in a Boat,* but the purpose of their journey had not been literary. It had been to get to Oxford on Saturday morning at half past nine and murder John Fernandez. They had got to the spot at the appointed time and found a man there who fitted the description they had. Probably they were hired assassins who had never met the man themselves. The planning that had gone into the murder was as intricate as an anarchist plot.

She approached the desk and asked for Sergeant Cribb. It was just noon; the bells had been chiming everywhere as she had come along St Aldate's. He ought to be available.

'Sergeant Cribb, miss?' said the constable on duty. 'I don't know whether I ought to—'

Constable Thackeray made a timely appearance at the door behind the desk. 'Miss Shaw! Good to see you, miss. Are you comfortable at that hotel?'

'I should like to speak to Sergeant Cribb if that is possible.'

Thackeray's expression changed. 'I don't advise it just now, miss. The air's blue in there—and I ain't talking about the cigar smoke. He's had a setback, you see. We should have charged our prisoners by now—you heard that I arrested 'em last night, did you?—but things have gone a bit sour. It's not so clear as it seemed. You'd be better off having your lunch first, really, miss.'

'Please tell the sergeant I have something that may be of the greatest importance to tell him,' Harriet insisted.

Thackeray departed, muttering something uncomplimentary about young women who wouldn't listen to advice, and presently put his head round the door and beckoned her into the office.

Cribb was speaking into the telephone. 'Definitely Goldberg? You've checked the naturalization papers? Well get on with it, man. I'll hold on while you do.' He put his hand over the receiver. 'What is it, Miss Shaw? I'm busy, as you can see.'

Harriet started expounding her theory. She had not got far when Cribb put up his hand and spoke into the telephone again. 'I told you the name. Fernandez. No, Goldberg. I'm getting confused. Nothing in the name of Goldstein? No, it's not helpful. It's no help at all. Good-bye.' He hung up the receiver. 'Where's Thackeray? I think I'll have that dog brought in. I feel like kicking it. Continue your story, Miss Fernandez. You have my full attention.' The telephone rang and he picked it up. 'Who are you? Yes, of course I'm Cribb. Who did you expect—Charlie Peace? Names? I gave you the names before. Humberstone, Gold and Lucifer. Thank you, Constable. I can do without your feeble attempts at humour.

I'm trying to investigate a murder here. What do you say? All employed in the Claims Department? Very well, I don't need to know any more. Is somebody checking with the Home Office as I asked? Habitual Criminals' Register. And the Convict Office? I know it takes time. I wasn't born yesterday, laddie.' He hung up the receiver. 'So you think it was all a mistake, Miss Shaw?'

Behind Harriet, Thackeray appeared again. 'I'm sorry to interrupt, Sergeant. I thought you ought to know straight away that P.C. Hardy has returned. He's ready to make his report.'

'Send him in and come in yourself. You don't mind, do you, Miss Shaw? No need to get up. You can stay and listen. We've all had a small hand in this investigation.'

Hardy was still in blazer and flannels. His boater was tucked under his left arm and he carried a notebook in his right hand. Seeing him again after an interval, and so soon after Cribb's tantrums on the telephone, Harriet was inclined to view him in a more favourable light than formerly. He turned a glance in her direction as he crossed the carpet to take his position in front of Cribb. 'Good mornin', Sergeant. Good mornin', miss.'

Cribb took out his watch. 'Good afternoon. It took you enough time to get here, Constable. We've had another murder and three arrests since we saw you last.'

'Moses!' said Hardy. 'Did you cop the

three—'

'They're in the cells. Make your report, man. We're not here to welcome you to Oxford.'

Hardy's stance stiffened. 'Very well, Sergeant. After leavin' Clifton Hampden, I took the train from Culham, changin' at Twyford Junction—'

'I'm not interested in the blasted train journey!' exploded Cribb. 'What happened about the dogbite?'

'Upon arrivin' at Henley, I reported to the mortuary,' Hardy implacably continued, 'where I had to wait for two hours for the police artist to arrive. I then climbed on to a slab and he made a sketch of the dogbite on my leg. He also made a sketch of the bite on the tramp's leg. I have them here in my notebook.' He extracted a loose sheet from among the leaves and handed it to Cribb.

The sergeant arranged the paper on the blotter in front of him. 'These aren't the same size. The top one's bigger.'

'That was my impression too,' said Hardy. 'I thought the artist must have got his proportions wrong. He said he hadn't and he produced a tape-line to prove it to me. We measured both bites again. The one on the tramp's leg was clearly made by a larger dog.'

'Not Towser?' said Thackeray in disbelief.

Cribb was speechless.

'If you look carefully at the drawings, you'll

see that there are half a dozen other differences of detail,' Hardy went on. 'It's mainly owin' to the sharpness of the teeth. The mortuary keeper said that Towser must have been a younger dog than the one that bit the tramp.'

'This means that Mr Humberstone and the others didn't have anything to do with the murder of Walters,' said Harriet.

'Or Bonner-Hill, for that matter,' added Thackeray. 'We only suspected them of that because the circumstances were alike.'

As the implications of Hardy's news fizzed and spattered like firecrackers in their minds, speech stopped in the room. For several seconds only their eyes communicated.

Cribb said, 'You knew this yesterday. What prevented you from coming back at once and letting us know?'

'I was acting upon your orders, Sergeant. After I'd finished at Henley, I proceeded to Marlow to examine the register of guests at the Crown. After the discovery about the bites, I fully expected to find the names in the register.'

'They weren't there,' said Cribb.

'No, they weren't,' said Hardy. 'I was flummoxed. The receptionist couldn't remember seein' three men of their description. It seemed to me that if their dog wasn't the one that bit Walters, they had no reason to pretend they were in Marlow on

Tuesday night if they weren't.'

'Eh?' said Thackeray.

'I decided to do some more checkin',' Hardy continued. 'I walked down the High Street to the town landing-stage and I was lucky enough to find a boatman there who remembered them tyin' up the *Lucrecia* there on Tuesday evening, towards nine o'clock. He remembered them exactly as I described them, even the dog, which they left on the boat to guard it.'

'Did he notice where they went after they tied up?' Cribb asked.

'Yes, he did, because it was the public house he spent the rest of the evening in, a little place close to the river, name of the Polecat. Time he got there, they'd already had a few drinks. They were sittin' at a table with three young women often to be found in the Polecat.' Hardy took a sidelong glance at Harriet, who continued to look steadily in his direction. 'The boatman remembers them leavin' with the, er, ladies at about half past ten.'

'This begins to sound familiar,' said Cribb.

'Well, Sergeant, having got as far as that in tracin' the movements of the suspects, I decided I should try to speak to the ladies'—he looked again at Harriet—'to establish for certain where Humberstone, Lucifer and Gold spent Tuesday night. I spent the rest of yesterday afternoon footin' it round the poor end of Marlow, tryin' to find them. In the end I knocked up a woman who said she knew them and they always spent Saturday nights in Maidenhead, because that's where all the, er, swells go. She even mentioned the name of the pub where I could expect to find them. Havin' got so far, I didn't like givin' up. I gave careful consideration to what you would probably order me to do in the circumstances and I decided it was my duty to go to Maidenhead. A bus left Marlow at seven and I was on it.'

'Did you find the women?'

'I found one of them, called Dinah, known in the Polecat as Dynamite.'

'Very whimsical,' said Cribb without smiling.

'And very dangerous it turned out to be, askin' her for information,' said Hardy. 'She had a man with her from London who formed the impression that I was tryin' to cut him out. He got quite ugly about it. What made things worse was that Dinah was under the same misapprehension, but she seemed to, er'—Hardy eased a finger round his collar—'prefer me to the man from London, which hampered my inquiries somewhat. Not to prolong the story, Dinah told me when I pressed the matter that she and her two friends took Humberstone, Gold and Lucifer to a house of accommodation in Marlow after they left the Polecat on Tuesday. They were there all night and left early next day. To make quite sure, I visited the house this morning. That's why I wasn't here before now, Sergeant. The woman who keeps the place confirmed that three men answerin' to their descriptions were in that house from eleven on Tuesday night until seven o'clock on Wednesday morning.'

The impact of Hardy's statement was devastating. When Cribb spoke, it was not to say the obvious, but to provide time to absorb the shock.

'That was it, then. You can see why they were so unforthcoming about their night in Marlow. A pilgrimage, they called it. It wasn't holy places they were visiting. Not the sort of thing that would go down very well in the Providential, I imagine.'

'Never mind that,' said Thackeray, grasping the nettle. 'It means that they definitely didn't murder Choppy Walters. They couldn't have. Are you going to release them, Sarge?'

'I shall have to,' Cribb bleakly said. 'From what we've just been told, it's clear that we've spent the best part of a week tracking down the wrong three men. It's a blasted nightmare. If Miss Shaw is right, even the corpse is the wrong man.'

CHAPTER TWENTY-NINE

A small shock in Merton Street—The Warden goes too far—Harriet delivers a letter

At lunch Melanie asked Harriet to go with her to Merton College that afternoon to sort through her late husband's things. The Warden had spoken to her about it after Morning Service. 'It will be frightfully boring for you, my dear,' Melanie said, 'but just having you with me is such a support. I don't think I could bear to be alone in that room surrounded by his things.'

'I shall be glad to come,' said Harriet. She would be of more help to Melanie than she could be at the police station. Now that the innocence of Humberstone and his friends was confirmed, there was nothing she could do to help Sergeant Cribb, unless hc produced three different men and a different dog. She just had to wait until somebody could be spared to escort her back to Elfrida College. Rather than spend a depressing afternoon thinking about what happened after that, she would be glad to go with Melanie.

She should have been prepared for the small shock that awaited her as they turned out of the hotel into St Aldate's. Some fifty yards ahead, walking away from them, were the distinctive figures of Humberstone, Lucifer and Gold, with Towser lingering behind to bark at a cabhorse. Of course they had to be released, but it still made her catch her breath to see them at liberty.

It was ironic after her unwillingness to identify them and confirm their guilt that she now had difficulty in accepting their innocence. When Bonner-Hill's body had been discovered, the horrid possibility that she might have prevented him from being murdered had dominated her thoughts. The idea had fixed itself so firmly in her mind that each time she tried to remember the scene in the water she could see only Humberstone and Lucifer at the oars, with Gold reclining on the cushions. The image her troubled conscience presented was more vivid than her recollection of the experience itself. In her worst moments she wondered whether what she had seen was a caprice of her imagination, induced by the tense excitement of that secret bathe. Yet Molly and Jane had seen the boat. They must have, to have taken fright as they did. What a relief it would be to summon them as witnesses and have their support! That was out of the question, of course. It would mean betraying them to Miss Plummer and ruining their careers as well as her own.

'Is something wrong?' Melanie asked.

'Nothing. I was thinking about College. Our Principal is a formidable lady. She even creeps into your thoughts when you are not expecting it.’

‘How very inconvenient. When I was your age I had the same trouble with young men, but that wasn’t a depressing experience. Isn’t there some nice young man of your acquaintance who might be called to mind to exorcise the lady?’

At Merton, the Warden drank tea with them before escorting them through the quadrangles to Bonner-Hill’s rooms. It was apparent to Harriet that there was something he wanted to mention; he tried to create an opening in the conversation once or twice over the teacups, but Melanie was unstoppable. The Warden said, ‘Perhaps this is the moment when—’

‘Is it?’ Melanie broke in. ‘I don’t know how you tell one moment from another. I lose all conception of time in Oxford.’ And she expanded on the strangeness of a city with so many clocks that they confused people.

Five minutes later the Warden said, ‘If I may be so bold—’

‘You’re going to suggest we have a second cup,’ said Melanie. ‘I never do, but don’t let me stop you, Harriet. Tea is a stimulant—don’t you find so?—but I think it isn’t good for me to drink too much. I’m too excitable already. I’ll let you into a secret. On stage I never drink tea. It’s always ginger beer in the teapot. Do you like ginger beer, Warden?’

At the door of Bonner-Hill's rooms, the Warden paused, key in hand and an expression of grim determination on his face. 'His books. We should like them for the library,' he said in a rush. 'That is to say, I could help you to dispose of Mr Bonner-Hill's collection of books if his Will is not specific in regard to them. So inconvenient, trying to deal with booksellers. You could leave them just as they are on the shelves for the librarian to sort—to catalogue, that is. Our library has benefited greatly from endowments,' he finished breathlessly.

'If that was Harry's intention, no doubt he will have provided for it in his Will,' said Melanie without enthusiasm. 'May we go inside now, or was there anything else?'

'But of course.' The Warden turned the key. 'There is no reason to hurry yourselves, ladies. If you would kindly return the key to the porter as you leave . . .'

'Did you ever hear anything so direct as that?' Melanie said, when the door was closed behind them. '"We should like them for our library", without so much as a by your leave, and poor Harry not even buried yet. I tell you, Harriet, there's a myth that people in universities have genteel manners. When they want anything, they're as blunt as beggars. Well, my dear, I wonder where his papers are. It's very tidy, isn't it? No wonder he despaired of me. There's his travelling-trunk in the corner. We'll pack things into that. His bedroom is through there. It would help me greatly if you would empty the wardrobe. I don't intend to leave his suits behind for the Warden.'

Harriet was no authority on gentlemen's bedrooms, but she doubted whether many came up to Bonner-Hill's in tidiness. Little in it suggested it was occupied at all. The furniture was all of the serviceable kind provided by the College. There were no photographs or pictures, no special ornaments or bric-a-brac. A pair of polished shoes symmetrically positioned on the mat beside the bed, and a bathrobe hanging on the door were more suggestive of a hotel room than a home. Oddly, she found the impersonality more poignant than a roomful of small evidences of occupation. She could see the lonely don, separated from the wife he had worshipped but failed to wean away from the stage, moving about these rooms like an overnight guest.

She opened the wardrobe and began lifting out suits and putting them on the bed. There must have been a dozen there. She doubted whether they would all fit into the trunk without creasing, and that would be a sin.

Melanie appeared at the bedroom door. 'You're doing splendidly, darling. Such a help! I say, here's a strange thing. I found this letter on his writing-desk. It's addressed to John

Fernandez. I wonder what Harry was doing with it. It's been opened, you see.' She held it between them, showing the torn edge of the envelope.

Nothing was said, but Harriet knew that Melanie was offering to take out the letter and look at it. She was pitting their friendship against decorum. It wanted only a whisper of encouragement to begin a conspiracy. The temptation was strong. Alone, Harriet might have yielded, but she was not ready to admit as much, even to Melanie. 'We really ought to return it to Mr Fernandez.'

The 'really' gave Melanie the chance, if she wished, of pressing the point, but she was not going to risk a stronger rebuff. 'You're right, my dear. Possibly he left it here when he was calling on Harry. Oh dear, I wish it wasn't addressed to him, of all the people in Merton, though. I suppose I could hand it to the porter to give to him, but it looks so pointed when his room is just across the passage.'

'Let me take it,' offered Harriet, hoping her eagerness was not too apparent. When Melanie had suggested spending the afternoon in Merton, the possibility of a second meeting with Fernandez had crossed her mind, but she had seen no way of taking the initiative. 'I met Mr Fernandez this morning.'

'Would you? What a thoughtful suggestion! I am not comfortable with the man, as I think I mentioned this morning. I should not go inside, my dear, even if he invites you.'

'I shall not,' said Harriet. 'It would not be proper.'

The card on the door read *J. Fernandez, M.A.,* but the envelope in Harriet's hand was less formal: *Mr John Fernandez, Merton College, Oxford.* The postmark was *London, 23 Aug. 89*—a week ago. She examined the neatly severed envelope, even put her fingers inside and satisfied herself that it contained a letter, but she did not take it out. That would have been too demeaning after the conversation with Melanie.

She knocked and held her breath, waiting to see if he was in. He might so easily have decided to go out for a Sunday afternoon stroll, making up on the fresh air now that his throat was better. How did she know it was better? In the Chapel he had sung more lustily than the Warden and the other Fellows together.

Footsteps ended the uncertainty. Fernandez opened the door, blinked in surprise, and said, 'How very delightful. Let me see. It's Miss Harriet Shaw, is it not?' His hand went to his hair and made sure that it was flat.

She smiled. 'Yes, I'm sorry to disturb you—'

'Not at all. Won't you come in?' He opened the door fully and stepped back with it.

'Thank you, but no,' Harriet firmly replied. 'I have just come to return a letter addressed to you which Mrs Bonner-Hill found in her husband's room. We are sorting through his things, you see.'

He took the letter, glanced at the writing on the envelope and pocketed it. 'Careless of me. I must have left it when I spoke to him on Friday evening. I wasn't my usual self at all. Had a confounded nasty bout of laryngitis.'

'You're better now, I hope?'

'Immeasurably, Miss Shaw, immeasurably. If I may presume to say so, I felt a distinct improvement in chapel this morning when I saw that our little congregation was not quite the same as usual. And when you mentioned afterwards that you had an interest in geography, my recuperation was complete. Is it physical?'

Harriet felt a tingling of her cheeks. 'I beg your pardon.'

Fernandez smiled. 'The geography, my dear. Is your interest mainly in the natural features of the earth's surface?'

'Oh. I understand. Yes, I particularly enjoy looking at maps.'

'A cartographer, too! We seem to have so much in common. Are you sure you won't step inside for a few minutes? I have a collection of maps which is certain to interest you, including, I may say, a copy of a sixteenth-century chart said to have been used by Magellan.'

'You are most generous, sir, but I must return to Mrs Bonner-Hill. I am here to keep her company, you see. She is likely to become depressed if I leave her for long.'

He nodded resignedly. 'Yes, from my slender acquaintance with Mrs Bonner-Hill, I would expect her to be easily agitated. Well, Miss Shaw'—he took a step towards Harriet—'I shall let you go upon one condition, and that is that you allow me to meet you tomorrow morning at eleven o'clock at the entrance to the Bodleian Library. It is not renowned for its maps, but I suppose I am the foremost authority in Oxford on those that are there, and I should be most honoured to show them to you.'

'That is very obliging of you, sir, but—'

'You cannot refuse,' said Fernandez.

'I shall have to see how Mrs Bonner-Hill proposes spending the morning. If she should require my company . . .' Harriet was already determined that nothing would stop her from keeping this engagement, but she was not so naïve as to let Fernandez know. It did no harm to introduce a little uncertainty into one's dealings with gentlemen.

'It would be kindest not to tell her of our arrangement,' Fernandez suggested. 'I should not like her to think that we discovered our mutual interest in geography as an indirect consequence of her husband's death.'

'I shall not mention the matter to a soul,' said Harriet, and meant it. Her cultivation of Fernandez was her own business. She was uniquely placed to find out why somebody had meant to murder him.

CHAPTER THIRTY

A tutorial for Sergeant Cribb—Jacks, piscatorial and homicidal—Uncle in the Steel

Twenty minutes after Harriet had left, Fernandez had a second caller: Sergeant Cribb.

Harriet, back in Bonner-Hill's rooms packing shirts into the trunk, did not look up as the sergeant made his way round the Fellows' Quad. If she had, she might have wondered what he was doing in Merton. That he was there to follow up her theory that Bonner-Hill had been murdered in error would not have occurred to her. At the police station, her contribution had been totally eclipsed by Constable Hardy's.

She did not understand that Cribb was a strict observer of priorities. First, he had done what was of paramount importance, released Humberstone, Lucifer and Gold, at the same time assuring them that no charges were to be preferred on *any* of the matters which had come to his attention. Then he had taken a solitary, ruminative lunch. Over the roast beef he had assessed the consequences of the collapse of his case against the three men. He was left with no suspects and, worse, no logical explanation for the murders. Over the apple pie with cream he had begun to think about what Harriet had said.

A strong black coffee, and he was on his way to Merton College.

Fernandez whisked open the door with such a winning smile that Cribb took half a step backwards.

Order was swiftly restored. 'I supposed you were somebody else,' Fernandez explained, frowning.

To make things absolutely clear, Cribb reminded him of their last meeting. 'I'd like a few words more with you, if that's possible, sir,' he went on. 'You know how it is—things come to you afterwards that you should have asked about before. Might I come in, sir? I wouldn't care to be overheard.'

In the sitting-room, Fernandez took a stance at the fireplace and motioned Cribb towards a chaise longue. The wall behind it fairly bristled with actresses and angels.

'I'll take the window-seat, if it's all the same to you, sir. I was wanting to talk to you about the late Mr Bonner-Hill.'

Fernandez shrugged. 'I hardly expected you were here to discuss the weather.'

'I was hoping you might know what led him to go out on the river yesterday morning.'

'Nothing *led* him there,' said Fernandez. 'He

went of his own volition.'

'It was the first time he'd ever been out like that, fishing on a Saturday morning quite alone.'

'True, but he was becoming interested in the sport.'

'How long had he been going out with you on your fishing expeditions, sir?'

'I told you that before,' Fernandez said, as if he were addressing an undergraduate. 'Two months. No more.'

'So you did, sir. But you've been doing this for two years yourself. Every Saturday.'

'Not every Saturday. Kindly do not put words into my mouth, Sergeant. In court, it is called leading a witness, I believe. On a number of Saturdays in the last two years I have been away from Oxford. I have obligations to attend to, besides my College duties.'

'The Royal Geographical Society. I remember, sir. But it would be true to say, would it not—I'm trying not to lead you—that you've established a routine of going out on Saturdays—most Saturdays—to look for that thirty pound pike you mentioned?'

Fernandez nodded warily.

'And do you always fish from the same spot, sir?'

'Not always,' Fernandez answered. 'We move about the back-waters. Those are the favourite haunts of the pike. They like it comparatively still, and thick with rushes and water-plants. I've caught half a dozen or more this year along Potts Stream and Hinksey, but they were jacks, all but one, and I returned them. The big one still eludes me. I've seen him more than once, actually.'

'Jacks, you said, sir?'

'Young pike, Sergeant. It's not sport to take them before they're full-grown.'

'It's much the same in my line of work, sir. We like to hook the big ones if we can. Funnily enough, the biggest of them all is known as Jack. When we land him, we won't be tossing him back.'

'The Ripper?'

Cribb nodded. 'But let's return to Mr Bonner-Hill. I'm a stubborn man, sir, and I would like to know what prompted him to go out on Saturday. He talked to you about it, I expect. He must have, when you said you wouldn't be going out yourself. When was that—on Friday evening?'

'Friday evening. Yes.' Fernandez paused, evidently calculating whether it was necessary to add to his answer. Cribb waited expressionlessly, letting the silence work for him, and it did. Fernandez continued, 'I looked in on him after dinner, about nine, I suppose. I could scarcely utter a word, my throat was so bad, so I went in to call if off. He said at once that he would go alone. He was adamant. I remember he remarked that it might be the very morning when the big one came by.' He gave a nervous laugh. 'If it had, I don't think he would have taken it, poor fellow. He was hopeless with a rod, but I was reluctant to discourage him. Pity I didn't, as it turned out.'

Cribb was not there to speculate. 'Another question, Mr Fernandez. When you talked to Mr Bonner-Hill, did you discuss the place where he would do his fishing?'

'We talked about it, yes. We decided that the back-water leading to North Hinksey—the one that links with Seacourt Stream—was a promising stretch of water. That's where the punt was found, I understand.'

'Yes, sir. Did any other person suggest that you might go to that particular spot on Saturday?'

Fernandez said cautiously, 'Why do you ask?'

'I'll tell you in a moment, sir.'

'Nobody suggested it, in fact. The choice was ours alone.'

Cribb got up from the window-seat. 'That's odd, sir. That's caught me by surprise.'

'I fail to understand why,' said Fernandez.

'This murder was arranged more than a week ago, sir, and probably before that. I thought at one stage that Bonner-Hill was done to death by some homicidal ruffians who didn't like the look of his face. Now I'm sure that there was planning in this. Last Tuesday night a tramp by the name of Walters was taken on the river at Hurley and murdered in just the same way as Bonner-Hill. We think the murderers—there were three of them—were trying out the method. It's a clever way to kill a man. Simple, but the cleverest ways usually are. You take him aboard a boat and render him insensible—with alcohol in the case of the tramp—and then you roll him over the side and hold his head and shoulders under till his lungs fill with water. Looks like drowning, of course. I think they might have used chloroform on Bonner-Hill. The post-mortem tomorrow may tell us. Could be traces in the lungs still. But you see my point, Mr Fernandez. The thing was planned. The killers knew where to find their victim. Bonner-Hill was murdered because he went to the backwater leading to North Hinksey on the day and at the time the murderers expected a man to be there.'

Fernandez folded his arms in a way that proclaimed how unimpressed he was. 'Pure chance. It must have been. But for my laryngitis we should both have been there. They could hardly have murdered two of us.'

'I don't suggest it, sir. They didn't plan for two. They expected one, and one came.'

Fernandez frowned. 'I trust you are not suggesting that I conspired with these desperadoes to cause Bonner-Hill's death.'

'Not at all, sir,' answered Cribb. 'If you want

it straight, I think they might have planned to murder you.'

'Me?' Fernandez tossed back his head and laughed. 'Murder me? Why should anybody want to to murder me?'

Cribb had turned to face the quadrangle. 'I don't know, sir. I thought you might have some ideas about that.'

Fernandez crossed the room and caught him by the shoulder. 'Turn and look me in the face, Sergeant. You must have meant what you just said in jest. This is too ridiculous for words.'

Solemnly, Cribb said, 'I mean it, Mr Fernandez. I'm not one for jokes. I don't know why they should want to kill you, but I believe they tried. They expected to find you there yesterday morning. You've been going out on Saturdays looking for that pike for two years, you said. It's common knowledge—must be, by now. They devised a means of killing a man from a boat and making it look like a drowning. They came to Oxford expecting to meet you in the backwater, but they met Bonner-Hill instead. Superficially, Bonner-Hill bore some resemblance to you. He was about the same age, his height was similar and he had a moustache like yours. They're all the rage, I know. Point is, that on a misty morning in September, the mistake was not impossible, particularly when he was dressed from head to foot in waterproofs. Did they belong to you, by any chance?'

'Certainly not. Bonner-Hill wasn't the sort to borrow other people's clothes. He wouldn't be seen—'

'Dead in them, sir? Of course, he was careful about his clothes. I should have remembered.'

'But really, the notion that he was somehow mistaken for me is pure speculation.'

'Perhaps you will hear me out, sir,' Cribb said quietly. 'I believe the murderers didn't know that Bonner-Hill had taken to fishing with you. This only started in the last six weeks, you said. Until you told me otherwise, I thought they must have known exactly where you planned to do your fishing yesterday. That's the part that baffles me. You stand by what you said, do you, sir—that the plan to go there was yours alone?'

Fernandez made a sound of impatience. 'For Heaven's sake! If you think an experienced angler would go to anybody else for advice on where to pitch his line, you betray a lamentable ignorance of the sport.'

'I'll admit to that, sir. What troubles me, you see, is that there are no end of backwaters around Oxford. The Thames alone—'

'The Isis,' said Fernandez in a pained voice. 'In Oxford, the river is known as the Isis.'

'Call it what you will, sir. It's still got Potts Stream, Seacourt Stream and Hinksey Stream branching from it. That's getting on for ten miles of backwaters, without adding the Cherwell. I cannot understand how the murderers knew where to find Bonner-Hill without prior knowledge. Unless, of course'—Cribb traced a finger thoughtfully round the line of his jaw—'unless they followed him from the boatyard. Where would he have hired the punt from?'

'The boathouse at Folly Bridge. But I hardly think your three assassins would risk being seen at Folly Bridge. The place is very well-frequented, even early on a Saturday morning.'

'Pity,' said Cribb. 'It brings me back to my problem. Putting myself in the murderers' place—and it sometimes helps to try, sir—if I wanted to make sure you took your boat to one particular backwater, I'd try to tempt you there, let you know that there was good fishing to be had in that locality.'

'I think you would do better to confine yourself to facts, not flights of your imagination,' Fernandez commented.

'I might send a message through a third party,' Cribb doggedly went on, 'or a letter, anonymous of course. Might even offer to take you to the spot, or meet you there. A dedicated angler like yourself would find it difficult to resist an offer like that.'

Fernandez inhaled sharply and audibly, and said, 'This is entirely hypothetical and I object to your implication that I am withholding information from you. If you have any other questions to address to me, my man, kindly state them now, in a decent, straightforward fashion, before I altogether lose my temper.'

Cribb looked contrite. 'I'm sorry, sir. Went beyond myself.' In his experience it was almost a law of interrogation that a straight apology evinced a magnanimous response.

'I must admit I'm not quite myself, either,' said Fernandez. 'It's a shock to be told that you were meant to be murdered, even if you don't altogether believe it.'

'Nasty shock,' Cribb agreed. 'You won't feel very comfortable in your boat for a while after this. Be looking over your shoulder half the time. Mind, I don't think Bonner-Hill was murdered in the punt. He was taken aboard another boat. Went freely, too, I think. There were no signs of a struggle on the punt. Makes me think of two possibilities—either he knew the murderers, or he was meeting them by arrangement.'

Fernandez brought his hands together with a muted clap. 'If he knew them, they must have known him, and they couldn't have mistaken him for me.'

'That's why I favour the second possibility,' said Cribb. 'The hired assassin baiting his hook, if I might borrow the expression, but catching Bonner-Hill instead of you. Can you think of anyone who bears a grudge against you? I think you might be in need of protection, you see. I can probably arrange for a constable to keep watch here, if you like.'

'In Merton? Good Heavens, Sergeant, this is in the realms of fantasy. No, I can't think of anyone who would like to kill me, and no, I don't want a policeman in the passage, thank you.'

Cribb rubbed the back of his neck. 'This is very awkward, sir. You must forgive me if I press the question further. You haven't any enemies, in Oxford, or anywhere else?'

'How does one know one's enemies? I shall begin to think I have, if you persist.'

'You're a single man, sir,' Cribb smiled. 'A ladies' man, they tell me, though.' He winked. 'No jealous husbands lurking in the shadows, I would hope?'

'Certainly not,' said Fernandez, without smiling.

'It's a conundrum, sir. It really is. I'm trying my best. What about your family? Are your parents alive?'

'Both dead. I have two brothers serving in the army and an uncle in London. If you're as desperate as you appear to be to find a motive, you may wish to speculate on the fact that he is Deputy Governor of Coldbath Fields House of Correction.'

'The Steel, sir?' Cribb's eyes lit up as if mention had been made of his school. 'I know it well. My word, this is a small world! You're right, though. It's not impossible for someone to have seen a way of taking revenge on your uncle by attacking you. Old lags get a lot of time to work up hatred, and to scheme. I'll think about that. His name is the same as yours, is it?'

'Matthew Fernandez. But I've no reason to believe—'

'Nor me, sir. I shan't discount it, though. You've been extremely patient with me. I'm an irritating sort of cove.'

Fernandez fumbled for an appropriately civil response. 'Not at all. Not irritating. Well you must admit it sounds deucedly far-fetched to suggest that three men came all the way from London in a boat to do away with a harmless don in modern history.'

Cribb smiled. The smile remained on his face as he passed through the Fellows' Quad to the Front Quad. It was still there when he started down Merton Street.

At no point in the interview had he suggested to Fernandez that the three men had started from London.

He marched into Oxford Police Station and announced to Thackeray that he was catching the next train to Paddington. 'I'm going to see the Deputy Governor at the Steel,' he said. 'If anything develops here, you can use the telephone set to leave a message at the Yard. I should be back tonight.'

CHAPTER THIRTY-ONE

Coldbath on Sunday evening—The treadmill treatment—A little rift within the lute

'Cribb, you don't look a day older than you did in the infantry,' said Mr Barry, warder-in-chief of Coldbath Fields House of Correction. 'Police work evidently keeps you young. What are you now—inspector?'

'Sergeant only,' Cribb admitted. 'Haven't done so well as you, Sam. I still speak out of turn too regular to please the high-ups. I'll tell you what I'm here for. I want to get a few words with a party named Fernandez—Deputy Governor, if my information's right.'

'One of *my* high-ups.' Barry put down his mug of tea and walked to the window. 'Take a look down there.'

The office was high at the top of the North Block. Cribb glanced down the shaft formed by adjacent buildings and saw something very like a string of pearls arranged in a box, except that they were moving, rotating slowly clockwise: the cropped heads of sixty convicts at exercise.

'How many have you got in the Steel?'

'Twelve hundred, give or take a few,' said Barry. 'That's three times the number in Holloway, and they've got twice the ground.

We arrange the exercise in shifts. Mr Fernandez, the one you mentioned, worked it out. He's a rare one for organizing. The treadmill's turning from eight in the morning till nine at night. Crank. Shot-drill. Everything's on the go.'

'Including the warders, I expect,' said Cribb, sensing acrimony.

'Keeps us occupied. Come downstairs and we'll find him. Likely as not, he's in one of the yards. He likes to keep an eye on the exercise.'

'Is he disliked in the prison?' Cribb ventured, as they started down a flight of iron stairs.

'He devised the system,' Barry tersely answered. 'What do you want with him?'

'I'm interested in his nephew. Oxford don. Has he ever mentioned him?'

'Never a word. He's too occupied with his own family, I expect. Five sons and eight daughters. They all appear in the prison chapel every Sunday. The two eldest girls are married.' Barry selected a key from the ring chained to his belt and let them through a door to another landing. 'They say that's how he worked out the shift system—spacing out the baths on Saturday night.'

After two more flights of stairs they reached ground level. More doors, more locks, and they were in the exercise yard they had overlooked from the office. The prisoners, unsuggestive of pearls at this level, trudged mindlessly round the perimeter, their boots rasping on the stone flags. A stench of sweat hung in the air. Any thoughts Cribb might have entertained of a career in the prison service were dispersed in that yard. 'It's known as the sorry-go-round,' Barry told him. 'I'm told Mr Fernandez is in the next block.'

He led Cribb up more stairs and along a catwalk between lines of cell doors, descending again to enter a yard no different on the ground from the other, with its own shuffling circle of misery watched by yawning warders. But here an activity was taking place in a gallery above the heads of the footsloggers. In twelve narrow stalls convicts were at the treadmill, forcing their feet to keep pace with steps that sank endlessly away as an unseen wheel turned, its revolutions fixed at a rate that took no account of aching calves and skinned ankles.

'He's over there,' said Barry. 'You'd better introduce yourself.'

He was conspicuous by being in a plain suit, but otherwise Fernandez Senior was a disappointment in appearance, smaller and more mild-looking than Cribb had expected of a man who had fathered thirteen children and reorganized the largest prison in London. He had a winged collar and spotted tie. He was hairless except for a thin, reddish moustache.

Cribb lifted his bowler. 'Mr Fernandez? The name's Cribb, sir. Detective Sergeant.

Scotland Yard. Might I have a word?'

'You are obstructing my view of the clock,' said Fernandez in a pained voice.

Cribb sidestepped. 'I shan't take up much time, sir.'

'I hope you don't, or twelve prisoners will tread a forty minute shift, instead of twenty, and they won't thank you for that. I am supervising an innovation in the exercise. The present group is due to be replaced at twenty minutes to the hour, but the order has to come from me. You have two and a half minutes of my time, Sergeant. What is it you require—an interview with a prisoner?'

'With you, sir. It concerns your nephew, John Fernandez.'

Cribb could not have been prepared for the reaction this provoked. 'Does it indeed? What did you say your name was?'

'Cribb, sir.'

'The Metropolitan Commissioner shall hear of this, Cribb. Reasonable inquiries are one thing, but this amounts to persecution, and I won't tolerate it. I was personally assured by Inspector Abberline that I should not be subjected to more questions about my nephew. It was conclusively established that he is unconnected with the matters under investigation. I *will* not have my family hounded by policemen. Have you spoken to Inspector Abberline?'

'No, sir, but—'

'I suggest you do. I have nothing more to say on the matter.' He turned his back on Cribb and pushed through the line of convicts to the centre of the yard. 'Odds!' he piped in a voice just strident enough to be heard above the mechanism of the treadmill. 'On your feet! Sharp now, unless you want a turn on the crank.'

Twelve convicts stood up in the stalls, which Cribb now saw were numbered from one to twenty-four. The odd numbers were about to start their shift. 'One, two, three, change!' called Fernandez.

The evens backed away from the mechanism and leaned on the sides of the stalls or crumpled to the floor. The odds took up the tread.

Cribb had eased his way through the chain and was speaking to the Deputy Governor at a rate that brooked no interference. 'Someone nearly murdered your nephew, Mr Fernandez. It happened yesterday morning in Oxford. A man was drowned. We think the murderers mistook him for John Fernandez. That's why I'm here.'

'Kindly modulate your voice,' said Fernandez. 'I would rather that the whole of Coldbath Fields did not hear about the misfortunes of my family. Somebody tried to murder him? Whatever for?'

'I hoped you might be able to tell me, sir. I've reason to believe that somebody travelled down from London to Oxford with the intention of drowning him.'

'Why question me about it?' said Fernandez. 'Naturally it causes me concern, but I know nothing about it.'

'Your nephew raised the possibility that released prisoners might seek revenge on you by attacking your family, sir.'

'Revenge?' said Fernandez, screwing his face into an expression of horror. 'What an ill-informed idea! These men bear no malice towards me. They have their term to serve and I am here to see that it is served as the law dictates. They have much to thank me for, if you want to know. I inaugurated many of the procedures which contribute to the general efficiency of this house of correction and, in consequence, the well-being of its inmates. The fact that you see me supervising treadmill exercises does not mean that I am not concerned with the things of the spirit, Sergeant. The improving texts displayed throughout these buildings are here on my initiative.' In case it had escaped Cribb's notice, he extended his hand towards a card above the treadmill bearing the legend *Be Sure Your Sin Will Find You Out (Numbers Ch. 32 v. 23*). 'As a matter of fact, they were chosen by my own dear wife and daughters. No, Sergeant, I have no fear of former prisoners, nor need my nephew be alarmed.'

'I'll try to reassure him, sir,' said Cribb.

'Perhaps he hasn't had the advantage of visiting the prison.'

'This is a house of correction. A man of your vocation ought to know that prisons are for long term convicts. No, my nephew has never been here. I have not set eyes on him for a year. The last occasion was his father's funeral. That is why it so infuriates me that I am plagued with policemen asking questions about him. The man has a slight imperfection of character, I concede—the "little rift within the lute", as Tennyson puts it—but to my knowledge it has never been more than that. They understand him at Oxford. I'm sorry, if what you say is true, that somebody tried to murder him. These are violent times, I am afraid. It could happen to any of us. The Queen herself, God bless her, has survived a number of attempts upon her life. Savage times. Now, if you will excuse me, I think I see a man shirking up there. An hour on the crank will do him good.'

CHAPTER THIRTY-TWO

A look at Suspects, Other—The file on Fernandez—Frou-Frou and an alibi

From Coldbath Fields Cribb caught a green Victoria bus to Whitehall and marched briskly into the Metropolitan Police Office in Great Scotland Yard. At half past eight on a Sunday evening the sergeant at the information desk was deep in his *News of the World.* Cribb's curt, 'Inspector Abberline—is he on duty?' got a less instant response than it warranted.

'Abbey what?'

'Fred Abberline, for God's sake. Where have you been for the past twelve months? The man in charge of the Ripper investigation.'

'Jesus!' The duty sergeant dropped his newspaper. 'Abberline's off duty. There hasn't been another . . . ?'

'No.' Cribb had conducted his conversation as he was moving through the information room to the registry.

The clerk on duty here was sharper to react. He had dropped his *Bicycling Times* into the waste paper basket before Cribb reached the counter.

'The Whitechapel murders,' Cribb announced. 'I'd like to look at the file on them.'

'File!' The clerk pulled a face. 'There's twenty altogether, Sergeant. One for each of the five victims; one for others murdered in similar circumstances; nine for correspondence; one for suspects, principal; two for suspects, other; and two marked miscellaneous.'

'I'd better take them all. Where do I sign for them?'

'You'll need a hand-cart to move them. The correspondence was coming in at the rate of a thousand letters a week last winter. We're still getting upwards of a hundred, mostly from lunatics.'

'Give me *Suspects, Other*, will you? I'll start with those.' He gave a long whistle as two bulging files tied with tape were dumped on the counter. 'I should think you've got the whole of London in there.'

In the adjoining office Cribb turned on the gas, placed his watch on the desk and unfastened the tape round the first file. He leafed through the contents carefully, not without excitement. Up to now there had not been much to get excited over in this investigation. Detective work held more disappointments than rewards, he knew, but occasionally, just occasionally, the shade of Sir Robert Peel, or whoever it was who interceded with the gods for detectives in despair, procured a small advantage for the side of law and order. Unless they were playing false, the gods had favoured Cribb when Fernandez Senior had mentioned Inspector Abberline's name.

With the possible exception of the sergeant at the information desk, nobody at Scotland Yard needed telling that Fred Abberline had been in charge of the Ripper investigation ever since the mutilated body of Mary Anne Nichols had been found in Buck's Row on the last day of August, 1888. As the tally of Jack the Ripper's victims had grown through the months of autumn, Abberline's name had become a by-word in the press. *Inspector Abberline, we are informed, is sparing no effort in his investigation, but we understand that he is no nearer to making an arrest.*

If Abberline had been to Coldbath Fields asking questions about John Fernandez, it must have been connected with the Whitechapel murders. That was not necessarily significant, for hundreds of men in the city and the suburbs had been questioned, and *Suspects, Other* contained more reports than Cribb cared to count.

It was not long before he found the one headed *Fernandez, John,* and began to read it.

University lecturer. Fellow of Merton College, Oxford. *Age* 38. *Height* medium. *Build* sturdy. *Hair* black, straight, uses pomade. *Eyebrows* thick. *Forehead* narrow. *Eyes* brown. *Nose* fine, straight. *Mouth* broad, finely shaped, red lips. *Chin* square. *Face* oval. *Complexion* swarthy. *Beard* none. *Moustache* thick, black, extends beyond ends of mouth. *Marks of peculiarities* none. *Previous convictions* none.

Suspect was interviewed at Merton College, Oxford, on June 9th, consequent upon information from an anonymous source that on a number of occasions he had violently forced his attentions on women, including the wives of other members of the University, interfering with their clothing in a manner that would have justified charges of indecent assault if the ladies concerned had not insisted that no complaint be made to the police. Suspect's tendencies are said to be known to his colleagues at Merton (this was subsequently confirmed by the Warden) and 'constitute no serious threat in a community which is exclusively male'. The informant suggested that the suspect had been visiting London during each of the nights when the Whitechapel murders took place, and that there were similarities between his handwriting and the script of the letters signed Jack the Ripper which had been reproduced in the newspapers.

The interview was conducted by Sergeant Holloway (H Division) in the presence of P. C. Stoner, 177H. Suspect first denied that he had molested women, but on being informed that there was no intention of preferring charges respecting the incidents at Oxford, he admitted three which had come to the notice of his colleagues, but advanced the opinion that the ladies concerned had encouraged his attentions by unfastening certain of their garments, but had grown alarmed when he had behaved 'with an excess of exuberance'. He admitted that in each case the lady had seemed distressed by the incident.

On being questioned about his movements at the times of the murders, suspect claimed that he was in London for a meeting of the Royal Geographical Society on August 31st (confirmed), and spent the previous night at the Oxford and Cambridge Club (not confirmed). On Friday, September 7th (the night of Annie Chapman's death) he was in London again, visiting the London Library, and passed the night at Bradley's Hotel in Jermyn Street (confirmed). On Saturday, September 29th (when the victims Stride and Eddowes were murdered) he again stayed at the Oxford and Cambridge Club (unconfirmed), having attended a committee meeting of the R.G.S. earlier in the day. On Thursday, November 8th (the night of Mary Kelly's death), he claimed to have been visiting his uncle, Mr Matthew Fernandez, who is Deputy Governor of Coldbath Fields House of Correction. This was later denied by Mr Fernandez (see below). On being asked about the frequency of his visits to London, suspect replied that the weeks before the start of term (which commenced in October) were the obvious time for conducting business not connected with the University.

Inquiries were put in train at the Oxford and Cambridge Club. The staff were unwilling to comment on the movements of a member, but confirmed that Fernandez had not signed the register for the nights of August 30th or

September 29th. Mr Matthew Fernandez, interviewed by Inspector Abberline on June 13th, stated that he had not seen his nephew for over a year. He confirmed that the suspect was 'unreliable on occasions with members of the fair sex', but he was strongly of the view that his nephew was 'not a homicidal type' and referred to his experience of such men in penal institutions.

The suspect was interviewed again, by Inspector Abberline and Sergeant Holloway, on June 14th, when it was put to him that his account of his movements on the nights in question had been confirmed in one instance only, and had been found to be false in another. Suspect admitted that his previous statements had been misleading. He had supplied a false account of his movements out of loyalty to a lady. On being questioned further, the suspect stated that he had spent the nights of August 30th and September 29th in the company of a Mrs Melanie Bonner-Hill, the wife of a Fellow of Merton College. Mrs Bonner-Hill, who is an actress, was appearing in *The Belle's Stratagem* at the Lyceum Theatre. They had stayed at a theatrical lodging-house in Kensington.

On November 9th, they had been in Windsor, where she was appearing in *Frou-Frou.* Mrs Bonner-Hill was now living apart from her husband. Suspect stated that after certain disagreements with Mrs Bonner-Hill he, too, had ended his alliance with her. He was not confident, in the circumstances, that she would confirm his account.

Mrs Bonner-Hill was traced to Windsor and interviewed by Inspector Abberline on June 17th. Contrary to the suspect's expectations, she confirmed that he had been with her on the dates in question, and verified the information from her diary. She stated that he was a man of 'ungovernable passion' and an adventurer, but she was confident that he was not murderously inclined towards women.

A handwriting expert, Mr Looper, reported that in his opinion there was no resemblance between a specimen of the suspect's handwriting he had studied and the 'Jack the Ripper' correspondence.

In the light of these findings, Inspector Abberline ceased to regard Mr John Fernandez as a serious suspect, and the inquiries were brought to an end.

P. Holloway
Sergeant
H. Division

Cribb sat for a minute in thought. Then he replaced the report in the file, tied the tape round it again, picked up his watch and hat and returned to the registry.

'That was quick,' said the clerk. He smirked. 'Are you off to make an arrest now?'

Cribb shook his head. 'Not on a Sunday.

Tomorrow, I think.'

The clerk's eyes opened wide. 'You don't mean it? Heavens! What's Inspector Abberline going to say when we tell him in the morning?'

He got no answer.

Cribb was already on his way to Paddington Station.

CHAPTER THIRTY-THREE

In which Thackeray works it out—Cribb delivers a lesson in geography—Japan's attitude is explained

'What's the matter with you, Constable? Moonstruck?' Cribb demanded. Having gone to the unusual length of providing his assistants with a detailed account of what he had learned at Coldbath Fields and Scotland Yard, he felt he was entitled to a response. He was not asking for a bouquet; two or three words indicating approval would have satisfied him. Frankly, he had not expected much from Thackeray, but Hardy he had come to regard as a sharp young constable capable of appreciating good detective work. He was obviously mistaken.

'I'm sorry, Sergeant,' Hardy answered. 'I was turnin' it over in my mind, like, thinkin' how clever it was.'

'Ah,' said Cribb, his confidence pricking up.

'Yes, we could do with Miss Shaw in the force. We would never have found out so much about Fernandez if she hadn't pointed out in the first place that he must have been intended as the victim instead of Bonner-Hill. She's an uncommon clever young woman, that one.'

'That's a fact,' Thackeray confirmed. 'And pretty with it.'

It was Monday morning. Cribb had arrived sufficiently early at the police station to use the telephone set for an hour before the Chief Inspector got in. Sharp at nine, he had hung up the receiver, blown his cigar ash out of the window, replaced the ashtray on the desk and moved into the charge room next door.

'Pity Miss Shaw ain't here to give us the benefit of her latest theories,' Cribb acidly said. 'I was planning to make an arrest this morning, but I might be wrong again.'

'An arrest?' Hardy looked more dubious than impressed. 'Who do you propose to arrest this time, Sergeant?'

'Work it out. Miss Shaw gave us a description. It must be useful, coming from an uncommon clever young woman like that.'

Thackeray scratched the side of his head. 'I don't follow you, Sarge. Do you mean the three men she saw on the night the tramp was killed?'

'Yes. What's the matter with that?'

'We arrested the only three men we've seen along the river, and they was innocent—well, innocent of murder, that is.'

'Quite right,' said Cribb. 'We released 'em.'

'Because they couldn't have been the three Miss Shaw observed that night,' contributed Hardy. 'They were in a house of accommodation in Marlow. If she didn't see *them*, who did she see?'

'Perhaps she made a mistake,' hazarded Thackeray. 'What do you think, Sarge?'

Hardy put in his answer first. 'Miss Shaw is a reliable witness. I'll stake my reputation on that.'

'She's cool-headed, I agree,' Cribb said. 'But don't be too free with that reputation of yours where this young lady is concerned. I don't suggest we can't rely on what she's told us, but I don't believe she's told it all.'

'What do you mean by that?' demanded Hardy.

'She led us to believe she was bathing alone when the boat came by. Bathing in the altogether isn't a solitary pastime, in my limited experience. It's a social activity. I'm told that undergraduates bathe naked here in Oxford. There's a place along the Cherwell known as Parson's Pleasure.'

'Do you mean that there might have been other girls with her in the river?' said Hardy, blinking at such a possibility.

'Not girls, necessarily,' Cribb wickedly

replied. Leaving Hardy to ponder that, he turned to his other assistant. 'Yes, Thackeray, the answer to your question is that it's reasonable to believe what Miss Shaw has told us. Do you recollect the description she gave of the men in the boat?'

'She likened them to places on a map, Sarge. It didn't mean much to me. Maps wasn't done when I went to school.'

'Let's remedy that deficiency, then.' Cribb got up and tapped on the Chief Inspector's door. There was no reply, so he let himself in and presently returned with a large revolving globe on a stand, which he placed on the table in front of Thackeray. 'The first man was like the Gulf of Bothnia, Miss Shaw informed us. You'll find that near the top, Thackeray. Should be marked in blue.'

Thackeray gripped the globe with his hands.

'There,' said Hardy, touching it with his finger.

'It doesn't look like anybody I know,' said Thackeray.

Cribb had his notebook out. 'The man was wearing a cap, according to Miss Shaw. Look at the top part of the Gulf. Do you see the peak of the cap, and the nose and chin underneath?'

'Blimey, yes. I do. Long, thin neck. Narrow chest. This don't look like an oarsman, Sarge.'

'I know. I took it for Mr Lucifer. Now take a look at the Persian Gulf. Down a bit and to your right.'

Hardy came to the rescue again.

'Good Lord!' said Thackeray. 'Blooming clever! It's just like a big fellow sitting in a boat, pulling at the oars.'

'Thicker in the neck, large head, wearing a hat,' said Cribb. 'Seemed good for Humberstone to me. Now for the third man. Miss Shaw wasn't very clear about this one, if you recollect. She said she found it difficult to distinguish his outline from the cushions.'

'And you suggested Japan,' said Hardy.

'Where's that, for pity's sake?' asked Thackeray, trying to turn the globe with his fingers still marking the Gulfs.

'Never mind,' said Cribb. 'That was only my suggestion. I didn't see the man myself. Japan has quite a bend in it, like someone leaning back against a cushion. Miss Shaw was positive the third person was a man, because of his attitude. I have her words here somewhere. "No lady would recline in quite the attitude this person did." '

'Mr Gold?' said Thackeray.

'Well, he was the third man of those we arrested, so I supposed it must be him. There was something wrong about it, though. Gold seemed to be the spry one of that threesome. I couldn't see him lying at his ease. Yet he didn't fit the description of either of the oarsmen. I began to think again about the third man, propped against the cushions. Was he asleep? I wondered. It made no sense, going out in a boat by night to do a murder and falling asleep on the way. Then I thought suppose the third man hadn't been a murderer at all. Suppose he were the victim.'

'Choppy Walters!'

'Already dead, Sarge?'

'No. He definitely died from drowning. He was breathing till they put him in the water. Dead drunk, I think. They could have met him in a pub and got him tight. They *might* have used chloroform, but I think gin is more likely.'

Thackeray was hacking his way through a jungle of tangled thoughts. 'Then we must be hunting for two men in a boat, instead of three.'

'But where do we start looking for them now the trail's gone cold?' Hardy dismally asked.

'We don't look,' said Cribb. 'This is 1889. We wait for a telephone call. If they're somewhere on the Thames, as I think they are, we've got 'em. I've alerted every lock-keeper up and down the river.'

CHAPTER THIRTY-FOUR

Rendezvous at the Bodleian—Some observations on chance occurrences—Fernandez leaves nothing to chance

Harriet's white muslin skirt embroidered with pansies had creased hardly at all in the travelling-case. Once she had decided on that for her appointment with Mr Fernandez, she was bound to put on her plain navy blue velvet jacket, worn with the blue striped blouse and the matching hat. Her thoughts strayed to the humming-bird hat, still in its box in her room at College. It would have been nice to have worn it this morning; after the things Jane and Molly had said about it she would never wear it again to church, but it was still a beautiful hat. She turned away from the mirror and buttoned her boots, high-lows that clicked noisily on the hotel steps as she went out. She hoped she had not been seen; Melanie would have guessed everything at a glance.

Fernandez greeted her at the Bodleian with a compliment about her clothes. He was well turned-out himself, in a biscuit-coloured suit and boater, although Harriet did not presume to say so.

He had arranged for a dozen or so books to be displayed on a table in a room adjoining the upper reading room. Most contained maps of great antiquity, scarcely recognizable as the outlines Harriet knew from her atlas. Great fish and sea monsters enlivened the maritime areas, looking capable of biting chunks from the land masses. Fernandez encouraged her to play the game of identifying countries, praising her successes and confessing that he would not have known the others himself unless he had spent years studying the history of maps. He went on to talk with quiet authority of the problems of early navigators, the impossibility of relying on the *mappae mundi* and the consequent development of the *portolani,* the pilot books of the Portuguese, and the less sophisticated *ruttiers* used by the English.

In the hour and few minutes they spent there, Harriet began to understand what it might mean to study at a great university with a tutor to guide her, not a Miss Plummer reciting her *Notes for Teachers in Training Colleges* on each topic decreed by the inspectors, but an authority with the ability to bring her close enough to a subject to apprehend its purpose and feel its power to inspire. Interestingly, Fernandez spoke without the tendency to arrogance she had noticed before in his statements. Instead of airing his expertise, he spoke with reserve, in terms calculated more to clarify than impress.

He ended by showing her one of the treasures of the Bodleian, Marco Polo's *Les*

Livres du Graunt Caam, with its lavishly illustrated pages. 'The first of the illustrated travel books, and still the best, I think,' said Fernandez, as he returned it to its box. 'And now, Miss Harriet—if I may call you that—I should be honoured if you would join me for luncheon.'

'For luncheon?' Harriet blanched. She had not been taken to luncheon by a gentleman in her life. She doubted whether it was proper. 'I was not expecting such a thing. Of course, it is exceedingly generous of you. You have already been uncommonly kind to me—'

'Then it is settled!' said Fernandez. 'The least you can do to repay my kindness is grace my table at the Clarendon.'

'A hotel?' said Harriet, hardly able to voice the word.

'The best in Oxford, my dear. Frequently patronized by royalty. Ah,' said Fernandez, touching his fingers on the back of her gloved hand, 'I should have realized. You are concerned about the propriety of visiting an hotel in the company of a gentleman. I shall take you instead to Mr Stanford's Restaurant in the High.'

It seemed unmannerly to refuse after he had been so considerate as to alter his arrangements on her behalf, so Harriet presently found herself sipping Chianti and telling Fernandez about the geographical excursion with the gardener and his son last summer, while a waiter helped her to an *Escalope de Veau au Romarin.* Nobody at Elfrida would believe this was happening to her. On Monday they always had cold beef and boiled potatoes.

'I was thinking how remarkable it is that I should have met the one person in Oxford who could show me the books I saw this morning,' Harriet told him. 'I suppose all the important moments in our lives are governed by chance. If I had not met Melanie—Mrs Bonner-Hill—and offered to accompany her to Merton College Chapel yesterday, I should never have learned what treasures the Bodleian contains.'

Fernandez smiled. 'And if I, in my turn, had not recovered from a bout of laryngitis, I should not have been at Morning Service, nor had the delight of your company now. A rationalist—and we have a number of those at Oxford—would tell you that these are chance occurrences, that life is a sequence of unpredestined events to which we are too often tempted to ascribe a significance. I prefer to think that such meetings as ours are governed by more than mere chance.'

'I am sure you are right.' Harriet blushed at the truth of this, thinking of the ways she had manipulated mere chance. She hoped Fernandez would suppose the wine was making her warm.

'To pursue the point,' he went on, 'if I had not had my laryngitis, I should have gone out with Bonner-Hill on Saturday morning as I invariably do—'

'And you might have been murdered!' said Harriet.

'I had not thought of anything quite so dramatic. I was projecting that poor Bonner-Hill might not have suffered the fate he did, because two of us would presumably have been better able to defend ourselves from attack. But then the chain of events which led to my meeting you would not have been forged. Even the death of a close friend has brought its compensation. Won't you have some more asparagus?'

Harriet remembered why she was there, realized that an opportunity was about to slip through her fingers. 'No thank you. Forgive me for suggesting such a thing, but has it not crossed your mind that whoever killed Mr Bonner-Hill may have intended to murder you?'

Fernandez put down his knife and fork. 'A chilling thought, my dear. What put it into your head?' He refilled Harriet's glass.

'Melanie told me about your custom of going fishing on Saturday mornings. She said her husband had only recently taken to going with you. He had not been out on the river alone before. It seemed to me that if that were the case, nobody could have expected to find him alone. If, on the other hand, they did not know Mr Bonner-Hill had started accompanying you, they would expect to find *you* alone. It suggests to me that they must have mistaken him for you.' She tipped a large amount of wine down her throat. 'Had it not occurred to you, Mr Fernandez?'

'I should be happier, my dear, if you used my first name, which is John. I am sometimes called Jack in Merton, but I prefer the name my parents gave me.'

'Then you must call me Harriet.'

'That will be a special pleasure. Well, Harriet, your perspicacity is remarkable. Of course, you are absolutely right. Mine is the body that should be undergoing a post mortem examination this morning. Bonner-Hill, unfortunate fellow, was murdered, as you correctly surmised, because he was mistaken for me.'

'But why, John? Why did somebody wish to murder you?'

Fernandez emptied the last of the wine into their glasses. 'That I shall explain, Harriet, but it is a story I should prefer not to relate in a public restaurant. With your permission I shall take you after lunch to Magdalen Bridge, where we can hire a punt and take it up the Cherwell to a place I know where a man might speak in confidence.'

'I'm not sure whether that is—'

'First, we'll have coffee with liqueurs. Have you tried Benedictine? Then you must.'

CHAPTER THIRTY-FIVE

Waiting for the ring—Melanie becomes perturbed—A curious report from Abingdon

After Cribb's eulogy on the convenience of the telephone, there was a chastening wait for it to ring. Privately, Thackeray and Hardy would have been happier doing something active towards an arrest, but Cribb's faith in modern technology was unshakeable. 'I have issued a description of the two suspects to each of the lock-keepers,' he said over the third mug of cocoa that morning. 'I have men posted at every railway station within ten miles, and a watch is being kept on all the roads out of Oxford. As soon as they are seen, a message will be conveyed over the wires to the telephone set in the Chief Inspector's office and we shall be in pursuit within seconds.'

'Suppose they cleared off yesterday, Sarge,' Thackeray injudiciously suggested.

'Sunday?' said Cribb, shaking his head. 'Too risky travelling on Sunday. People would notice. They'll have waited for today, when everyone's moving about the country.'

'What about Saturday?' Thackeray persisted.

'If you recollect,' said Cribb with a glare, 'there were uniformed police all over Oxford looking for Humberstone and his friends. Mark my words, the ones we're after will have gone to earth until today.'

'I suppose,' he said an hour later, 'they could be lying low until tomorrow.'

At noon he found a pretext for going into the Chief Inspector's room to make sure the telephone receiver was on its hook. At one, Thackeray persuaded him to think about lunch. Hardy was sent for a cold chicken from the shop next door. 'I could fetch some beer from a pub,' Thackeray volunteered. 'Cocoa doesn't really go with chicken.'

'You stay here,' growled Cribb. 'The call could come at any minute.'

The only call in the next hour was not from the telephone. Melanie Bonner-Hill was shown in, plainly in an agitated state. 'I know how busy you are,' she told Cribb, 'and you will probably think I am being hysterical, but I am dreadfully concerned for the well-being of Miss Shaw.'

'Harriet?' Hardy was on his feet.

'This morning I was planning to show her some of Oxford's places of interest in return for her kindness to me. I said nothing about it last night, thinking it might make a small surprise this morning. But when I called her room she had already gone out. I found one of the hotel staff, a chambermaid, who had seen her go out. She was wearing a muslin skirt she showed me yesterday, calling it the best she had. She had sat in the hotel lobby watching the clock until five to eleven, when she looked in the mirror, powdered her cheeks and went out. Sergeant, she is a stranger to Oxford. I think she had an appointment to meet somebody, and the only person she has spoken to other than me in the last forty-eight hours is John Fernandez.'

'Fernandez?' Hardy clapped his boater on his head. 'That's the man they thought was Jack the . . . Sergeant, I must find her!'

'Steady, Constable,' cautioned Cribb. 'Mrs Bonner-Hill, you say that she has spoken to Mr Fernandez. I presume this was at Merton College. How could she have had a conversation with Fernandez without your overhearing it?'

'It was when we were clearing my husband's rooms yesterday afternoon. I found a letter posted from London addressed to John Fernandez. It had been opened. To save me calling on Mr Fernandez, whom I didn't wish to see in the circumstances, Harriet offered to return it. She was gone for long enough to have been persuaded to meet him. He is very difficult to refuse.'

'This letter,' said Cribb. 'It would be helpful to know what it said. You didn't, by any chance . . .?'

Melanie nodded. 'I might as well admit that I did. Before I called Harriet I opened it. It wasn't a proper letter at all, for there was no address and no signature. It seemed to be about fishing—an arrangement to meet at half past eight on Saturday near a railway bridge.'

Cribb brought his clenched fist down on the table with such suddenness that Melanie started in surprise. 'Got 'em!' he said. 'Mrs Bonner-Hill, you know Fernandez. Where would he take a lady for lunch?'

'The Clarendon Hotel,' she said at once, and blushed. 'Just over the road in the Cornmarket.'

Cribb took out his watch. 'Ten to two. Past lunchtime. Better hurry, Constable.'

Hardy was already through the door. As an afterthought Cribb shouted, 'You might find 'em in—'

The door slammed.

'—the coffee lounge,' Cribb finished, practically to himself.

'She's completely inexperienced,' said Melanie. 'He'll take advantage of her. I know him. Oh dear, I feel so responsible.'

'No more than I do, ma'am,' said Cribb, remembering Miss Plummer. 'Hardy's the right man for this. Good in emergencies. Nicely mannered, too.'

'But what if they have *left* the coffee lounge?' Melanie's eyes opened wider at this dire possibility.

'I dare say the management would be of assistance in that case, ma'am. Duplicate keys, you know. All's not lost.'

Melanie was unconvinced. 'On an afternoon like this he is more likely to have taken her on the river.' She blinked twice. 'He's not to be trusted in a punt.'

'The river? Do you mean the Isis, ma'am?'

'The Cherwell. And I know exactly where he likes to go. I shall go after Constable Hardy at once and tell him.'

Somebody had to escort Melanie across Carfax to the Clarendon. Consequently, when the telephone rang loud and clear three minutes later, Cribb was deprived of the satisfaction of seeing Thackeray's jaw sag in surprise, as it surely would have done. More irritating still, he had to walk to the Cornmarket and seek out the two constables to announce the news to them. They were just leaving the Clarendon with Melanie. And Thackeray spoke first.

'Nobody's seen Fernandez or Harriet here, Sarge. They must have gone elsewhere to lunch.'

'It doesn't matter where they had lunch if they went on the river afterwards,' chimed in Melanie. 'We must go to Magdalen Bridge without delay.'

'We'll take a cab,' Hardy announced, starting out towards the road with his left hand held high. 'You've decided to join us after all then, Sergeant.'

'I have just been speaking on the telephone,' Cribb said in tones measured to combat the distractions of Cornmarket Street. 'The keeper of Abingdon Lock was on the wire to me. Only a few minutes ago a paddle steamer travelling from Oxford to Reading passed through the lock and the captain remarked to him that two passengers had been noticed behaving oddly, standing at the aft end of the boat, away from the other passengers on the upper deck, which has a sun canopy. As one of these two was a lady, carrying no sort of sunshade of her own, although the sun was particularly hot at that time, another passenger very decently went to the deck and offered her the use of his wife's parasol. She simply turned her back on him and made no reply. Supposing they must be foreigners who had misunderstood his meaning, he addressed the man in French and was told in very forthright English to mind his own business. He was so insulted that he reported the incident to the captain. After taking a discreet look at them, the captain decided not to pursue the matter. But he related it to the lock-keeper at Abingdon, who was sharp enough to put two and two together and pick up the telephone. They can't escape us this time.'

'Well I never!' said Thackeray. 'A man and a woman. Who would have thought—'

'*You* wouldn't and that's plain,' said Cribb ungraciously. 'You're coming with me to arrest 'em, Thackeray. Hardy can cope with

Fernandez.'

Hardy had made his priorities patently clear before Cribb had got to the end of his speech, by stepping into the road and whistling for a cab he had seen. It pulled up beside the curb.

'This will do,' said Cribb. 'What are you waiting for, Thackeray? There's another one behind for you, Hardy. Whistle him up, man, or he'll pass you by.'

CHAPTER THIRTY-SIX

Jolly boating weather—Confidences on the Cherwell—Harriet unbalanced

Harriet reclined against the cushions watching clusters of foliage drift across her vision. She had the interesting sensation that the punt was stationary and the trees were travelling over her head in the direction of Oxford. Common sense dimly insisted that John Fernandez was poling the punt upstream, but common sense was a poor match for dark leaves moving against a blue sky after Chianti and Benedictine.

She should not have accepted the drinks. How many times had she heard Miss Plummer articulate the perils of insobriety? One sip, she would say, one sip will seep into your veins, depriving you of the will to resist the devil and all his works. And she was right! The dear old Plum was right! Harriet on her cushions was unable to resist even the glass of champagne John Fernandez had poured for her after they had pushed off from Magdalen Bridge.

Bubbly, Molly always called it when she talked about it in college. Molly, *naturally,* knew about champagne, the devil and any of his works you cared to mention. But had she ever shared a bottle of Pommery and Greno's Extra Sec on a punt with a Fellow of the University of Oxford?

'We shall stop under the willow there,' announced Fernandez, so distantly he might still have been at Magdalen Bridge. 'The leaves will form a natural canopy. Do not be alarmed if they brush your face as we pass underneath.'

She closed her eyes and enjoyed the coolness of the shade. Fernandez thrust the pole into the mud below and looped the painter round it. Then he brought the champagne bottle to Harriet's end of the boat and sat level with her knees. 'Before I begin, will you have another glass, Harriet? Of course you will.'

She held her glass unsteadily under the neck of the bottle.

'You must be asking yourself, my dear, how I was able to confirm so confidently that Bonner-Hill was murdered in error. It will interest you to know that you have held the evidence of this in your own pretty hands.'

'My own pretty hands?' Harriet repeated, wishing she could think of something more intelligent to say.

'I refer to the letter you found in Bonner-Hill's rooms and so kindly returned to me. I still have it in my pocket.'

Harriet saw him take it out and open it. It was pale green in colour. She had remembered the envelope was white. She moved herself up on the cushions and saw that not only the envelope, but his hands were tinted green. With some relief she realized that it was due to the effect of the sunlight filtered through the leaves.

'Shall I read it?' he said. 'It is only a note and there is no address and nor is it signed. It says *"If you would care to hook one of thirty pounds or more, take the backwater on the Osney side of the second railway bridge at 8.30 a.m. on Saturday 28 August and proceed toward North Hinksey. Bring live-bait and hooking tackle. You will be shown the place. I promise you this is no jack".'*

'I don't understand it,' said Harriet. 'Have I drunk too much champagne?'

Fernandez smiled indulgently. 'It would make sense only to an angler, and a pike man at that. It promises to reveal the haunt of a pike of prodigious size. The person who wrote it knew precisely how to secure my interest.'

'I think I should be suspicious of a letter

nobody had signed.'

'So was I, my dear—up to a point. The truth of it is that my curiosity was stronger than my suspicion. When you have been searching for two years for a large pike, a letter such as this is difficult to dismiss. The person who wrote it obviously knew something about pike fishing.'

'He knew something about you,' added Harriet, and thought it rather a profound remark.

'True, my dear. Oh, I considered the possibility of an undergraduate prank, but the students were still on vacation. Term doesn't begin for another week. The trunks are starting to arrive, but not their owners. I ask you, where would be the amusement of a jape with nobody about to appreciate it? The more I thought about it, the more likely it seemed that the letter was serious in intent. What I could not fathom was the reluctance of the writer to identify himself. The only explanation I could hazard was that somebody for his own malicious reasons wished to frustrate another angler who had traced the fish to its lair and was planning to take it. The pike, you see, is a fish that favours particular haunts. The backwater mentioned in the note happens to lead into Hinksey Stream, where the largest pike in Oxford was caught. In short, the letter was too convincing to ignore.'

'You decided to carry out the instructions?'

'That was my intention until Friday evening,

when I felt so wretched after dinner that I knew I should be unable to get there on Saturday. I went to Bonner-Hill's rooms and showed him the letter. I had made no arrangement with him to come with me because it seemed to me there was some question of confidentiality in the business, and I did not want to risk antagonizing my mysterious correspondent. Bonner-Hill read it carefully and agreed with me that it would be a pity to ignore it. He offered at once to go in my place, and I agreed. He would say, if he were asked, that he was John Fernandez. Neither of us realized what a fateful decision we had made. You may imagine how I felt when I learned that Bonner-Hill's body had been found.'

Harriet took hold of a willow leaf and traced her fingers along its stem to the bough. 'Did you tell the police about the letter?'

'I did not, I confess. I shall explain the reason, Harriet. As recently as last June I had a profoundly disturbing experience at the hands of the police. The Warden called on me one afternoon and said that a detective sergeant had come to Merton and wanted to ask me certain questions. He had travelled up from Scotland Yard, so I gathered that it must be something important, although I couldn't imagine what. I hold the view that we have a duty to cooperate with the functionaries of law and order, so I admitted this detective and a constable who had come with him, and the Warden very decently withdrew.'

'What did they want?'

Fernandez moved closer to Harriet. 'My dear, I am sure that a young lady such as yourself can have had no experience of the police, except perhaps to ask for directions in some unfamiliar neighbourhood. Allow me to tell you that they are by no means so courteous or considerate as they may appear. These officers began at once to question me in a manner that was so far from being civil that I had to remind them more than once where they were and who I was.'

'How very unpleasant,' Harriet commented, at the same time moving more to the side of the punt so that her legs were less in danger of touching his.

'I would not describe myself as a gregarious person, Harriet,' he went on, 'but I am fortunate in having a modest circle of acquaintances, including some of the fair sex. I am a bachelor, as you must know, and my position in the College necessarily reduces my opportunities of meeting ladies, but that does not mean that I do not enjoy their company. Without being indiscreet, at the risk of even sounding a little conceited, I would add that from time to time ladies have demonstrated more than a little interest in making my acquaintance.' He paused, as if to give Harriet the opportunity of making her own position clear, but she was dipping the willow leaf in her champagne and moistening the tip of her tongue with it. 'If this bores you, my dear . . .'

'Not at all. Please go on.'

'If I may speak frankly, then, a gentleman—even a cloistered gentleman such as myself—does not reach the prime of life without noticing that certain ladies—and I speak of respectable married ladies—are disposed at times to encourage a gentleman to—how shall I put it?—'

'Flirt with them?' suggested Harriet.

'You have it.' Fernandez put his hand over hers to confirm the fact. 'These are the games wives of an adventurous spirit occasionally like to play. Mild diversions from the solemn business of matrimony, quite harmless if they are not indulged in to excess. The secret smile, the touch of fingers, the contact of legs under a table—of course, you would have no experience of such things.'

'I am learning,' said Harriet, withdrawing her hand from his with a smile that would go usefully with a mild reproof in the classroom. 'Did the policemen ask you about your games?'

'They did, Harriet. I might not have objected to that if they had been discreet, but they were not. They referred to them in terms that could only be described as coarse, portraying my part in the business in the most lurid colours imaginable. I supposed that they hoped to provoke me into revealing names, but I was determined that I should not.'

'That was gallant,' said Harriet.

'Yes. Imagine my surprise, then, when the sergeant made it crystal clear not only that he knew the names of the ladies, but that he was actually in possession of a letter claiming I had perpetrated an assault on one of them.'

'Oh!' Harriet drank the rest of her champagne in a gulp.

'That was my response exactly, Harriet. I was bereft of speech for several seconds. Won't you have some more? There's enough for another glass each.' In upending the bottle, Fernandez drew himself to Harriet's side and stayed there. 'I hope, my dear, that you do not take me for the class of person who forces himself on defenceless ladies. The detective sergeant obviously did, you see, because of the libellous contents of this letter he had received. He had been persuaded that I was a veritable satyr. He was investigating certain incidents concerning a number of women in London and he wanted me to state where I had been on four separate nights last autumn. I gathered that the writer of the letter had maliciously linked my name with the events in question.'

'How very unfair!' said Harriet.

Fernandez took her hand in his again. 'The deuce of it was that by coincidence I had been out of Oxford on the nights he mentioned. On two of the occasions I had been with a lady.'

'Melanie?' The champagne must have sharpened Harriet's intuition. She was certain he was talking about Melanie. Or had cold logic told her that something like this must have happened for Melanie to hold Fernandez in such contempt?

'Why keep it from you?—yes. Naturally, I did not at first reveal her name to the police. I fabricated a story instead. One of the nights I had passed at my club, I told them, and the other with an uncle of mine, a man whose position in the world ought to have impressed a policeman. That was a miscalculation. I thought the mention of his name would be enough, and that they would not presume to approach him on the matter. Unfortunately, it seems they did, and he denied having seen me. They were back within a few days and I was compelled to admit the truth—that I had spent both nights in the company of Melanie Bonner-Hill. It was ungallant, I know, and she has not forgiven me, but Harriet, my predicament was extreme. They actually suspected I was that monster who murdered all those women in the East End last autumn.'

Harriet felt her hands jerk in his, but he seemed not to notice.

'Of course,' he went on, 'I could not be sure that Melanie would be willing to confirm my story. To her lasting credit, she did, and the suspicion was lifted from my shoulders.

Harriet, I cannot convey the relief I felt when I learned she had told them the truth. The mental torment I had been through, wondering if she would shrink from the shame of it! Now do you understand my feelings when the police came to my rooms again on Saturday inquiring into Bonner-Hill's death? They were not the same policemen, but I was terrified that they would link the tragedy in some way with the matters they had tried to connect me with before. That was why I said nothing about the letter that sent Bonner-Hill to his death. I could not face the ordeal of having my private life investigated again by the police, as it must be if they discover I was the intended victim.'

'But if you have done nothing to be ashamed of—'

'That is not the point, my dear. One's reputation becomes tarnished. Things are said about one. It was dreadful enough having to walk about Merton with people knowing the police had visited me twice. Imagine the investigations that would be set in train if it became known that someone had wanted to murder me. All my friends, acquaintances, people who scarcely know me even, would be interrogated, invited to speculate on anything I had done which might have given offence to my supposed murderer. Too horrible! I'll tell you what I shall do, Harriet—I shall destroy the letter.'

Harriet sat up. 'I don't think you should do that.'

He had already taken it from his pocket again and was preparing to tear the envelope and its contents in two. Impulsively, Harriet tried to snatch it from him, but he jerked it clear of her grasp. As her fingers came ineffectually together she found to her dismay that she toppled clumsily against his chest. There seemed to be something amiss with her sense of balance, for willow leaves started drifting across her vision like bits of glass in a kaleidoscope. Or was he tearing the letter into confetti and scattering it over her? Impossible to tell.

The only certain thing was that she was lying with her back against his chest, unable to sit up. Close to her ear she heard Fernandez say, 'So *you* like playing games, Miss Harriet Shaw. I thought you might.'

CHAPTER THIRTY-SEVEN

A cabman gives advice—Detectives on the wagon—The view from the saloon

The cab journey was shorter than Cribb or Thackeray expected. Instead of heading south along the Abingdon Road, the driver turned right at the police station and took them up

Queen Street, New Road and Parkend Street, to halt outside the railway station.

'What's the game?' Cribb called up to the cabman. 'Clifton Lock, I said, not Oxford bloody Station!'

'Aye, chum, and you said you wanted to get there quick. It'll take me an hour on them roads, whippin' my horse into a lather. If you get out now, you've got two minutes to buy your tickets for the 2.45, and that'll get you to Culham inside fifteen minutes. From there you can walk to Clifton quicker than I can drive you, easy.'

A cabman so selfless as to sacrifice a good fare to the Great Western Railway had to be believed. Cribb gave Thackeray a prod, planted a shilling in the cabman's proffered palm and led the way across the station yard to the booking office.

Just as promised, they handed in their tickets at Culham as the clock at Clifton faintly chimed the hour. The ticket-collector who doubled as head waiter was on duty.

'Can we get a cab from here to Clifton Hampden?' Cribb asked.

'It's only a mile.'

'I know that. We want to ride.'

'No cabs here, sir.' The ticket-collector paused, letting the bad news sink in. 'I might be able to arrange something if you could wait ten minutes. They serve a nice cup of tea in the Railway Hotel across the road.'

So that was it. 'There's a shilling in it for you if you can get a cab here in the next five minutes,' Cribb recklessly promised. Eyebrows would be raised at Scotland Yard when his statement of expenses went in, but somewhere below Culham Cut was a steamer with two murderers aboard. If it reached Clifton Lock before he did, there was no chance of boarding it before Day's, three miles downriver.

The ticket-collector squinted at the station clock and came to a decision. 'Might be able to fit it in before the 3.35,' he said. 'Wait here a moment.' He closed the ticket barrier and moved at a trot out of sight behind the station building. In three minutes he reappeared on the box of an open cart hauled by an ancient white horse. 'I'll take you myself on the station wagon for half a crown,' he called.

'At least somebody's got a head for business in these parts,' Cribb commented as he arranged a sack to furnish some sort of upholstery at the back of the cart. They turned out of the station approach and bowled quite briskly along the Clifton Road.

Near Clifton Hampden the courses of road and river approach each other. Cribb stood up in the cart hoping to be reassured by the sight of a funnel across the quarter of a mile or so of flat fields.

'Some of them paddlers go at no end of a lick,' Thackeray cheerlessly remarked. 'Can you see anything, Sarge?'

Cribb waited at least two minutes before replying. 'There she is. We've done it!'

At that the ticket-collector pulled on the reins. The wagon stopped. 'That'll be half a crown as estimated, sir.'

'This isn't Clifton Hampden. We're not there yet,' protested Cribb.

'Clifton Lock, you said. Lock's across the fields. If you want to catch that steamer, you'd best be footing it over the plough. I could take you on to Clifton if you like, but you'd still have to walk back to the lock from there. I can't drive my wagon along the towing path.'

So for the second time that afternoon Cribb was forced to concede to local knowledge. Poorer by half a crown and muttering unspeakable things about cabmen professional and amateur, he clambered over a gate and his boots sank to the laces in freshly ploughed earth.

'You'll always be welcome at the Railway Hotel, gentlemen,' called the ticket-collector as he turned the cart.

After three minutes of hard footwork and blasphemy, Thackeray, too, sighted the steamer's funnel. It was within fifty yards of what had to be the lock-keeper's house, because it was the only building in view. 'Sarge, we're not going to get there in time,' he breathlessly told Cribb's obdurate back.

'We will if the lock's against them,' answered Cribb without turning his head.

By degrees the river itself flashed its presence and they saw the steamer slowing at the approach to the lock. Smaller than the pleasure steamers on London's water, it had the spruced-up look the steamboat companies annually applied with a coat of white paint on the paddle-box, lifebelts and funnel. The rest was brown in colour and had not been touched for years. Behind the funnel, under a faded green and white striped awning, a dozen or so passengers sat facing each other on what the company would have called the saloon deck, sited about the main cabin. At the level of the main deck a cluster of passengers had gathered at the fore end of the boat to watch the operation of the lock. On the aft deck a couple stood alone, leaning on the rail, studying the water or the river traffic behind. They could not have noticed the panting representatives of Scotland Yard who tottered aboard seconds before the paddles began to power the boat out of the lock, towards Clifton Hampden Bridge.

The captain could not have been more delighted if one of the royal family had patronized his trip. 'Detectives, are you? By Jesus, it's a famous day for the *Iffley Queen*. Will this be in *The Times*? We were in the *Berkshire Post* when Henry rammed Wallingford Bridge last summer, but I've had nothing so grand as this. Have you got handcuffs or would you like a length of rope?'

'That shouldn't be necessary,' answered Cribb. 'I'd like to take a look at the couple first. Should we go on to the top deck?'

'I can show you something more interesting from the saloon,' offered the captain. He beckoned to a deckhand. 'Take the wheel, Henry. Centre arch, mind. Hold her steady and you shouldn't go wrong.' He opened the door of the main cabin of the boat, a carpeted room with seats and windows on either side and at the farther end. 'Very cosy on a cold day,' he said. 'We sell more beer on the bad days. If you ever thought of bringing your detective department on a day's excursion, you could do worse than this. You can have a minstrel band for five pounds extra.' He threaded a passage round bentwood chairs and tables to the windows at the end. 'What do you say to that, then?' he said, pointing through the glass.

The saloon was sited some four feet lower than the aft deck, which was level with the windows. All that could be seen of the couple who had behaved with such unwonted incivility were their lower halves, the man's white flannels and his partner's navy blue serge skirt. 'You've missed it,' said the captain. 'You need a sharp eye. It's a favourite game with the fast lads, coming down here and looking along the deck for a glimpse of a well-turned ankle. Keep looking. You'll see something in a moment.'

Thackeray was as partial as anyone to a pretty ankle, but he had not traversed a ploughed field to indulge in this sort of thing. 'Sarge, if we want to identify these people, shouldn't we go upstairs, where we can see them properly?'

'There you are!' said the captain. 'How about that?'

'Bless my soul!' said Thackeray.

The wearer of the skirt had changed position, leaning far enough forward to reveal not a shapely calf, not the trimming of a petticoat, but the ends of a pair of white trousers and a very unfeminine pair of boots.

'That's good enough for me,' said Cribb. 'I'm obliged to you, Captain.' He returned upstairs and made his way between the files of interested passengers on the upper deck and down the steps at the end.

The couple turned at the sound of his approach.

'James Hackett,' he said. 'I am a police officer, Detective Sergeant Cribb of Scotland Yard. I have reason to believe that the person with you is a man by the name of Percy Bustard. I should like to put some questions to you both in connection with the death of Henry Bonner-Hill.'

'And may the Lord have mercy on our souls,' intoned Jim Hackett.

'It's all up, then,' said Bustard, pulling off the beret toque which, with the rest of his boating costume, had contrived to make him quite a passable female. 'How the devil did you cop us?'

'I reasoned that Jim Hackett was the Persian Gulf and you were the Gulf of Bothnia,' Cribb unhelpfully replied. 'What are you doing now, man?'

'Unbuttoning the bodice. You've no idea how hot it is in this dress. I'm fully clothed underneath.'

'I know that,' said Cribb, 'but *they* don't.' He jerked his thumb in the direction of the saloon deck. A dozen faces paraded expressions suggesting everything from open lechery to apoplectic shock. 'Lord knows what they're liable to do. Come below and you can take off your dress in private. I want no scenes aboard this boat.'

He might have saved his breath. Not on Bustard's account, but his companion's. It was Jim Hackett who chose that moment to shout 'Jesus saves!'—and leap over the rail into the river.

'Blasted clown!' said Cribb. 'One of us will have to go ashore and pick him up when he reaches the bank. Thackeray, you'd better warn the man at the wheel.'

'I wouldn't bother with that,' said Bustard.

'Why not?'

'Jim Hackett can't swim a stroke.'

'Lord help us!' said Cribb. 'Take off your boots, Thackeray, and get in after him. Two drownings in a week is quite enough for me.'

CHAPTER THIRTY-EIGHT

The wind in the willow—From Magdalen to Mesopotamia—A knife for Harriet

Possibly the champagne had something to do with it. When the punt had first glided under the willow's shade, Harriet had been grateful for the coolness, but in the last quarter of an hour she had become quite as warm as she had been in the sunlight. The collar of her blouse had the clamminess of a poultice.

'I think I should like to take off my jacket.'

'I shall assist you, my dear.'

She sat upright and the willow leaves blurred, and for two or three seconds became swathes of green chiffon, pretty, but disquieting. She blinked twice and brought the leaves sharply into focus again.

She withdrew her arms from the velvet jacket. Fernandez folded it and got up to place it out of range of their feet, which gave her the chance to recline against the cushions instead of his chest. Before he turned, she unfastened the two top buttons of her blouse. The cool air on her skin was blissful. 'You don't mind?' she inquired. 'I felt uncomfortably warm, and this seems quite private, under the tree.'

'We shan't be disturbed,' he assured her. 'Won't you take off your hat as well? It has gone a little askew, if you'll pardon me for mentioning the fact.'

'Really?' Her hand went to where the hat should have been. She laughed, located it, and handed it to him.

He turned it over in his hand. 'It's a charming hat.'

'Not my favourite. I left that behind. Please take your jacket and boater off, if you wish, John.'

'Would you mind if I unbuttoned my shirt?'

'If that is more comfortable. After all, you are the one who has taken all the exercise. It would be unfair of me to refuse you the liberties I have taken myself.'

Harriet's words produced a quick response from Fernandez. He returned to his position beside her at the end of the punt, scattering hat, jacket and cravat untidily behind him as he came. 'Perhaps it is time I initiated some liberties. What do you say to that, Harriet?'

'I am not entirely clear as to your meaning, John.'

* * *

The boatman at Magdalen Bridge listened carefully to the description Hardy and Melanie Bonner-Hill provided. Yes, more than one couple had hired punts that afternoon. He supposed it might run to as many as six. He couldn't say whether one was a young lady in a white muslin skirt and a blue velvet jacket, because he didn't usually notice the ladies. The men arranged the hiring. Now if they could remember what the man was wearing, it might jog his memory. Was it a striped blazer by any chance?

'We don't know,' said Melanie despairingly. 'We haven't seen him this afternoon.'

'He's much older than she is,' said Hardy.

'That's no help, with respect, sir, if I don't know the lady's age.'

'About eighteen.'

'The man must be nearly forty,' added Melanie.

'I'm no judge of ages, ma'am. You say he's dark-haired with a moustache. Can you remember anything else to help me? You see a lot of moustaches these days. To be personal, you've got one yourself, sir.'

'Anything else?' said Hardy, glaring at the man. 'Mrs Bonner-Hill, can you think of anything else to help this man decide whether he has seen Fernandez?'

'Fernandez?' repeated the boatman. 'Do you mean Mr Fernandez from Merton College? Why didn't you mention his name before? Of course I've seen him! One of my best customers. He's down here at every chance he gets. Always brings a lady with him, too. Yes, he collected a punt half an hour ago.

Must have got to Mesopotamia by now.'

Hardy's jaw dropped.

'It's a meadow,' said Melanie. 'I know exactly where he'll have taken her. Boatman, we shall want a boat at once.'

* * *

Well, she had permitted him to kiss her. *That* would be something to tell them at Elfrida. A proper kiss on the lips with one hand under her head pressing her face to his and the other . . . Well, the other had not stayed in one place. Even now, when it appeared to be resting on her waist, she could feel small movements through her clothes.

If she was honest, kissing was not so exquisite as Molly and Jane had led her to believe. His lips had been damp and his moustache had tickled her nose distractingly. By all accounts including his own he was not inexperienced in such things, so perhaps the fault was hers. She was not sure whether it was prudent to allow him a second one. It was certainly not proper, but she had stopped being proper when she had accepted his offer of luncheon. Perhaps one more could be justified, so long as she made it quite clear that the liberties ended there. If there *was* anything in kissing, she would like to find out while she had the opportunity.

His hold on her waist tightened and his face

came close again, more slowly and confidently this time, the water's reflection glittering in his eyes.

Just as she parted her lips, the bells of Magdalen broke into a chime. Bells all over Oxford began sounding the hour. Harriet turned her head away and giggled.

'I'm sorry, John. That was so unexpected. I thought we were miles from anywhere and then the bells started.'

'They say it's the best place in Oxford to listen to the bells,' said Fernandez without enthusiasm. 'Great Tom is the last you hear.'

'What are they striking? Is it four o'clock? I ought to be back by now.'

'What is it? Are you afraid of me? Do you think I want to hurt you?' For the first time that afternoon, he looked as if he might.

Harriet was alarmed. 'Of course I don't, John! You have been more than kind to me, but if I am late in getting back, people will wonder where I am.'

'*People?* What do you mean by that?'

She was on the point of naming Sergeant Cribb and his assistants, but checked herself in time. 'People in the hotel. Melanie and others I have met. Afternoon tea is at half past four. If I am not there, somebody will notice.'

'Afternoon tea? I gave you an expensive luncheon and champagne.' Emboldened by this, Fernandez placed his hand on her throat and drew it down, forcing open another button of her blouse. 'I shall take you back in good time, Harriet. We were on the point of exchanging a kiss, if you remember.'

She remembered, but her curiosity was not so strong as to consent to a kiss in her present predicament. 'If you would take away your hand, I should like to fasten my blouse. Then you may kiss me.'

It was a brave offer, and it impressed him enough to move his hand back to her throat.

'I should prefer to fasten my own collar, if you don't mind,' said Harriet firmly. She took hold of his wrist and planted the hand firmly where it had formerly been, on her waist.

As she leaned forward to attend to the buttons, something dropped from above her, something small that passed close to her face, touched the soft skin below her throat and lodged against the lace trimming of her chemise. 'What was that?'

'A small caterpillar. It must have dropped off the tree. Shall I remove it?'

'Oh no!' She jerked away from him and the movement caused the caterpillar to fall between her breasts. 'Oh, how horrid! I can feel it moving! It's inside my clothes!' She forced her finger and thumb down the front of her stays, but was unable to reach it. 'I cannot bear it!'

Fernandez turned and picked up his jacket. From the pocket he took out a clasp-knife and opened it. 'Turn round!'

She was on the edge of panic. 'What are you doing?'

He grasped her shoulder and forced her to face the water. She felt her blouse tugged from under her belt and wrenched up her back to the shoulders. She drew in her breath in a gasp, preparing to scream.

'Quiet, for God's sake, and keep still! I'm going to cut your laces.'

She should have realized it was the quickest way to loosen her stays and stop the tiny trespasser. She submitted, and felt the constriction ease with each cut. The torment inside her chemise increased. She would have writhed against the side of the punt if it were not for the touch of the knife on her spine.

The last lace snapped. Harriet succeeded in scooping her hand down the front of her clothes and extracting not a caterpillar, but an old brown catkin. It must have held fast to the tree for the whole of the summer. 'A pussy-willow!' she said.

Pandemonium followed.

Without warning, another punt coursed under the tree, with Constable Hardy aboard, crouching at the front, shouting, 'Get away from her, you devil!'—and Melanie seated at the other end, screaming.

Fernandez turned, knife in hand, as Hardy leapt aboard and crashed a paddle over his head, knocking him insensible. The punt jerked against the bank and Harriet tipped headfirst into the water. Fortunately, it was only waist deep.

She had started to stand up when she realized that her blouse was open to the waist and her stays jutted horizontally in front of her like a breakfast tray.

She hesitated only briefly. With style she had not dreamed she possessed, she pulled the stays free and dropped them into the water. Then she opened her arms and let Hardy lift her into the punt.

'You have rescued me, Roger,' she said. 'You have rescued me again!' She held him tightly.

The empty champagne bottle, dislodged, like Harriet, from the punt, followed her stays downriver.

CHAPTER THIRTY-NINE

Cribb reveals the truth—To say nothing of the dog—Swing, swing together

Jim Hackett's suicidal leap from the *Iffley Queen* had various consequences. It earned Thackeray, his rescuer, a column of tribute in the *Oxford Times* and a cold that stayed with him for a month. It inspired a question in Parliament about the safety of lifebelts, after the one Thackeray had carried to Hackett had proved incapable of supporting him. And it gave Percy Bustard time to consider his position.

'Drink your cocoa, Jim, and don't say a word,' he advised his accomplice, now swathed, like Thackeray, in a blanket, but with one arm handcuffed to a table in the saloon. 'There's no evidence against us. A decent lawyer will see us through. We can answer any charge they bring.'

Cribb smiled. 'Feeling more confident, now you're out of your skirts, Mr Bustard? He'll need to be a very good lawyer. I made a bad mistake early in this case—spent the best part of a week tagging after the shirt-tails of three gentlemen interested in other things than murdering university dons—but this time I don't think I'm wrong. You murdered a tramp by the name of Walters on Tuesday night at Hurley, and Henry Bonner-Hill on Saturday morning in Oxford.'

'We were not in Hurley on Tuesday night.'

'Miss Harriet Shaw—a young lady you've met more than once—observed three men in a boat above Hurley Lock in the early hours of last Wednesday morning. The passenger was Walters, probably drunk, and the two oarsmen answered your descriptions—one much larger than the other.'

'That's not much of a description,' commented Bustard. 'If Miss Shaw persuaded herself that she saw Jim and me, she's mistaken. We slept in the boat at Wargrave on Tuesday night. I don't know whether you're familiar with the River Thames, old sport, but Wargrave is a good ten miles upriver from Hurley and, more to the point, there's Hambleden and Marsh Locks in between. The locks are closed at sundown. We couldn't have brought the boat to Hurley without shooting the weirs.'

'Yes, I'm familiar with the story,' said Cribb. 'You were careful to mention that you bought a veal and ham pie in the George and Dragon. But Jim Hackett corrected you, said it was the Dog and Badger.'

Bustard shrugged his shoulders. 'Perhaps it was.'

'The only Dog and Badger for miles around is in Medmenham,' said Cribb. 'It happens to be P.C. Hardy's local pub. There's no Dog and Badger in Wargrave. I've checked the county gazetteer.'

'Slip of the tongue,' said Jim Hackett.

'Stow it!' ordered Bustard immediately. Then, affecting unconcern again, he asked Cribb, 'Why do you suppose we should have wanted to murder a common tramp?'

'Not for his money,' answered Cribb. 'We found three hundred pounds on the body. He was killed to practise the method. You reasoned that nobody would take much interest in a tramp who drowned in the river. You met Walters somewhere in the neighbourhood of

Medmenham—quite possibly the taproom of the Dog and Badger—filled him with liquor, walked him to the river and took him aboard the boat. He was nine parts drunk by then, and I dare say you gave him some gin or whisky to do the rest. You rowed towards Hurley and heaved him over the side, taking care to hold his head and shoulders under long enough to fill his lungs with water. Pity you gripped him so tightly. You left some bruises round the neck. There was also a dogbite on his leg.'

'A dogbite!' said Bustard. 'That's ridiculous! We haven't got a dog.'

'Not now, Mr Bustard, but you had one at the time. Fox terrier, I think. Miss Shaw noticed it sitting at the front of your boat. A nice domestic touch, that. Pity it got too excited when you were struggling with Walters' body and fastened its teeth on his leg, because you had to get rid of it after that. It's no good asking what you did with the poor animal. I suppose it went the same way as Walters. Nobody's going to get excited about one more dead dog in the Thames.'

Jim Hackett started to say, 'We didn't drown the—' when Bustard nudged him so sharply that cocoa spilled over the blanket.

'If you didn't drown it, then I've a theory that it's buried on Phillimore's Island,' said Cribb. 'You lit a fire there. If we dig underneath the ashes, I reckon we might find what's left of that unfortunate dog. A fire is a useful way of covering freshly dug earth. Yes, I think we'll send a little exhumation party to Phillimore's Island.'

'A dead dog won't prove much, even if you find one,' said Bustard.

'On the contrary,' said Cribb. 'If its teeth match the marks on Walters' leg, that's evidence strong enough to hang you.'

Bustard was unmoved, even if Jim Hackett winced at the mention of hanging. 'You really haven't explained why we should have gone to so much trouble to kill the tramp.'

'I told you. You were trying out the method. You were going to Oxford to do a job of murder and you wanted to be sure of getting it right. And you did, of course, apart from the fact that you killed the wrong man. Bonner-Hill, poor man, came to the rendezvous instead of Fernandez.'

'Rendezvous? Fernandez? This is all a cipher to me, old boy.'

'It was to me until I realized you were sent to kill Fernandez, and not Bonner-Hill,' said Cribb. 'Fernandez had been fishing for pike on Saturday mornings for two years. Anyone who wanted to kill him must have known they could rely on him being on the river on a Saturday. Just to make sure, a letter was sent from London telling him to be in a certain backwater if he wanted to be shown where a large pike could be found. You were waiting there for him, but Bonner-Hill arrived instead.

Thinking he was Fernandez, you murdered him. I'll make a guess and say you used chloroform or ether instead of alcohol, to render him insensible first.'

'Make as many guesses as you like, old sport,' Bustard airily said. 'You've still got to find a reason why Jim and I should have wanted to kill this fellow Fernandez.'

'That took a little trouble to establish,' said Cribb. 'Even after I'd convinced myself Fernandez was intended as the victim, it wasn't easy. A philanderer like that makes no end of enemies—jilted ladies, jealous husbands and the like. Someone got so agitated about him three months ago that they wrote to Scotland Yard suggesting he was Jack the Ripper. Nasty thing to do. They must have known the Yard would have to investigate. Detectives came to Merton to question him, and when he unwisely gave a false account of his movements at the time of the Whitechapel murders, they began to consider him as a serious suspect. He had claimed to be visiting his uncle, who is Deputy Governor at Coldbath Fields, on the night of the Ripper's fifth murder, but when asked, the gentleman said he hadn't seen Fernandez for a full year. Inspector Abberline, the man in charge of the Ripper investigation, visited Fernandez himself and put some sharp questions to him. It turned out that he wasn't Jack the Ripper. He had been trying to preserve a lady's reputation.'

'Very reassuring for Oxford University,' commented Bustard, 'but I fail to understand what connection it has with Jim and me.'

'So did I, until I looked into it,' said Cribb. 'On Saturday, we found you beside Bonner-Hill's body, if you remember.'

'Attempting to resuscitate him,' Bustard pointed out.

'I don't deny it. By then you'd realized that you had murdered the wrong man. You must have taken his pocket-book before you tipped him in the river, thinking it would hinder identification. After the body had floated away with the current, you opened the pocket-book and found Bonner-Hill's name inside. In a panic you rowed after him and got him on to the bank to try resuscitation. At the time, I had the idea fixed in my mind that we were looking for three assassins, not two, so I put it down to coincidence that you were there beside the body. Later I saw it in a different light. And I understood why you had been in such a hurry to get to Oxford that you had abandoned your boat at Benson on Friday afternoon and completed the journey by bus. You had to be sure of being in Oxford for the meeting with Fernandez on Saturday morning.'

'Ah yes. The rendezvous,' said Bustard sardonically. 'I suppose you think Jim and I wrote the letter telling Fernandez where to meet his murderers.'

Cribb shook his head. 'Not you, Mr Bustard.

The person who gave you your orders. Oh, I considered carefully whether you or Mr Hackett had a motive for murdering Fernandez, and I couldn't find one. But when I put together everything you had told us about yourselves, I understood your part in this conspiracy.'

'Everything we told you? What do you mean?' Bustard was speaking more guardedly now.

'Well, you told me yourself that you met Mr Hackett when he was working for your father-in-law, but you didn't tell me the nature of the business. As that policeman commented on Saturday, it looked more like labouring than business from the state of Jim's hands.'

Jim Hackett turned his palms and studied them as if he had never noticed them before.

'The curious thing about Jim Hackett,' Cribb went on, 'is his habit of quoting from the Bible. He's plainly not the sort to have been a theologist, or a vicar. And the texts he quotes are all of a kind. Improving texts, I think they might be called. "Be sure your sin will find you out." '

'Numbers, Chapter 32, Verse 23,' said Jim Hackett, automatically.

'Stash it, you loony!' ordered Bustard.

' "Every idle word that men shall speak, they shall give account thereof in the day of judgement," ' said Cribb. ' "Man goeth forth to his work, and to his labour until the evening."

I'm sure you recognize them, Mr Bustard. They are the texts your father-in-law, Matthew Fernandez, displays on the walls of Coldbath Fields House of Correction. Jim is a graduate of the Steel. He's seen those texts so often that he quotes them all the time. The labouring Jim did was hard labour. Five years of it altogether. He's a ticket-of-leave man. I've checked by telephone with Mr Barry, the warder-in-chief. No wonder his hands are rough, after five years of turning the crank and picking oakum. Yet he's a good man to have in an assassination party—strong, obedient and experienced in violence.'

Jim Hackett beamed at the compliment.

'Jim's muscle and your head were a useful combination, as Fernandez Senior decided when his thoughts turned to murder.'

'Good Lord!' said Thackeray.

'It had shocked him to the marrow being visited by Abberline and questioned about the Whitechapel murders. He knew his nephew had a fast reputation, but it had never caused him serious embarrassment before. This was too appalling for words—the police, coming to the Steel to interrogate him about a false alibi. Unendurable. Whether his nephew was Jack the Ripper or not, it couldn't go on, for the sake of the family—that family he parades so proudly in the prison chapel every Sunday. Now that his nephew was known to the police, they'd be back every time a woman cried rape within twenty miles of Oxford. It would be common knowledge in the Steel in no time at all. After that the Home Office. He'd be asked to resign. You can't have a Deputy Governor related to a man who could be Jack the Ripper. For the sake of his reputation, his job, his family, he had to wipe John Fernandez off the face of the earth.'

'And you really think the Deputy Governor of the Steel arranged for his nephew to be murdered!' said Bustard. 'That's a little hard to credit, if you don't mind me saying so, old boy.'

'Not at all,' said Cribb. 'In my experience, a man like that is quite capable of murder. Prison is a world on its own, as Mr Hackett will tell you.'

'For a prisoner, maybe,' said Jim Hackett, 'but not for the Deputy bleeding Governor!'

'Don't be so sure. Fernandez has his life centred on the Steel. He's in his element with his systems and routines, doing everything by numbers. The beauty of it is that it's so tidy. Nothing can go wrong for long, because he's got it all under control. If a man holds up the system, he puts him on the crank. It soon brings him round. There's a remedy for everything. For a man like Fernandez it's a perfect way of life, until something threatens it from outside. What does he do then? He looks round for his remedy. The fact that it means murdering his nephew is of no account. That's the solution to his problem, so he applies his mind to achieving it. Being the methodical man he is, he works out a way to do it that will seem like an accident, or suicide at worst. He knows his nephew's custom of fishing, so he devises a plan to dispose of him by drowning. He writes a letter making sure that he will come to the appointed spot. Of course, he can't risk going to Oxford himself, so he calls in his son-in-law and explains what needs to be done for the sake of the family. You are to travel up to Oxford by boat like all the others doing the thing in the book. You're splendid for this purpose: one of the family, but without a jot of sentiment. You've never met John Fernandez, so he won't recognize you when you come face to face. Unhappily for Bonner-Hill, it works in reverse—you don't recognize him. Have I got it right this time, Mr Bustard?'

Bustard gave a joyless smile. 'I'm afraid you have, old sport.'

'Strewth!' said Jim Hackett. 'We're blown! "God be merciful to me, a sinner." St Luke, Chapter 18, Verse 13. If you and I swing for this, somebody ought to go with us.'

'We'll make damned sure he does, Jim, old boy,' said Bustard.

CHAPTER FORTY

A college reunion—Sugar from the Plum—Harriet's arrangement

'Naked?' asked Jane and Molly together.

'Not *completely*,' Harriet conceded. 'But my stays were gone and my blouse was unbuttoned to the waist. It was all on account of a catkin.'

'Harriet! Do you expect us to believe that?'

'I'm not sure. I really don't mind what you believe. Roger—he's my policeman—believed he was rescuing me from a fate worse than death. He was terribly sweet.'

'What happened to Mr Fernandez?'

'He opened his eyes after Melanie had bathed his temples for a few minutes. She agreed to stay with him on the punt until he was well enough to take them back to Magdalen Bridge. Do you know, I think she rather likes him, in spite of everything? Isn't that amazing?'

'But what happened to you?'

'Roger took me back in the other punt. My clothes were much more dry by the time we got there. He drove me to the hotel in a cab. This morning Sergeant Cribb called for me and brought me back by train. And here I am.'

'What did the Plum say? Is she going to

rusticate you?'

Harriet smiled. 'Not this time. Sergeant Cribb told her I had been a credit to the college, and he gave her his copy of *Three Men in a Boat* as a present. She gave him the most sugary smile in return and suggested I went to my room and unpacked. She didn't even warn me about breaking bounds again.'

'Would you do it again?'

'Break bounds?' said Harriet. 'If the need arose.'

'You'll never see your policeman again unless you do.'

'Not so, my dears. There's going to be a trial, and I'm one of the witnesses. Roger is another, so we are sure to meet. Murder trials go on for days and days, he told me, especially as Matthew Fernandez is going on trial with the other two. Tomorrow afternoon I'm going to Medmenham Police Station to check the statement I first made. Roger will be there, because he has been copying it out.'

'So you'll see him as soon as that,' said Molly wistfully.

'He'll be on duty,' Jane pointed out. 'It's not the same as walking out with him.'

'You're quite right, Jane,' Harriet admitted. 'It's not the same at all, in a stuffy old police station with the sergeant looking over his desk at you. That's why I shall arrange that Roger walks back with me afterwards.'

'Harriet! How can you possibly arrange

that?'

'I shall remind him that he left his bicycle here last week. It's still propped against the gardener's shed.'